HIGH TOLERANCE

A Novel of Sex, Race, Celebrity, Murder... and Marijuana

"The wry and knowing Mike Sager has written a saucy and kinetic L.A. novel; celebrity gets fully toasted in this engaging romp about show business and the clash of cultures high and low, where the talk is tough before the shooting starts. The spotlight, it seems, can sometimes be a very dark place."
— Ron Carlson, author, *Return to Oakpine*, on *High Tolerance*

"Mike Sager writes about places and events we seldom get a look at — and people from whom we avert our eyes. But with Sager in command of all the telling details, he shows us history, humanity, humor, sometimes even honor. He makes us glad to live with our eyes wide open."
— Richard Ben Cramer, author, *What It Takes: The Way to the White House*

"Mike Sager writes with uncommon grace and, always, with respect for those who give him their time. His stories cut to the bone of our common humanity."
—Paul Hendrickson, author, *Hemingway's Boat*, on *The Someone You're Not*

"You know those engrossing books that keep you up all night? Don't pick this one up if you have somewhere to be the next morning."
—E Online.com on *Scary Monsters and Super Freaks*

"Like his journalistic precursors Tom Wolfe and Hunter S. Thompson, Sager writes frenetic, off-kilter pop-sociological profiles of Americans in all their vulgarity and vitality. He writes with flair, but only in the service of an omnivorous curiosity. He defies expectations in

pieces that lesser writers would play for satire or sensationalism... a Whitmanesque ode to teeming humanity's mystical unity."
—*The New York Times Book Review* on *Revenge of the Donut Boys*

"I can recognize the truth in these stories—tales about the darkest possible side of wretched humanity."
—Hunter S. Thompson on *Scary Monsters and Super Freaks*

"This collection of pieces by Mike Sager is just brilliant—brave, written with soul and beauty, and unflinching in the depiction of a real America that needs to be revealed. Bravo to Sager for being one of the few writers left willing to do it."
—Buzz Bissinger, author, *Friday Night Lights*, on *Wounded Warriors*

"Mike Sager's keen, journalistic eye and unique voice transfer to fiction with highly entertaining results...Deviant Behavior is a street-level, symphonic portrait of an American city."
—George Pelecanos, author and producer, *The Wire* and *Treme*, on *Deviant Behavior*

"Like a silver-tongued Margaret Mead, Sager slips into foreign societies almost unnoticed and lives among the natives, chronicling his observations in riveting long-form narratives that recall a less tragic, less self-involved Hunter S. Thompson and a more relatable Tom Wolfe."
—*Performances*

"Mike Sager is the beat poet of American journalism, that rare reporter who can make literature out of shabby reality. Equal parts reporter, ethnographer, stylist and cultural critic, Sager has for 20 years carried the tradition of Tom Wolfe on his broad shoulders, chronicling the American scene and psyche. Nobody does it sharper, smarter, or with more style."
—Walt Harrington, dean emeritus, College of Media, the University of Illinois, Urbana-Champaign

HIGH TOLERANCE

A Novel of Sex, Race, Celebrity, Murder... and Marijuana

By Mike Sager

THE SAGER GROUP

Artifex Te Adiuva

Dedication

For Marvin M. Sager, MD

"... for your life to be worth anything you must sooner or later face the possibility of terrible, searing regret. Though you must also manage to avoid it or your life will be ruined.

"I believe I have done these two things. Faced down regret. Avoided ruin. And I am still here to tell about it."

—Richard Ford, *The Sportswriter*

HIGHTOLERANCE

PART THREE

EPILOGUE

PART ONE

1

Don't Nobody Own Us, Mothafucka

The CEO of Roots American Productions thumbed the remote and the projection screen went dark, leaving the room in pregnant silence.

At six foot four and 160 pounds, Thomas Washington Curry was a whippet of a man, wearing his trademark cornrows and diamond-encrusted dental grills. Other than his mother, who called him Tommy, and his banker, who called him Mr. Curry, he was known around the world as Chilly T, a shortened form of his original and somewhat controversial handle, Chilly Tom Neegrow. He'd broken into hip-hop nearly a decade earlier, a former drug dealer and convicted felon who promoted himself as a *political* rapper—a truth teller who made people uncomfortable, like his heroes Dick Gregory, Gil Scott Heron, Richard Pryor, and Ice Cube. Recently he'd again altered his public moniker, part of the "ongoing personal evolution," which these days included yoga, meditation, and a strict vegan diet, according to a recent fawning profile in *Jet*. Henceforth he was to be known simply as Chill—the brand name he was using for his new line of household furnishings, available exclusively at Target.

He leaned back expansively in his leather chair, put his vintage Jordan sneakers up on the desk, adjusted his shades, the mirrored lenses of which reflected the trio of young Mexican American rappers fidgeting on the suede sofa before him. They called themselves *Los Vatos*. They were decked out like original gangsters in Pendleton shirts and khaki pants; one of them wore a hair net.

The meeting was being held in a penthouse office atop a newly renovated mixed-use conversion at Sunset Boulevard and Vine Street, at the heart of Hollywood. At the touch of another button, the floor-to-ceiling curtains swept open with a motorized hum, revealing a south-facing panoramic view, stretching from snowcapped mountains to shimmering sea, with forests of skyscrapers dotting the landscape between: Downtown, mid-Wilshire, Century City, Santa Monica. Twenty stories below, tourists plied the Hollywood Walk of Fame, visiting Grauman's Chinese Theatre, the Hollywood Wax Museum, and Ripley's Believe it or Not—meanwhile fending off the homeless Goths, tweakers, and other assorted mental cases who haunted the Boulevard of Broken Dreams.

Chill allowed the silence to marinate. He studied the rappers before him, taking measure of their will, meanwhile fingering the carefully sculpted moustache element of his facial hair—the outline of a beard so thin it appeared to have been drawn with mascara. To attend to his elaborate personal grooming needs, he kept a hair stylist and a barber on call 24/7. As part of his general philosophy of promoting economic self-reliance, he didn't just employ them—he'd helped them open a high-end salon on the first floor of this building. In return, Chill claimed a 10 percent share. Under this same plan, he had interests across the globe; like a one-man NGO, he gave out micro loans wherever he met worthy people in need.

Chill raised his chin slightly, giving him the proud aspect of a king. With his eyes shielded, his dark-chocolate face seemed totally devoid of expression; you could never tell where you stood with him in negotiations. During a meeting, he was liable to read a magazine, chew paper, toss spitballs. He always had a blunt lit; his favorite strain of sativa was called Abusive Kush Private Reserve. He purchased it specially at a marijuana collective called Malibu Green's Farmacy. There was a limited supply, a secret list of subscribers. Only the most fabulous were included.

Now Chill removed his sunglasses—the slang of the moment was Hater Blockers—a gesture of peace and interest, a move that said, *I'm keepin it real.*

He leaned forward, ashed the tip of his blunt in a Baccarat candy dish. Then he issued to *Los Vatos* what the hosts of *Entertainment Tonight* liked to call his "one hundred thousand dollar smile"—theater-quality, upper and lower prosthetic dentures crafted of platinum and liberally encrusted with blood-free diamonds, the two incisors cut to resemble vampire fangs. That he could spit his complicated rhymes—his verse was known as much for its humor and erudition as it was for its rawness and filth—while wearing the unwieldy accessory was probably Chill's most undervalued talent. No one undervalued his ability to produce hit songs and make money. Whatever he did, the market followed. He seemed to know instinctively what to give the peeps, as he liked to call his audience, which by some accounts was nearly 80 percent white and Hispanic—the reason *Los Vatos* was in the house this afternoon.

The mogul nodded in the direction of the giant screen where they'd just watched *Los Vatos'* demo. "This some cool shit," he told them. "Who own y'all?"

"Don't nobody own us, mothafucka."

His name was Sleeper. Well-muscled and strikingly handsome, he spoke in an edgy, Cali-Mex sing-song. He had coal-black hair, slicked back from a widow's peak, and wore a long, cartoonish, Pancho Villa moustache. The way he said *mothafucka*—you could tell he was deeply offended.

As if programmed to respond to profanity, a pair of large black men, one on either side of the room, rose simultaneously from the stools on which they'd been sitting. Clevon and Eddie had once been members of the Fruit of Islam, the paramilitary wing of the Nation of Islam. In their day, they'd guarded Minister Louis Farrakhan, Johnnie Cochran, even Michael Jackson. Now they guarded Chill. After two seasons on Chill's reality television show, *Chillin with Chill,* nearly everyone in American knew Clevon and Eddie. There'd been meetings about a spinoff.

Sleeper had his own backup, Yogi and Roc, sitting on either side of him on the sofa. They'd all seen every episode of Chill's show. Beneath the bravado, none of them could believe they were actually sitting here in this office.

We chillin wit Chill, ese!

Are those cameras in the ceiling?

I wonder if we'll be on the show?

They'd driven here from the Oakwood section of Venice, a fifth-generation barrio of shotgun clapboards surrounded by tony rehabs, just blocks from the famous and eclectic boardwalk. The three had grown up together, part of the same *cliqua* of the Venice Gang, the Lil' Locos. Since he was young, Sleeper had a reputation for being a Romeo and a hothead. If he liked it, he fucked it. If he wanted it, he charmed it out of you. He'd bullied his way through life with the gall of the beautiful—like a guy at a skate rink who has never before skated but is determined to go fast, he seemed to enjoy being dangerously out of control. When he fell down, there was always somebody willing to pick him up. Usually she was hot.

Chill waved a hand in the air, an informal signal to his bodyguards that said, *I got this, no worries.* This kid Sleeper was the real deal. The camera loved him. He could spit. He could flow. He could write his own dope rhymes. He could even sing, a dreamy crooner's falsetto that made for sweet hooks.

"So who shot y'alls video?" Chill asked.

"We did," Sleeper said, still playing hard.

Chill laughed and threw his hand dismissively. "Man, you *bullshittin.*" There was a little bit of hot sauce on the epithet. "This professional quality. Where you get the money?"

"Where *you* get *you* money?" Sleeper shot back.

Everyone knew the answer to that.

Chill eyeballed the *Vatos* appraisingly. They were perfect. They already had a look. They had rhymes and tracks, almost enough for a first album, and a unique sound—a mélange of hip-hop, old school R&B, and traditional Mexican mariachi—sort of like Reggaeton meets Usher meets Public Enemy. He would stake his conglomerate empire on it: these little beaners were gonna blow the fuck up. There was a huge crossover potential. *Note to self: a vato-style line of clothing?* They could push fashion in that direction—Pendletons and khakis and hairnets. They could do motherfuckin *zoot* suits. Latin Pride. *Latina* Pride—that's where all the money was, according to a marketing study he'd commissioned. Latino females, fifteen to forty-six. In market tests the numbers on Sleeper were off the charts—Justin Timberlake numbers.

The only thing the group lacked, really, was a some polish and direction, a little more layering in their songs—something Chill could do himself in the studio in a couple of weeks, tops. He already had ideas. Like a new car he'd been hankering for, he was ready to sign them up and take them for a spin in the studio. He'd even said as much in their earlier phone conversations—the paperwork, a deal, was waiting on the credenza behind him. A check had already been cut. All that remained was the pacification. These idiots were so fresh off the street, they didn't even know when to start playing nice.

"So you tellin me I got me some big time playas up in here?" Chill said.

"We do what we do, you know what I'm sayin?" Sleeper folded his arms across his chest, raised his own chin a notch. Yogi and Roc crossed their arms, too.

"It like *dat?*" Chill asked, clearly amused.

"It like *dat*," Sleeper said defiantly.

There's the album cover right there, Chill thought. He looked over at Clevon, thinking, *this little motherfucker don't know when enough is enough.* He issued a huge smile; the blood-free diamonds caught the recessed lighting like a disco ball. He addressed Sleeper with all of the passivity and good will a man of his station could possibly be asked to muster.

"Listen, yo. I wanna fuck with you guys—if you'll let me. I think you're going places. But with the tone y'all got, I'm not sure y'all know what a good deal even look like."

Sleeper issued his own saccharine smile; his teeth needed work. "We don't need nobody to launch us," he said. "We already got our *own* label. All we lookin for is a mothafucka who can give us some kind of distribution deal. We lookin for a partnership, *ese*."

"A *partnership*," Yogi repeated. He was three months younger than Sleeper. They were first cousins on his mom's side; when they were babies, they'd often shared a crib.

"Cause we got other acts comin up behind us," Roc explained.

"You know what I'm sayin?" Yogi said. He sounded unsure.

Sleeper: "We can deliver. We can be makin hit records, but we can also be bringin in other acts, we can be producin hit records for *other* artists. We got the hookup to the *brownside*. It's an untouched demographic right now and we got the connect, you feel me? Maybe you can give us an *umbrella* deal, somethin like that. Maybe you got another office in this building—" He wheeled his finger around in the air above him like an old West wagon master, indicating his ultra-plush surroundings, a gesture of unmitigated entitlement that made Chill's stomach cramp.

"You could write it off or whatnot," Sleeper concluded blithely. "The suits can work out the numbers. You feel me?"

Chill issued a theatrical frown. The tips of his fang-incisors showed in the seam between his meaty lips. "Oh *mannnn*," he said, shaking his head mournfully. "I don't think *nobody* gonna give you no deal like that, homeboy."

"That not what Fat Sam say," Yogi shot back, maybe a bit prematurely.

"Es la *verrrdad*," Roc added, rolling the R for emphasis.

Chill remained calm. He was worth in excess of $6 billion. He didn't need this group or any other. "If you wanna fuck wit Fat Sam, go on across town and piss on *his* leg. You feelin *me*?"

Sleeper stood abruptly. "It like dat?"

"It however you want it to be, my brother," Chill said evenly. "I was tryin to give you some money today. I was tryin to give you a ca-reer. Can't nobody turn you out like I can. But obviously you have some kind of social disease or whatnot cause you don't know what the fuck is good for you. You done thrown away your whole future in the space of five minutes."

Sleeper's handsome face twisted. "Why you wanna disrespect me for?"

Yogi and Roc rose in sync beside him.

"Disrespect *you*?" Chill said, incredulous. "You lucky even to be in this *building*. I got ten more just like you down in the lobby who are *begging* to come up here and suck my dick."

Sleeper's black eyes turned wild. He'd spent a few years in juvvie, where his striking good looks were not an asset. "Suck your dick?" he repeated. "Suck on *this* mothafucka."

He pulled back the front of his plaid shirt to reveal a chrome-plated Beretta 9 mm pistol sticking out of the waistband of his kakis.

Without a moment's hesitation, Clevon and Eddie opened fire—twin Glock 9 mms, stealth black, pulled from the ample folds of their own oversized clothing.

All three members of *Los Vatos* crumbled to the floor, dead instantly.

Their blood mingled on the ecologically sound bamboo hardwood planks, also available exclusively from Target as part of Chill's new line of home furnishings.

2

What If Some Wacko Has a Gun?

Angelika Collette limped across the unfinished concrete floor like a streetwalker who'd lost a shoe in a sketchy getaway.

The studio was darkish and the music was blaring, a monotonous techno trance beat that made you feel spaced out whether or not you were high. The place smelled of fresh paint, hair spray, food service, and roasted coffee, the last courtesy of the authentic Italian barista stationed in the vaulted lobby.

The Robert Rothman Studio had been open for only a few months, part of a gallery conversion project that had reinvigorated Bergamot Station, a former stop on the Red Line Trolley, which ran until the early 1950s from downtown Los Angeles to the Santa Monica Pier. The sun was setting. Workers in blue uniforms streamed in twos and threes out the front gate of the recycling plant across the street, past a colorful mural, a child-like depiction of the life cycle of reclamation.

Parked at the curb in front of the studio was a Lincoln Town Car that had ferried the starlet this morning from her secret new digs in Malibu. As stipulated, it had remained on station throughout the day at the usual hourly rate. Angelika was fifteen when she'd first arrived in Hollywood with her mom, Missy Collette. They'd lived in their car for a time, a Delta 88 appropriated from Missy's third husband—he'd stayed behind in Portland, Oregon, in the family's double-wide trailer. Angelika slept in the front seat of the car. Missy took the back. Every morning they'd drive to the public beach near the Santa Monica Pier to shower. They found a button somewhere that said "Working Actress" and pinned it to the sun visor. "We'd rub it for luck when I went to auditions," Angelika would later recall in an interview.

After five years of bit parts and audition CDs, she'd broken into the public consciousness at age twenty with her first movie role, a spot-on performance as a heroin-addicted model in the much-bally-hooed indie film *Skag,* for which she won an Oscar. From there she'd become such a phenomenon that *Time* magazine featured her on the cover. With her edgy asymmetrical hairstyles and her six-pack abdo-men—a trademark diamond solitaire winking out from the shallow cavern of her navel—Angelika was iconic worldwide.

Now she was twenty-five. Besides the Oscar, she had two dou-ble platinum albums waiting to be hung on the wall of her new home office. A third record was due soon, featuring duets with many of the great artists of the day, including Stevie Wonder, Maroon 5, John Mayer, and Snoop Dogg. The producer on the project was the hip-hop impresario known as Chill.

Thanks to the ruthless efforts of the celebrity press . . . the in-satiable maw of twenty-four-hour-a-day cable programming . . . the dangerously codependent relationships between civilized people and their various electronic screens . . . and the apparent absence of more creative interests and methods of killing time . . . people from Des Moines to Dubai knew everything about Angelika's life—or at least they thought they did.

Every day, in village squares and mall commons, over fence posts, desktops, and cups of Starbucks, Angelika's career and person-al life were discussed and analyzed and gossiped about as if she was an intimate acquaintance, a sister or a relative or a neighbor. Who she was dating, how much money she was making, where she was eating or partying or vacationing, what she was wearing, the terms of her divorce settlement and child custody arrangements ... not to mention her occasional practice of going commando, the fleshy evidence of which had been caught on film and auctioned to a wire service for millions of dollars—all of it was open for discussion. Her entire life was an open book. Or so everyone believed.

As she sang in her popular dance hall anthem, "U Only Think U Know (Me)":

> *Hashed and rehashed/fried and refried*
> *Served up like a side/hear my side*
> *Let me entertain/then look away*
> *U only think u know (me)*

The photos from today's shoot were to be featured on the cover of *Vanity Fair's* annual Hollywood issue. Angelika had a movie upcoming, the postapocalyptic *Ozone Jungle II,* a budding sci-fi action franchise showcasing her martial arts abilities, a skill set she'd developed to augment her work in more serious films. (As Missy liked to say, "Always have something to fall back on besides your keister.")

Angelika had specifically requested this photographer, Rob Rothman. He'd worked with the superstarlet many times before. He knew her body canvas so well that he had this way of making all of her flaws totally disappear: The way her left eye was a little bit smaller and lower. The way her nose curved slightly to the right. The way her shoulder blades stuck out like chicken bones—she could go on and on about her myriad imperfections. Thanks to the digital technology, immediately after each set-up was completed, she was able to view Rothman's photos on a huge monitor. He even let her delete the ones she didn't like.

Rothman's crew had worked for a solid week to build the set, a re-creation of director Peter Black's haunting cinematic vision for *Ozone Jungle II.* There were huge faux I-beams and papier mache rubble, trashed appliances, car parts, oil drums, and even some scattered body parts, all of it painted and otherwise theatrically distressed to look authentic. Throughout the day, as the shoot had proceeded, the crew had been increasingly blown away by Angelika's spontaneous routines and fluid poses—a series of balletic, gymnastic, and martial-arts-inspired splits and jumps and maneuvers that brought to mind Cirque du Soleil.

"Somebody turn up the AC!" said Troy the publicist at one point, fanning himself with a fey hand.

At the moment, Angelika was on the move from her dressing area to the set proper for the final shots, what they hoped would be the cover. Limping on one strappy heel, she kept her arms folded across herself, holding closed a long, black cashmere robe. Troy supported her by one elbow, a willing but insufficient crutch—he was a small man with a high-and-tight marine-style haircut to match his high-and-tight little butt, which switched to and fro as he walked. Around these two hovered a trio of beautiful handmaidens—one white, one Asian, one black—the stylist, the agency rep, and the makeup artist, this third a big girl with dark skin wearing camouflage Capri pants with cargo pockets and a utility belt stocked with various cosmetic tools, giving her the appearance of a mercenary beautician marching off to battle. Following closely behind was a tall, rubbery guy holding a comb and a can of hair spray. He skated along on his stocking feet, a style of locomotion reminiscent of the cartoon character Gumby.

At the caboose of this little celebrity train was Charlie the tailor, a wizened Asian man wearing a silver thimble on his fingertip. It was his job to sew Angelika into—and to cut her out of—the assortment of sheer microfiber bodysuits that had been Rothman's vision for this shoot. At the moment, Charlie was cradling in both hands Angelika's defective Manolo Blahnik, having just repaired the four-inch heel with Superglue, an ample supply of which he always stocked for emergencies.

Reaching the ready area near the set proper, a sort of satellite dressing room, Angelika stopped and submitted her lips and face to the makeup artist for retouching; she seemed no more self-conscious about giving over her anatomy to someone else's care than did a prize thoroughbred having its hoofs cleaned. From day one she'd been a natural. That first time on *Friends*—her inaugural experience on camera, one line as a guest star in the wildly popular weekly television sit com—she'd hit her mark and delivered her line in one fluid and perfect take . . . and completely stole the scene. At that moment, everyone else in the ensemble cast, all of them making nearly $1 million an episode, seemed to disappear from the soundstage. A hush fell over the set, a knowing silence. Everyone made a mental note. *This is where I was when a star was born.*

Angelika allowed the robe to fall. The graphite-colored microfiber clung to her like a second skin, revealing at once everything and nothing—a three-dimensional silhouette. She was firm where a woman was supposed to be firm, ripe where a woman was supposed to be ripe. Though she was not tall—only five-foot-four in bare feet—there was a monumental quality to her, a sculptedness, a tensile strength. She looked as if she'd just as soon fight you as fuck you, and that she'd be the one to decide which.

Rothman fitted the camera to his face and assumed a position that put one in mind of a college wrestler—feet wide, knees bent, shoulders hunched. He moved in a wary circle around his opponent/subject as she herself moved and posed and vogued across the scrim-covered floor. With each digitized click of the shutter the lights popped; there followed immediately the ascending whine of the batteries recharging. The hypnotic thump and drone of the music cast a spell.

Back walkover into handstand into forward roll.

Angelika's heart beat faster, a thin sheen of perspiration moistened her skin. Adrenalin and natural opioids flowed through her brain; her muscles engorged with blood.

Cartwheel into round-off into split.

A sense of well-being traveled to every corner of her body; her face seemed to glow with otherworldly light. Gone were her worries about the big interview upcoming with Larry King, the lines yet unmemorized for her next movie, the fabrics yet unchosen for her clothing line. Gone for the moment were her worries about all the boxes yet unpacked, the new contract for her perfume deal yet to be vetted, the five songs for her next album yet to be recorded. Gone were her worries about Eleanor's weekly spelling test, about watching her weight, about growing old alone, about what people were going to think when they found out she had a secret new man in her life. Already there were rumblings. How long would it take for them to discover her new address?

Spring board to I-beam. Walk, walk, walk, spin, scissor jump.

She concentrated on her physicality—the movement, the nerves firing, the muscles working together, all of it motor memory, stuff she'd been doing since gymnastics as a little girl. The constant inner monologue, the third-person self-commentary, the ever-present litany of questionings and fears and doubts and concerns that never let her rest . . . all of that began to disappear.

The flash popped. The recharger whined.

"Yes . . . Yes . . . *Yes!*" groaned Rothman, a lumbering man, sweating profusely.

Her mind became a still pond, a pristine beach, a humid bank of clouds. She was an Eskimo girl under a fur blanket in an igloo. She was a calla lily in an art deco vase. She was a baby born at home in a Jacuzzi tub . . . like her precious Eleanor, floating calmly upward through the warm water toward her first terrestrial breath.

Angelika jumped up onto a thrashed Viking stove and then launched herself through space—assuming as she flew a perfect *arabesque*, an outward physical translation of the sheer joy she was feeling inside, her neck and back arched just so, her arms and legs extended in proper academy form, her toes perfectly pointed.

Pop. Whine.

And there it was: the cover shot.

The headline would write itself: "Angelika in Flight."

She stuck the landing, careful not to break the heel again.

The whole set broke into applause.

Thirty minutes later, Angelika's coterie of attendants—Troy the PR guy, the three handmaidens, the Gumby guy, and Charlie the tailor—reassembled itself one last time to see her out of the studio.

They surrounded the superstarlet in the vaulted lobby, sharing the giddiness well known to people in the biz, that show-is-over, too-excited-to-go-home-feeling that keeps people chasing the dream. The starlet was wearing an emerald green Juicy-brand tracksuit and flip-flops. Her ankle was wrapped with an icepack—officially diagnosed a "slight sprain" by the on-set physician, duly noted on the union paperwork.

Bowing fatuously, Troy pulled open the elaborate and beautiful door, fabricated of native woods and scavenged metals by a young artist from Tijuana. With a sweeping hand, he bid Angelika to precede them outside into the night . . .

Whereupon she was ambushed by a horde of waiting press.

Microphones and sound booms with big furry covers, whining motor drives with stroboscopic flashes, phallic telephoto lenses, shoulder-mounted videocams and high-tech digital cams, hand-held microcassette tape recorders, the odd pad and pen. They oozed around Angelika and her party like quicksand, like ants, like so many white blood cells attacking a foreign microorganism in the body, surging and bumping and jostling, shouting hysterically—the press was hungry and tired, they'd been waiting for hours, sitting in their cars, looking at their watches, taking calls from their stressed-out bosses, considering deadlines and air times, needing something . . . anything . . . from this young woman, who somehow continued to be one of the biggest ongoing stories of her day, even when there was nothing to report.

"Who's the new man?" somebody shouted.

"When will you get engaged?"

"Was that a baby bump we saw at the AMFAR awards?"

"Is it true you had an abortion?"

Flashes popped. The crowd jostled.

"Could you *please* stand *back*?" Troy pleaded impotently.

Angelika stood like a statue, unblinking. *What if some wacko has a gun?*

3

The Average Annual Family Income in Mali Is $380

Nathan Sulcov padded down the hallway wearing his customary morning outfit of mismatched sweatgear, the hood deployed for warmth, giving him the appearance of a tall and gawkish monk.

He opened the front door, peered out tentatively through the curtain of his thick eyelashes. Ever since he was small, women had fussed over his eyes, a genetic gift from his mother, a gorgeous woman whose only real mistake was wagering her prime on Sulcov's father, Marv, a Brooklyn ob-gyn who was a charter key holder of the Manhattan *Playboy* club during the free-love seventies. On those occasions when Sulcov was standing before the bathroom mirror as a person will do, taking stock of his face—his mother's Maybelline eyes; his father's prominent nose and deep nostrils; his maternal Uncle Irving's slightly receding chin, shored up nicely with a trim beard—he sometimes wondered if it was possible that his ancestors, men of the Middle East, had actually evolved from the camel. His wife had once suggested, in a not-unflattering tone, that he was more likely descended from the chameleon: wherever he went, Sulcov exhibited a talent for fitting in. Arabs assumed he was Arab. Greeks took him for Greek. Ditto Jews, Italians, and gays. How many times had a flirty male clerk at Barneys thrown in a belt or a tie for free? In Hollywood, if you aren't going to be the richest or most famous or most powerful person in the room, it pays to be a little Zelig-like—not so strongly one thing or another, a version of yourself that reflects the prevailing sentiments held by the richest or most famous or most powerful person in the room. From these towering trees came the windfall that nourished people like Sulcov. It made sense to get along; they could always hire somebody else.

He retrieved from his stoop two copies of the *Times*, LA and New York, the twin suns around which his personal solar system revolved. Scanning the headlines—*Dow Dives on Barrage of Bad News. Israel Raids Gaza. Lakers Continue Win Streak. Writers' Strike Continues: Parties Appear Deadlocked. Horror Film Hostess Vampira Is Dead*—he proceeded down a hallway, in a northeasterly direction, toward the great room, skirting as he went the glassed-in courtyard, designed by the noted architect Arnold Stevenson to incorporate an enormous Banyan tree planted a century ago at the exact center of the property by an eccentric railroad executive.

Entering the kitchen, he turned off the low-wattage nightlight and turned on the under-cabinet fluorescents. Owing to the glass wall that formed the rear of the house, the views carried out through the great room to the pool, to the pool house/office and then to the canyon beyond. The city had recently ordered the brush cleared from the slope. It had cost nearly fifteen grand—including the terracing, gravel, and French drains made necessary by the removal of the natural soil-erosion control system . . . the brush. The job would not be complete until fire-retardant ground cover was planted, another couple thou by the time he paid the small army of day laborers the gardener would be recruiting to assist, all of them no doubt his relatives.

Don't forget to order the ice plant from the nursery. He walked over to the desk and found a pad and wrote it down. If he bought the ground cover in person, he'd avoid the gardener's markup—the Westside tax, a kind of reverse *noblesse oblige*, where providers assumed that rich people could afford to pay more for the same goods and services. The rainy season was fast approaching. There was danger of a mudslide—and a large fine if the work was not completed by February 1, according to the pink paperwork stapled to the front door by a passive-aggressive city functionary. *Who the fuck staples a notice to your front door?* The estimate to fill the holes and resand and refinish the vintage oak door: two grand.

Ask Bave to borrow truck, he scribbled.

He dumped yesterday's coffee grounds into the compactor, rinsed the plastic filter-holder and the glass carafe, opened the cupboard, removed the box of recycled paper filters, licked this thumb and forefinger, counted out four brown, flat-bottomed baskets—his secret for robust coffee.

Seven heaping scoops of Starbucks Kenya. Fill carafe with tap water. *The coffee would probably taste better if I used the Pure Flo water,* he told himself, as he did nearly every morning.

It's outrageous to have to pay for drinking water.

He thought about a show he'd seen recently on the Discovery channel. *The average family income in Mali is $380 a year.*

Our bill for drinking water last month was $40.

Soon they'll be selling bottled air.

Maybe you should invest?

He poured the carafe of water into the mouth of the coffee maker. The plastic grid was crusted in spots with white mineral residue, the leavings of their "heavy" California water. *I wonder how much mineral residue has built up inside of me?* He imagined for a moment a cross section of his insides, everything crusted with powdery crystals. Every few months, the showerheads would become clogged and they'd have to pay the handyman to delime all the little holes.

It would probably be healthier to use the Pure Flo.

The coffeemaker slurped and wheezed. Sulcov went about the kitchen securing the various items necessary to breakfast. Birds twittered outside and in the courtyard. The sixties-vintage schoolroom clock set high on the wall went *tick . . . tick . . . tick . . .* the second hand pausing so diligently at each and every hash mark, then moving on to the next.

Already he could hear the rising din of rush hour, two blocks away on the Pacific Coast Highway, a white noise that drowned out the thunder of the waves. Standing there at the kitchen counter, staring off into space with a knife in his hand, Sulcov thought about the millions of commuters across the Los Angeles area, all of them driving to work at that very moment in their various and self-defining vehicles—all of them individuals with singular and complex lives, their sensible pumps or wingtips or Adidas alternating between brake and gas pedal, or in some cases riding the clutch . . . checking the clock on the dash, worrying about today's presentation or lesson plan, rehearsing a speech to the boss or the spouse or the client or the kid's teacher, bargaining with themselves about their next cigarette, five more minutes.

My commute is only thirty-two steps.

For the first twelve years of his working life—how quick it had flown!—Sulcov had ridden a subway to work. In sun and rain, heat and cold, first from uptown and then from downtown and then from Brooklyn. During all that time, he'd been a slave to other people's hours and necessities, a minion of the great editorial We at *NewsSource,* America's oldest newsweekly magazine.

In his West Coast incarnation, he worked primarily from home. Aside from the usual family obligations—his wife, his son, his aging father—Sulcov served only one master: his name was M. Kelley Elizondo. Zondo had been his freshman-year roommate at Columbia. It was he who'd come up with the concept for *High Tolerance;* it was he who'd goaded Sulcov into camping out on his couch in Toluca Lake and "helping" to write the pilot. Sulcov was thirty-three at the time. Against character, he'd arranged a three-month leave of absence from *NewsSource* (meanwhile retaining his health insurance). Like his immigrant great grandfather, he'd left his wife and young child in the old country (in this case Brooklyn) and flown off to the New World to seek his fortune.

Now he was facing forty and *High Tolerance*—think *Law and Order* meets *Broadcast News*—was one half-season short of eligibility for worldwide syndication, the residuals from which would leave Sulcov permanently flush.

Of course, there was no telling if the Emmy- and Golden Globe-winning show would ever again see the bright lights of production. On this Monday in mid-January, during the year 2008, the Writers Guild of America strike hung over Los Angeles like kudzu, like Spanish moss, like a toxic algal bloom choking all life from a beloved pond. Well into the third month of the work stoppage, there was a general malaise everywhere you traveled, a sense of suspended animation. Everyone was blah and kind of semi-permanently annoyed, if not outright angry. Businesses all along the Hollywood food chain were devastated, from dry cleaners to craft services to new car sales.

To Sulcov, the money wasn't so much the problem. It was the uncertainty. The not knowing. The lack of control. The lack of gainful labor. The lack of a project about which to obsess. Doing a story one time for *NewsSource* about senior citizens, he'd interviewed a ninety-two-year-old who was still working as a columnist for a weekly newspaper. "You have to find something to be important to," the old man had said, the dangling preposition intended—meaning that a full and happy life needed to include something that couldn't exist without your efforts. Without a storyline to haunt him, a script to write, Sulcov had nothing to occupy his mind beyond his own foibles and needs and routines—and those of his immediate family, who actually seemed to be operating pretty well without him these days, except for the constant demand for his services as a driver and errand boy.

Not to mention the guild bylaws, which demanded four hours on the picket line every day.

Meaning he had to leave the house on a regular basis.

Upstairs a toilet flushed. The water Dopplered through the plumbing like beans in a Peruvian rainstick. The circular staircase vibrated with heavy footfalls.

Jake appeared, a thirteen-year-old wearing his own hoodie, his face a mask of sleep.

"How's the ankle?" Sulcov sang, delivering a quartered blueberry muffin on a plate with an allergy pill, a vitamin, a calcium tab, and two strawberries on the side.

Mumbling inaudibly, eyes askance, the boy took his customary seat at the dining table, his back to the canyon view, facing the tree, and opened his laptop.

The whooshing of the traffic on the PCH grew steadily louder. The neighbor's dog commenced howling, wanting back in. The two Sulcov males ate in convivial silence—Jake scanning his Mac, Sulcov turning the pages of the *New York Times*.

Another flush, slippers scuffling down the hallway from the master suite.

Leticia Harris Sulcov, known to all as Tish, had been raised in Baldwin Hills, the luxe part of south central Los Angeles, known as the Black Beverly Hills. At USC, her Alpha Phi sorority sisters had nicknamed her Mulatto Barbie—a preppy goddess cast in a darker hue, with an extra half-portion of junk in the trunk. A graduate of the Annenberg School of Communications, number two on the Trojan tennis team . . . from the moment she'd arrived at the Manhattan headquarters of *NewsSource* for a summer internship, every male in the place had coveted this exotic creature.

She was wearing her usual oversized fuzzy robe, her heels crushing the backs of her expensive Ugg slippers. On their occasional weekends at her parents' Malibu beach house, her mother—a Lena Horne look-alike with perfect finishing-school diction—would give her youngest daughter endless grief about the way she "insisted on shufflin around the house like Stepin Fetchit." That Tish persisted made Sulcov love her even more—a minor fist-in-the-air from an otherwise dutiful child, her daddy's favorite, the jock son he never had. Sulcov liked to think of her as his Fresh Princess, though he'd dared call her that only once.

She poured herself her usual—half coffee and half hazelnut soy creamer, two Equals. Her chair at the rectangular table was across and one down from Jake's, facing outward toward the canyon and the lightening sky. Sulcov sat to her right, at the head. She opened the *LA Times* and removed the Calendar section.

"Oh, look," she said, scanning the gossip on the second page. "Angelika Collette has a new *mystery* boyfriend."

"Anybody's better than that *what's-his-name*," Sulcov said.

Tish looked at him archly. "You know very well what his name is."

Sulcov raised his hands in surrender.

She gave him a look: *don't even go there.*

"That guy is totally *gay*," Jake said definitively.

"Don't say *gay*," Tish scolded. "Uncle Brooke would be *so* offended."

Jake spidered his fingers across the keyboard of his Mac. After an interval, he turned the screen to face his parents.

An image of Angelika's ex-husband, Christopher Stone. He was riding a white horse, his shirt open to his navel, his golden hair flying. Like its rider, the horse was large and muscular and appeared to have gone through considerable hair and makeup preparation for the photo shoot.

"Look at those *moobs!*" Jake howled—a righteous bay of teen vindication.

"I think they call those pecs, son." Sulcov's tone lampooned a teachable moment.

Tish: "They're no worse than Angelika's *fake* ones."

"You got a problem now with fake boobs?" Jake guffawed.

Sulcov: "Her *foobs?*"

"*Foobs!*" Jake laughed uproariously, cupping an imaginary pair.

Tish's brow furrowed. "You *know* I am soooo against plastic surgery," she said, her own teachable moment. "It creates false standards for women. So many of the women I—"

Just then a humming sound, emanating from the vicinity of Jake's person.

HUMMMMMMMM!

Like a robot drone called suddenly to service, the boy lost all focus on the present moment and reached into the pocket of his hoodie, retrieved his Blackberry, read a text . . .

"*Oh my God!*" he exclaimed. "There was an assassination attempt on Chill!"

"Chilly the Negro?"

"*Dad!*"

"That's his name, isn't it?" Being the father of a half-black child, he was allowed to assume at times the sensibilities of a black person—up to a point.

"Chilly *Tom* Neegrow." Jake corrected. "Tom as in *Uncle Tom*, with its obvious historical connotations." The boy had assumed a scholarly tone that impressed Sulcov with its confidence. "It's spelled "N-e-e-g-r-o-w. It's wordplay, get it? It's *political*. It refers to his desire to help African Americans evolve and 'grow.' " He used his fingers like quotation marks.

"And it's not *Chilly* anymore, either," he added, by now supremely annoyed. "It's *Chill*, okay? He *changed* his name, like, *six months* ago!"

"He continues to evolve," Sulcov quipped . . .

And regretted his *bon mot* even as it left his mouth.

Jake stood abruptly. "Why are you even *talking* to me about this? What do *you* care what happens to *Chill*?"

"It's 7:10, gentlemen," Tish announced. "Are you planning to make it to school today?"

4

Niggaz on My Dick

Chill and his posse waited like wannabes on the large sectional sofa in the lobby of Roots American Productions, the floor of which was also done in Chill-endorsed bamboo. For visual warmth there were several faux-oriental rugs, also from Chill's Target signature collection.

The atmosphere was funereal. Since the shooting 24 hours earlier, all work in the office had come to a standstill as police and fire officials combed and catalogued the scene. Given the amount of damage, the process was laborious. Cops and evidence technicians tracked in and out of Chill's private office. Every time the door opened, napkins and papers and empty Starbucks cups scattered like autumn leaves. A cleanup crew was on hand, chins on broom handles, awaiting the all-clear.

"Somebody bring me a slice of that veggie pizza," Chill commanded to no one in particular.

Simultaneously, a dozen homies cut their eyes to the floor.

"Y'all done ate all the pizza," Chill announced, not so much a question as a conclusion. Everyone in his posse was handpicked—except TBone, who was married to his little sister. Discounting the bodyguards, Clevon and Eddie, everyone had connections back to the rough Long Beach neighborhood where they'd all grown up. He loved them, he needed them, he knew their limitations; his greatest weakness was probably keeping them around. Every article and in-depth broadcast always mentioned his posse. The takeaway was that this big celebrity needed his ego stroked constantly, that his people were meant to function as his full-time amen chorus. To some extent, that was accurate. But the deepest truth was this: Chill hated to be alone. He'd grown up in a bustling matriarchal household overseen by his grandmother, full of aunts, cousins, and men friends. Until he was sixteen and went to jail for the first time, he'd shared a bed every night of his life.

"The police mighta ate some pizza," TBone offered. As Chill's major domo, TBone was the last wall of defense around the star. His job was to do and say whatever needed to be done and said.

The problem with TBone was not his work ethic. Since he was young, he'd always had a job. He'd delivered newspapers, mowed lawns, scooped ice cream, slung burgers. He'd worked in a warehouse, a candy factory, a butcher shop.

He just couldn't *keep* a job.

Like the time he worked as a security guard in a Beverly Hills jewelry store. Ordered to shadow the black customers who came into the place, TBone decided to shadow *everyone*.

It was only fair, right?

Now Chill gave him a sideways look, a buckshot scatter of con-flicted emotions. "All y'all niggaz on my dick," he said ruefully. He reached into his pocket, peeled off some bills from a healthy wad, thrust them in the direction of his personal assistant, a buck-toothed kid with a cylindrical tower of hair that rose off his head like a fez.

"Go downstairs and get *two* mo pies." Chill ordered. "Tell 'em it for *me*. And don't let them Dagos undercook the crust, you hear?"

"They ain't no Dagos in that shop no more," TBone said. "They got nothing but Mexicans making the pizza now."

Chill fingered the fine outline of his beard, processing this new information. When he was just out of prison and working in the mailroom at CBS records (a state-funded internship for young felons), he used to go to Giuseppe's Pizza at least twice a week for lunch. Years later, when he bought the building as a headquarters for RAP Records, the first-floor storefront restaurant conveyed with the property. It had been years since he'd enjoyed the simple pleasure of walking into a pizza shop and buying himself a slice. Venturing into public was not really an option anymore. Even driving a car was difficult during the day—other motorists tended to become overly excited. At a red light on Sepulveda Boulevard near the Getty Museum one afternoon a few years back, a woman in a Range Rover became so taken with the sight of him that she forgot to put her foot on the brake. As she mugged and waved at Chill, her car rolled into the intersection. She was killed instantly by a bus.

Chill still suffered from occasional nightmares about the incident—he had seen everything in gruesome detail. Insomnia was listed as the primary diagnosis on his license to ingest medical marijuana—his prescription indicated the use of calming indica strains to help him sleep. The Abusive Kush PR, however, was a powerful sativa, speedy and energizing—at the collective they called it "cerebral." Sometimes he wondered who else accompanied him on the exclusive list. There were rumors; some of the biggest names in Hollywood were always mentioned, high-profile stoners like Brad Pitt, Jack Nicholson, Bill Maher, and Woody Harrelson. It was also said that the original hipsters Peter Fonda and Dennis Hopper co-owned a share. Chill had no problem getting on the list; he was an icon of pot use, a vocal public proponent of medical marijuana who smoked openly in all his videos. He did wonder sometimes who it was who'd been eliminated to accommodate him. It was a measure of some sort, he imagined. Sometimes even *he* couldn't believe how rich and famous and powerful he'd become.

"When I was workin at the studio," Chill said nostalgically, "there used to be this grandma who always worked the register at Giuseppe's; she was straight-up gangsta. I'd pay her with a twenty. And she *always* gimme change back for a *ten*. And I'd be like, 'Scuse me, lady, I just gave you a *twenty*.' "

Chill laughed. "And she would never deny it. She would *never* fuckin deny it! She'd always act all surprised and shit." He threw his hands in the air, lampooning an Italian accent. 'Mama mia! I'm soooooo sorry!'

"And then next time I'd go in . . . bitch would try me *again*."

"Ain't *that* some shit," TBone said.

"Didn't she start recognizing you after a while?"

This voice belonged to the lone white guy in the room, a reporter from *StarNews*, a popular if lowbrow title that brought under one umbrella a tabloid newspaper, a website, and a TMZ-style celebrity gossip show. His name was Calvin Scott. He wore modish square eyeglasses and a backward Kangol cap. His pale, freckled skin looked out of place; his relaxed posture said otherwise. He'd been hanging around the rap mogul and his posse for some time now, collecting material for a major profile—an exclusive all-access deal brokered by the higher-ups.

"Don't you know that all niggaz look alike?" TBone asked pointedly.

"Grandma had *mad* game," Chill said. "I always used to wonder how many times a day she must be pullin that stunt. She prolly *retired* behind that shit right now."

"She lounging beside her pool in Beverly Hills," TBone said.

"Far as I'm concerned," Chill said seriously, "you can run your game, know what I'm sayin? I'll respect a nigga for his skill. Just don't try to run that shit on *my* ass no more after I done *caught* you."

Everyone in the room laughed uproariously—slapped thighs and *um-hummed* and shook their heads . . . *Yes, yes, emphatically yes!* Chill was the sun and the moon and the stars. The leader, the sugar daddy, the big mammary. From him all things flowed.

The door to Chill's private office opened, touching off a minor twister in the lobby. Out stepped L.A.P.D. detective Kenyatta Ducksworth. Thirty-five years old, with a rugged mahogany complexion, he was wearing a fashionable, narrow-cut suit with a white handkerchief peeking out from the breast pocket. Clearly a man who took care with his wardrobe, he looked like he'd just stepped out of a men's magazine, which is where he'd first seen this Band of Outsiders suit. Shooting his cuffs, he addressed the music mogul with polite respect. "Mind coming with me for a few minutes?"

Chill refitted his Hater Blockers. "Can't talk without my lawyer present, yo."

"I just have a *few* more questions."

"Who's the victim here, detective?" Chill looked to his amen chorus for support and was not disappointed.

"Well, the quicker I finish up here . . ." Ducksworth ventured.

"I said everything I had to say at the press conference this morning. Can we just get you a transcript? Or we can burn you a DVD? However you want it, my brother."

"I was hoping to go over a few details."

"I'm not really prepared to say any more without my lawyer present." He issued his hundred K smile.

Ducksworth: "You know the next line from TV, right?"

"The next line? What do you mean?"

" 'We can talk here, or we can talk down at the station house.' "

"You sayin you gonna *arrest* me?"

"I'm saying I can hold you as a material witness for up to 24 hours."

With a grunt of contempt, Chill rose and followed Ducksworth down the hall toward his own office.

The journalist rose and casually followed. He was halfway across the lobby when TBone reeled him back in. "Where you think you going, *StarNews?*" Even after two months, nobody knew Calvin Scott's given name. Or cared. He was the guy from the magazine.

Ducksworth shouldered the door with some effort; once inside, the two men stood and surveyed the carnage.

It looked like the scene of a house-clearing firefight in Fallujah, Iraq—bullet holes, plaster leaking from drywall, couch stuffing everywhere, blood drying on the floor. Two of the floor-to-ceiling windows had been shattered; the curtains billowed theatrically. The bodies had been removed late last night. The day shift at the coroner's office had just finished preliminary identifications and was shuffling the paperwork. Notifications of next of kin would follow shortly.

Ducksworth produced a notepad. "At the press conference you said the members of *Los Vatos* came through the door shooting."

"I said I was standing behind my desk, facing *away* from the door. I was looking on my credenza for some paperwork—some contracts."

"Your *credenza*," the detective repeated. Kenyatta Ducksworth's father was the son of a sharecropper, the grandson of a slave. He'd worked his whole life in a tire factory in North Carolina. After middle school, Ducksworth had attended a mostly white prep school on a basketball scholarship; he'd gone on to become the first in his extended family to earn a college diploma. With several full scholarships to law school on the table, the criminal justice major had opted to join the nation's highest profile—and most notoriously bigoted—police force.

Which hadn't exactly pleased his father, who had ridden him mercilessly growing up. "When you black you gotta be *twice* as good," the old man would admonish—an uneasy sentiment branded into Ducksworth's character the way the Greek letter Omega had been seared onto his shoulder when he was initiated into his fraternity at historically all-black Florida A&M. To this day, the old man couldn't understand why his son had thrown away his fancy education to become a *cop*.

But Ducksworth had his own ideas. Today this country bumpkin who grew up hunting and fishing and playing soldier in the woods was living in a renovated loft space in LA's hip Fairfax District, eating bagels for breakfast and Ethopian carryout for dinner. He pronounced every word clearly, dressed painstakingly, read *Esquire* and *GQ* for fashion, food, and lifestyle tips he believed would help define him as a successful modern man.

Which meant he knew very well what a fucking *credenza* was.

He had one in his home office, part of a home office suite he'd purchased online from Designs Within Reach.

The truth was, he resented the shit out of Chilly Tom Neegrow and all he stood for—another braggadocious *nouveau riche* rapper, filling up young black kids' heads with so much bullshit.

"What sort of contracts were you looking for?" Ducksworth asked.

"We were gonna offer them motherfuckers a *deal*. That's why they came up here in the first place. They had an *appointment*."

Ducksworth flipped a few pages in his notebook. "What I'm curious about right now is how the bodies ended up in front of your desk. Did they come through the door shooting and then leap over the sofa?"

"It's like I tole the press conference: My instincts took over. I didn't stop to think or observe anything—I dove for cover behind my desk. That's why we bought it."

He walked over to his unusual-looking ultra-modern desk and rapped it with a knuckle. "It's constructed entirely of Lexan—check it out. There's a roll-down door. It's bulletproof—even has a landline and supplies. In case of emergency, our MO is duck and cover. That's why we employ security. *They* supposed to think and observe. Ain't no heroes up in here, detective."

Ducksworth consulted his pad. "Beside the TEC-9, one of the vics was carrying a chrome-plated Beretta 9 mm. His name was Chauncey Garcia? Also known as Sleeper?"

"That kid was the real deal." The rap mogul's face arranged itself into a look of genuine regret.

"The Beretta was still in his waistband," Ducksworth said. "It appeared it hadn't been fired; I'm sure ballistics will confirm."

Chill shrugged.

"It just seems a little odd that these three experienced gang bangers—all of whom have pretty extensive criminal records—would bum rush your office with only one serviceable weapon between the three of them. Sounds more like a *suicide* mission than a hit."

"Maybe they Al Qaeda, looking for they virgins in the afterlife."

Ducksworth gave him a look.

"Listen, detective. I got wannabes here every day trying to get a contract. Obviously, these guys was fuckin crazy. Who the fuck comes up in here with a fuckin TEC-9?"

"A TEC-9 with no fingerprints on it," Ducksworth added. He stared into Chill's sunglasses, seeking his eyes. A distorted image of himself stared back.

"Like I said—"

"I know. You were underneath the desk. Meanwhile, your body-guards throw down with handguns against a TEC-9 and neither of them even gets a scratch."

"Clevon and Eddie the best. That's why we hired them."

Ducksworth flipped a few more pages. "You said you were interested in signing *Los Vatos*. Was there a dollar figure attached to the contract?

"The advance check was already cut. One million dollars—you'll find it in accounting."

Ducksworth's eyebrows rose. "One *million?*"

"I guess they weren't happy with my offer."

5

The Magneto That Powered Him

Nathan Sulcov took a seat on the lowest bleacher in the gymnasium at Santa Monica Prep.

The aging and cavernous structure smelled nostalgically of floor wax, dryer lint, wrestling mats, and bleach. Championship banners hung from the ceiling. Sneakers squeaked, whistles trilled, voices rose and fell, balls pounded the polished hardwood—the familiar sounds echoed off the familiar glazed concrete blocks that formed the inner walls.

The Heston Arena was named for its famously conservative benefactor, the actor Charlton, whose children had attended Prep. Like many traditional high school facilities, the building served multiple purposes. There were fixtures in the floor for volleyball poles; a heavily curtained stage occupied the north end. An industrial kitchen facility qualified the structure as an emergency shelter.

At the moment, each of the six basketball rims was occupied by a team from a different age group—a graduated array of players, from peewee to near-man, all of them dressed in identical uniforms . . . it looked like someone had disassembled a shipment of Russian nesting dolls and rearranged the inner pieces around the floor according to size. At each basket was a different coach, a different skill station. The scoreboard ticked off minutes. At the next buzzer, they'd rotate.

Sulcov had been a gym rat his entire life. Growing up in Brooklyn, you played seriously or you got off the court. How many empty hours had he filled with a bouncing ball? Even now, his dirty little secret was this: the highlight of his week was his hoops game—a rotating cast of twelve to fourteen writer/ball players who met at the Sports Club in Santa Monica. Most of them were East Coast Jewish transplants. All of them suffered from the same characteristic overabundance of self-esteem—especially when it came to their *mad skilz* on the court.

He spotted his boy—thirteen years old, five foot seven, one hundred and twenty-eight pounds, a stick figure with a decent Jewfro, his overlarge shorts hanging stylishly low. Enrolled as a seventh grader, Jake played up with the eighth graders on the U14 squad. What a difference the year made. Some of his teammates were already sprouting moustaches. By next season, the taller ones would be dunking.

It was hard to believe that only a year ago Jake was spending a lot of his time playing with G.I. Joes. He had the Humvee, a rocket launcher, a Black Hawk helicopter, everything done in desert camo. The coolest Joe figurine was always called Jake; he was outfitted with the best weapons, commanded the starring role in the unendingly varied battlefield dramas. The second coolest doll, the sidekick, was always called D-Nate—the D was for Dad. Jake would spend hours in his room narrating in a loudish but unintelligible soprano, adding sound effects—automatic weapons fire and explosions, the cries of the dying enemy. Hard into a story line, he'd refuse to come to dinner or to go to bed. He'd beg for extra time to see his battle to conclusion.

One evening at bedtime, Sulcov arrived at the doorway of Jake's room to find the boy boxing up all his Joe paraphernalia. From the expression on his face, Sulcov could tell something had happened. Some switch had been thrown; something had changed for the boy—some event, some occurrence, some monumental . . . *something* he would never know.

You don't expect to see the line in the sand as you're crossing it, but there it was. This helpless thing whose ass he'd wiped was moving ever closer to the exit. It was the oldest story. That he could see it coming made it no less wrenching.

Now Jake crossed over his dribble from his left hand to his right, evading a tallish orange traffic cone. He gathered his feet, set himself, launched a jump shot—his stroke culminating in a textbook, gooseneck follow-through ... arm overhead like an eager student's, wrist bent gracefully, hand splayed forward, a gesture at once so strong and so fey, like something from dance.

The ball traced a high arcing parabola through the chilly and aromatic atmosphere, meanwhile rotating sweetly backward, the product of the follow-through, the so-called shooter's touch. In his effort to put the nine-and-a-half-inch diameter ball into the eighteen-inch diameter basket—from a distance of about twenty feet—Jake's face expressed the entire realm of human possibility. With each attempted shot, whether in practice or in a game, the epic and elemental conflict of sport was once more recreated: either the ball finds its mark or it doesn't. You win or you lose, no discussion.

Every shot Jake attempted was thus a link to every other shot he'd taken before—a link to the thousands of similar shots already taken over the relatively short course of his lifetime. The three-foot Playskool basket in the nursery. The five-foot molded-plastic basket in the bedroom. The adjustable "big guy" basket delivered to the new back patio for his seventh birthday. They'd started with the rim at seven feet, adjusted it one foot upward every year. By age ten, having run away with the rec league at the local Y, Jake and his lovingly built jump shot were given over to professionals.

Swish. The ball fell perfectly through the iron rim, barely rippling the net ... setting off a palpable wave of relief and pride inside Sulcov's chest. It didn't matter how far he had to drive, or how long he had to sit on a hard bleacher seat. It didn't even matter how many shots Jake took or how many he made—though watching your kid go *off* during a game was unparalleled. Just being there was enough.

Lately, as Tish had become ever more busy with her charity work, with her myriad causes and obligations, he'd found himself focusing more and more on his child—a child he'd argued bitterly against conceiving. Now more than ever, Jake was the center of his universe, the magneto that powered him—his muse, his focal point, his area of concentration, the most important element of his life's work. He'd loved no one as deeply, not even Tish.

Often he asked himself: *what will you do when he goes to college?*

At last the entire group gathered at center court. After a team cheer— *Go Prep!*—Jake ambled over in the manner of a ballplayer, loose limbed and physically confident, a lanky, coltish, sore-legged strut he shared in common with all the others, as if the walk had been issued along with the uniforms.

Beside him was his best friend, Ezekiel "Z" Garcia. Twelve years old in seventh grade, he was six foot three, 195 pounds. According to his mom, the doctors said he'd eventually reach six foot ten. She was counting on him to become the first in his family to go to college. A lot rested on his broad shoulders.

Jake half-nodded to his dad and dumped his Adidas bag on the floor. He took a seat on the bleacher to the right of Sulcov and proceeded to change his shoes. Z sat on the far side of Jake and did the same with his size 15s. "How you doin, Mr. Sulcov?" he asked politely.

"Can we give Z a ride home?" Jake asked.

They'd met Z in the Under-6 rec league, Sulcov's first season coaching. Drafted unseen, Z turned out to be a head taller than everyone else his age—the beginning of a long and auspicious association between this point guard and this center, the one and the five, a special symbiosis of little man and big, on the court and off. Years later, the Sulcovs would be instrumental in landing Z a scholarship to Prep. The varsity football coach had him in his crosshairs, too; college recruiters were already sending letters.

Despite his mature first impression, Z was the baby of his extended family. He liked to snatch Jake's basketball or his cell phone and gallop away, initiating a rangy game of catch-me-if-you-can, annoying the crap out of Jake, who himself was six months older (and already a *teenager!*) and tended to lord it over the bigger boy.

Z lived with his mother in his grandmother's modest house in the heart of the westside territory claimed by the Venice gang. He took public transportation to school most days. His mother was on some type of government assistance. His father, a second- or third-generation gangbanger, was doing an extended sentence at a prison in Northern California. His brother, Chauncey, also known as Sleeper, had followed his father into the Venice gang. Until recently he'd managed a string of street-level crack dealers; with the profits, he'd built *Los Vatos*—a studio in his grandma's garage; a self-made album of killer songs; a modest-but-growing Mexican American following that stretched to Tijuana and beyond.

When encountered, Z was nearly always smiling. Everyone liked him instantly, even the refs—he got more love than any basketball big man Sulcov had ever seen. And while he handled all of his difficult challenges like a trooper—the practices, the strength and conditioning, the remedial classes, the boatloads of homework—the basics continued to elude him. He hardly ever changed his clothes. He hated taking showers. His fancy cell phone was always out of juice. Tish had wondered out loud on several occasions if Z let his phone die on purpose . . . maybe he felt that being disconnected telephonically somehow distanced him from his home life? Why else was he always wanting to sleep over?

It was only twenty minutes by bicycle between the two vastly different worlds inhabited by the boys' respective families. Taking the Strand, the wide concrete boardwalk that followed the coastline, it was an easy ride. Usually the boys met at the Venice basketball courts; they knew every weight lifter, sword swallower, homeless dude, and busker who haunted Venice's eccentric stretch of beach. That the two families' homes and lifestyles could be so different had not been lost on Jake. It was one of the reasons Sulcov had fostered the relationship—despite the real dangers of Z's neighborhood. You could tell knowing Z had made a huge difference in Jake's life.

Now the younger Sulcov reached into his gym bag and extracted his cell phone and turned it on, looking for updates on Chill.

"The assailant used a friggin *TEC-9*," Jake announced.

"That's fully automatic, dude," Z declared.

Jake imitated machine gun fire; both boys laughed maniacally. Sulcov smiled to himself. As often as not, Z had been right next to Jake on the sand-colored Berber carpet, playing G.I. Joe.

"It's amazing he wasn't wounded," Sulcov said. Remembering the morning's tensions, he took care to assume the proper note of gravity.

"He got an S on his chest," Z rapped, quoting "Superman," one of Chill's more famous songs, written as the theme from another of Hollywood's endless action hero remakes.

"What else does it say?" Sulcov asked.

As he'd been programmed during his years at private school, Jake assumed his best classroom reading voice: "At a press conference, the billionaire rapper/producer/entrepreneur credited his own quick reflexes with saving his life. When the assailants entered the room with weapons blazing, the former All-County receiver from Manhattan Beach Country Day School dove beneath his desk.

"'Instinct took over,' Chill told a capacity crowd at the hastily-called press conference outside the offices of his production company near Sunset and Vine. 'I made like I was diving into the end zone.'

"His bodyguards returned fire. A heated gun battle ensued. All three assailants were pronounced dead at the scene."

Sulcov to Jake: "Wow. You might want to rethink your dream of becoming a record producer. Sounds a little *dangerous*."

"Music is a lot like drugs," Z said matter-of-factly. "There's nothing else you can do to make money that fast and easy. People get greedy."

"I'll get bodyguards and shit," Jake said. "I'll hire some guys from the frickin Mossad."

"Aren't Chill's guards from the Fruit of Islam?" Sulcov asked.

"They used to be with Minister Farrakhan," Z confirmed.

"*Holy fuck!*" Jake exclaimed. He resumed reading. "The assailants have been identified as members of an up-and-coming Mexican American rap group called *Los Vatos*."

6

Boyz in the Hood

The kids jumped out of the Bimmer before Sulcov could finish parallel parking. Leaving the doors open, they hustled around the side of Z's grandma's sagging white clapboard house and disappeared.

Sulcov unfolded himself from the car and surveyed the street. The crime-deterrent mercury vapor lamps bathed the entire area in a blanched-salmon shade of fictive daylight, revealing a ramshackle collection of bungalows in various states of repair. Walls and fences were covered with riotous graffiti. Over the years, Z had delighted in pointing out the authorship of the various tags, each one as distinctive and meaningful to his eyes as Chinese characters would be to a native speaker in Chinatown.

Nobody knew how or why an enclave of Mexican Americans had come to populate this part of Venice. Their one square mile of territory was part of a district listed as Oakwood on official maps. The older families dated back six or seven generations—though the concept of a generation around here was somewhat foreshortened. Z's older sister was sixteen. She had an eighteen-month-old daughter. Z's mother, Graciela, was forty-three. *Her* mother, Z's *abuela*, the owner of the house, was sixty-five—*her* mother had only recently died at eighty.

For decades the Venice homeboys had been at war with surrounding gangs. There were rival Latinos from Santa Monica and Culver City, and black gangs everywhere else, the closest of which was the Shoreline Crips, just across their western border, one reason why most of Z's neighbors rarely went to the beach or boardwalk—to get to the ocean they had to pass through Crip country.

According to Sulcov's careful Internet research, from the fifties until the early eighties, the V-13 was known for its control of the heroin market in Los Angeles and beyond. Back then the homies lived large. It was the best and worst of times—great prosperity and constant violence. Their product, smuggled from Mexico, was a gummy, black, low-grade variety known as *chiva*, Spanish for female goat. The customers, *los pinche pendejo gringos* (whites) y *las miatas* (blacks) called it black tar. The homies wore fresh Pendleton shirts and hairnets and carefully starched and pressed khakis; they drove fancy restored Chevys and custom lowriders. After a local councilwoman was robbed at gunpoint, police assigned extra details and began cracking heads. The *Los Angeles Times* devoted a special section to the neighborhood: DEATH, DRUGS, DAILY VIOLENCE BECOME WAY OF LIFE FOR NEIGHBORHOOD. Dozens of local soldiers went to prison.

By the mid-eighties, crack had replaced heroin as the hot commodity in the shadow economy. (Black tar, meanwhile, would be supplanted by the more highly refined and potent white lady, imported from the Golden Triangle area of Southeast Asia.) The LAPD's infamously brutal and corrupt CRASH unit descended upon Venice. One twist of fate: the cocaine/crack trade was controlled by the *black* gangs—descendants of the very same addicts whose misery had financed the lifestyles of so many Mexican Americans. Except for the rare and enterprising homeboy like Sleeper, who was tough, ambitious, and charismatic enough to carve out a curb for himself, the homies were now the customers. As they said in the neighborhood: the *fedia* was in the other pocket now. And the monkey was on the other back.

More recently, rising property values seemed to be doing in Oakwood what public officials could not. Or maybe the search-and-destroy police work could be credited. Either way, streets like Abbot Kinney and Washington Boulevard, once outdoor drug bazaars, now housed chic boutiques and restaurants. Like an irradiated tumor, V-13's territory was shrinking every year. Sulcov was standing at the epicenter of what was left—old cars up on blocks in driveways, kitchen appliances discarded alongside houses, sagging rooflines, and rusty iron burglar bars. Here and there, neighbors could be seen gathered on porches and in yards. There was the look of a crisis in the body language of all.

Casually he went about shutting the doors of his car and placing Jake's athletic bag—and anything else of value—in the trunk. Though he'd been coming here for years, and though most everyone knew him very well as Z's coach and *patrón*, he could never quite shake the feeling that he didn't belong in this neighborhood, that he wasn't wanted, that he should have left five minutes ago, if not sooner.

As he neared the house, he passed a beautifully restored vintage Impala convertible, three *vatos* standing a casual guard. *I'll bet it's a '63*, Sulcov told himself. *I wonder if Jake noticed?* Years ago, on a rainy Sunday afternoon, father and son had purchased and assembled a scale model of a '63 Impala; it still had a place on Jake's bookshelf, the right back tire a little cockeyed, inexpertly set. He nodded respectfully toward the men as he passed. They looked at him with stony faces.

Sulcov entered through the front door; a delegation of Z's family members came forward and welcomed him. As usual the confines of the household were dominated by the women folk—all of them small and big at the same time, teapot shaped, short and stout. After much hugging and pressing of hands, he was escorted over to Z's mom.

Graciela Garcia was sitting in a comfortable chair in the living room. She rocked back and forth inconsolably, holding a framed publicity portrait of her eldest son, Chauncey, also known as Sleeper. To her right, in another comfortable chair, was her younger sister, the mother of Sleeper's bandmate/cousin Yogi. The third group member, Roc, was an orphan. His father had been killed long ago in a drive-by shooting; his mother died from an overdose of *chiva*. Raised from house to house, Roc's neighbors were his only kin. His photo sat on the mantle—a shot of him squatting in the visitation room at the county jail in an orange jumpsuit. A candle flickered in memoriam.

In the same fashion, Sulcov squatted and offered his hands to Z's mom, as he'd seen others do. His heart was in his throat. What can you say at the loss of a child?

Out back, the men milled around a crude fireplace in the Garcias' small backyard. If you didn't know what was going on—that two female Hispanic LAPD officers, accompanied by a Catholic chaplain, had visited the neighborhood less than two hours ago to inform *Los Vatos'* next of kin—you'd have thought you were attending a family cookout, complete with festive lantern lights strung around the yard.

Holding paper plates of beans and rice, Jake and Z joined an energetic tangle surrounding an original gangster called Big Gato. Despite his name—Spanish for cat, referencing his leonine eyes—he very much resembled a pitbull, albeit one dressed like a modern-day Venice homeboy: shin-length cutoff shorts, high black socks, bulbous skater shoes by Vans.

His given name was Higinio Fernandez. Growing up, he was best friends with Z's eldest brother, Big Juan. A large chunky customer with the same XXL frame as his hoop-star little bro, Big Juan would have been twenty-eight had he not been gunned down some years ago outside a convenience store by a rival gang member. As Yogi was to Sleeper, Big Gato was to Big Juan—a friend since the crib.

Barely an inch over five feet tall, with a shaved head and a thick handlebar moustache, Big Gato was covered with tats. "Somebody gotta be paid back," he was telling the assembled. His husky, sing-song cadence suggested the Frito Bandito. He was holding a forty-ounce bottle of malt liquor. "Sleeper and Yogi and Roc. They *hermanos*. It's up to us to revenge them." He pounded his chest with his fist three times for emphasis.

Jake remembered this this guy instantly—a full-color, Jesus-on-the-cross tattoo dominated the entire left side of his face, complete with Roman soldiers, citizen witnesses, and in the foreground, looking out beatifically, a tiny rendering of a Latina-inspired Mary Magdalene, inked to resemble his baby momma.

When the boys were about nine, the Sulcov family was at Z's for a cookout, one of many they'd attended over the years. After the sun went down, Jake and his dad ended up behind the shotgun shack belonging to Big Gato's *abuela*. There was a concrete patio illuminated by a porch light. The basket was dialed down to eight feet, common in Latino neighborhoods. A friendly game of three-on-three ensued. Sleeper, Big Gato, and another homie vs Jake and Z and Sulcov.

Talented youngsters that they were, cocky at times the way athletes can be, Jake and Z put on a little show . . . most of it at the expense of Big Gato, who had taken it upon himself to cover Jake.

Feared and respected for his rep as an old-school enforcer, Big Gato was never much given to thoughtful moderation—the reason he'd landed in prison in the first place. Discovered in the basement of a house in the middle of the night, most experienced criminals would have fled from whence they'd come, in this case a window. Fortunately, his lawyer was able to plead down the charges from attempted murder to aggravated assault.

Anyway, as the rubber match turned into a grudge game—as Big Gato continued to overcompensate for his lack of basketball skill with brute force—Jake pulled a sweet crossover and Big Gato stuck out his foot and tripped him, sending the boy sprawling on the concrete.

When Sulcov followed on the next rebound with a sharp elbow to Big Gato's solar plexus, a heated exchange ensued. The fireplug of muscle and the gawkish string bean stood toe-to-toe, cat eyes to camel face, pit bull to chameleon.

Jake was scared. *Really* scared. (But he was also proud, in the way boys can be, to know his father was his champion.)

At which point Big Gato's *abuela* came out of her back door with a large pail of cold water, threatening to cool things down.

After serving four years of an eight-year sentence—the standard deal, time off for good behavior—Big Gato had just returned to the neighborhood. Gathered around him now was a collection of neighborhood soldiers of varying ages, initiate to OG.

"How long we gonna let these *miatas* disrespect us?" Big Gato asked rhetorically. His obsessive prison yard workout regime had rendered him bigger and scarier than ever.

"They taken everything from this neighborhood. Everything, *ese*. When we was young—" He spat on the ground for emphasis. "The V-13 ruled the streets with an iron fist."

"And a pocket full of fedia," somebody said.

Everybody laughed.

Big Gato scowled. "Sleeper and them was just reaching the top of the mountain. There was nothing gonna stop *Los Vatos*. They was just about to blow up! The *miatas* killed them 'cause they couldn't handle that shit, *ese*. Just like back in the day. When *everybody* was gunning for us. Can't nobody handle no brown man getting his due."

"*Claro que si!*" somebody called out.

"Fuck the motherfuckers!"

"*Putos!*"

"Cheese eaters!"

"They act like they invented this life," Big Gato continued. "The Crips and the Bloods. *Shiiiit*. They go back, what? Ten years? Fifteen? Before crack there wasn't even no *miata* gangs—ain't that right, Pablo?" he indicated with his beer an older homie with a big belly and a gray moustache.

"Just a bunch a sorry niggers fiending for some *chiva*," Pablo laughed. His belly quaked.

Everyone cheered and chorused their approval.

Z mopped his plate with the last of his tortilla and looked abashedly at Jake.

His best buddy, after all, was half *miata*.

7

The Love That Can Have No Name

Angelika Collette paused in the doorway of her daughter's room. A sliver of light fell across Eleanor's porcelain-doll face; her fabulous golden ringlets were arranged around her head like sunbursts, the legacy of her Swiss-German daddy. No matter what Angelika thought of Christopher Stone—a loathsome plastic action-hero figurine whose skills as a man failed to live up to the promise of his packaging—she could not find fault with his genetic material. Together they'd made an absolutely gorgeous child. How this towhead came out of her was another question. Had she not been present for the birth, she might not have believed it herself.

Eleanor would soon be three. Angelika had been a single parent literally from day one. Missy filled in as birthing coach; there was no way that jerk was getting into the delivery room. He'd said he was going deep-sea fishing. His exact words: "I'll bring you back a big Blue Marlin for the wall, baby girl." (Missed warning sign: what white man calls his wife "baby girl?")

Did he think the paparazzi wouldn't follow? Had he never heard of a super-telephoto lens? Had he forgotten the helicopters circling like vultures at their wedding on Molokai?

There she was, in their condo-in-the-sky in Century City, thirty-four weeks pregnant, feeling like a watched pot.

And there he was, doing it doggy style with a nineteen-year-old stripper on the poop deck of a private yacht off the coast of Cancun . . . his primal O face beamed across the planet.

The gall! The idiocy! The utter disrespect!

ANGELIKA'S TRAGEDY, trumpeted *The Globe.*

HER BROKEN HEART, sobbed the *National Enquirer.*

STONE'S FISHY ALIBI, sniggered *The Star.*

Anonymous close friends were quoted. The usual corps of lurking paparazzi increased three-fold as the story went viral. Prescriptions for Ambien and Lunesta ordered under her name were retrieved from a pharmacy's trash bin; the fax from the prescription had not been shredded, per normal operating procedures. There was public debate about her need for rehab; there were rumors of a nervous breakdown. At one point, all daytime programming was interrupted for an O. J. Simpson–style car chase as she drove up the coast toward Ojai to visit her spiritual mentor.

As the press became ever more invasive, as further extramarital bimbos surfaced—over the course of time, Stone's cheating would be revealed to be epic; there was even a child conceived—the public seemed to step forward collectively and embrace her. America's sweetheart, round with child, had been utterly, horribly, indecently betrayed. She was hurting. The people took it personally. One commentator called it "an outpouring of pity and concern unlike any ever seen since the death of Princess Diana."

For his part, Christopher Stone was universally vilified. After a woman in a minivan pelted his vintage GTO with eggs, he went into hiding at the Hotel Chateau Marmont, the musty celebrity hideout set into the hillside above the velvet rope of the Sunset Strip.

Just as everything was dying down, the *Star* had trumped all with a grainy digital photo taken *below* the decks of the carnal yacht— apparently there was an optical monitor in the master cabin that could be accessed through the ship's onboard computer. That shot couldn't even be *shown* on television, even with censorship bars . . .

And everybody pushing her to make her usual appearances at the Grammys and the Oscars and the Golden Globes and the VMAs?

Thank Goddess, all of that was behind her now. It's true what Missy said: "You feel better one day at a time. Except on the days you don't."

Sure, maybe she should have waited a little longer. Waited for marriage. Waited to have a child. Maybe she rushed a bit, trying to create for herself the stable family she'd never had. Flush with the victories won by her own hard work—the recurring role on *Friends*, the first platinum album, the *Skag* nomination—she'd gotten a little cocky, trusted her judgment a little too far. When you're that young and everyone is telling you what you want to hear, how could it happen otherwise?

But there was no sense beating herself up . . . any further. She'd done a good job at that, thank you very much. At the end of the day, she knew that two things were true:

Out of her union with Christopher had come Eleanor, the love of her life, a little person who surprised and entranced her every single day.

Out of the ashes of her marriage had come . . . herself.

That was the key—the true lesson she'd learned. ("I Have Myself," the title track of her second album, debuted at number one on the charts.) She'd gone through this terrible disaster and had come out whole. She knew now that whatever had to be done, whatever problem came up, she was totally capable of dealing with it. Of course she wasn't perfect. But she was *working* in that direction, making tiny steps every day, moving forward. She kept reminding herself, *I am only 25 years old.*

Like Missy always said: "Life takes time. You can't know things before you know them. So give yourself a break, cupcake."

Angelika limped down the hallway into the great room, a fresh ice bag secured to her offended ankle with a bright pink ACE Bandage. Her dark chocolate velour Juicy sweatsuit complemented nicely her milk chocolate eyes. She loved the weight and feel of the material;

she always said it was like walking around naked, only better because you weren't. The little hoodie was nice too, especially on these chilly nights at the beach.

"Sorry to keep you waiting, guys," the starlet called out wanly.

Sitting on opposite ends of a large sectional sofa were her closest pals, Kisha and JamieLynn. Kisha you've already met, the confidant/makeup artist with the camo Capri pants. JamieLynn was Angelika's personal assistant and major domo, an officious Jewish girl from Birmingham, Alabama. For nearly a decade, she'd run a craft services truck with her husband—until he decided he'd rather be gay. For the last eighteen months she'd been with Angelika. Her legs were crossed, Indian style. Her sensible, nude-polished nails worked the keyboard of the Mac computer in her lap.

The western-most wall of the room was constructed entirely of glass sliders, affording a breathtaking view of the deck, the pool, the ocean. At night, a powerful spotlight on the roof illuminated the breaking waves, which crashed upon the beach with a foamy apocalyptic rumble that took some getting used to. As far as her security team could tell, her new location was still secret. But it would only be a matter of time before the paparazzi found her and she was on Star Maps again, and those chopped-top buses full of *tourons* were once again rumbling by her house—if you listened closely as they passed, you could sometimes hear them talking about you over the loudspeaker. "It's something you have to learn to live with, like a disability, only with great fringe bennies," she told the *New York Times*.

"Is that a new color from Juicy?" JamieLynn asked. Because of the noise of the ocean, you had to speak loudly to be heard.

"It's from next year's new fall line, I think," Angelika said. During the ten years she'd been working in Hollywood, the starlet had worn many show-biz hats. She'd acted and sung. She'd guest hosted, guest starred, won coveted awards. She'd built a profitable flowchart of businesses. She'd even been recognized by the Barbara Bush Foundation for her ongoing charity work with school kids around the country.

But there was one thing she was known for above all else.

It had begun with a photo taken après ski in Vail, Colorado, by a freelance photographer. Angelika had been wearing a pair of hot pink sweatpants. As was the fashion, the company's logo—JUICY—was emblazoned in four-inch-high letters across her toned and perfect posterior.

Shot from a low angle, cropped and enlarged to frame, the photo broke all records for Internet hits.

"The Ass of the Ages," trumpeted *Esquire*.

"A derriere that has launched a financial juggernaut," according to the *Wall Street Journal*.

"One of the places we'd most like to build a condo," declared the editors of *Maxim*.

As of last January, there was a sponsorship deal and a semi-permanent billboard on Sunset Boulevard. No doubt Christopher Stone passed it every day going to and from the Chateau. (Missy: "A great ass is the best revenge.")

Angelika crossed the room and retrieved her cell phone from the mantle. A gas flame danced around the ceramic logs in the fireplace. She let out an audible sigh.

"I can't believe it's almost eleven o'clock," she groaned. "This day has felt like *two* days."

Kisha yawned sardonically. "Time flies when you having fun."

Angelika pointed her carefully manicured fingernail at her trusted friend/employee. "You're sleeping over, right? Is that okay?" She turned to JamieLynn. "Did somebody make up a guest room for my girl?"

"Maria was already gone, but it got taken care of," JamieLynn said, a tad annoyed. She resented doing menial chores; she was no mere handmaiden, after all—if you wanted to see Angelika, you had to go through her. The agent, the manager, the lawyer, the nanny, the trainer . . . even Missy herself went through JamieLynn if she wanted to talk to Angelika. Her lilting, falsely friendly Southern accent evoked a plantation owner's difficult wife. Everyone in town knew of her; she had a license to bitch . . . at everyone *but* Angelika.

The mistress de la casa issued an exaggerated mommy-frown.

"Do you wanna just call it quits for tonight, JamieLynn? I know it's been a long day."

"I'm good," JamieLynn said stoically.

A tiny moth of guilt fluttered in Angelika's tummy. *Look at those bags under her eyes. She's gained back the weight—she must be hitting the chocolate again.* Angelika demanded a lot from her people, she knew that. But people demanded a lot from her. Like Missy always said, "Shit rolls downhill—either duck or get a big shovel."

"What if you come in late tomorrow?" the starlet offered. "I'm taking the day off—" she looked gravely at JamieLynn. "The day *is* cleared, correct? I'll *kill* myself if it's not cleared. "

"X-ed out on the whiteboard in the office," JamieLynn assured.

"A big, huge, monstrous, red X?"

"For all intents and purposes, tomorrow does not exist in the world of Angelika Collette."

"Planet Angelika," intoned Kisha.

Angelika dropped gingerly to her knees and began picking up Eleanor's cyclone of dolls, doll clothes and accessories. There was a large, expensive antique steamer trunk beside the fireplace. Everything lived in there. "So tell me—where are we with our charity stuff?"

JamieLynn half-stood awkwardly, holding the Mac, uncertain whether to help pick up toys or to start reading from her notes. Angelika waved a Barbie in her direction, bidding her to continue.

"We were talking about possibly looking into some ecological initiatives," JamieLynn said, resettling, "perhaps sponsoring some research. You said you were kind of interested in something more scientific since all the so-called 'touchy-feely areas' were pretty well-spoken for, including breast cancer, the rainforests, recycling, that stuff. As one subject for study, you brought up your concern that oil consumption would," and here she read from her notes verbatim, " 'cause a drastic change in the weight of the earth, thereby altering the earth's orbit around the sun.' "

"You're saying you're worried that the earth is losing too much weight?" Kisha asked.

There were plenty of airheads in Hollywood; Angelika wanted desperately *not* to be one of them. That she had dropped out of ninth grade to pursue her career in entertainment was something that haunted and shamed her; how do you command respect as a woman and a dealmaker in this industry when you haven't even graduated from high school?

To compensate, she read the *New York Times* and the *Los Angeles Times* every day online, listened to NPR, subscribed to the *Atlantic* and the *New Yorker,* TIVOed Jon Stewart and Rachel Maddow. An avid follower of current affairs, she was always happy to lend her name to a good liberal cause—twice already she'd appeared on Bill Maher's smart and cutting-edge political chat show. On the tour bus (or plane), or in her trailer on a movie set, she always had several books going. Her tastes ranged from Oprah picks—*Bee Season* and *The Kite Runner*—to more eclectic writers like Charles Bukowski, William Burroughs, Hubert Selby, Paul Bowles . . . she'd just finished *The Sheltering Sky*, which had become a movie with Debra Winger. She was considering starring in a remake—though her dermatologist had cautioned against it, citing the possibility of skin damage while on location for the required six months in Morocco.

"It just strikes me," Angelika explained, "that if we pump all the oil out of the earth and then burn it up—all those millions and billions of gallons . . . don't they weigh a lot? Doesn't burning all the petroleum—converting it from a liquid state to a gaseous state—mean that the earth itself becomes lighter? Liquids are heavy. Have you ever carried a big bucket of water? My grandmother had a well pump in the back yard. If the earth is lighter, isn't that going to effect our orbit? The sun's gravity would start pulling us closer, right? Maybe *that* has something to do with global warming—we're getting slowly pulled into the sun. It seems so *obvious*. Why don't you ever hear anyone discussing it?"

". . . pulling us closer to the sun," JamieLynn repeated gravely, fingernails clicking.

"Have you started smoking pot again?" Kisha laughed. Her plump lips formed a smirk. She was supposedly Angelika's closest confidant, but JamieLynn thought she always sounded a little mean. Each sentence she uttered, each random passing comment, seemed to conclude with an extra, unspoken clause, something along the lines of *you spoiled white bitch.*

"I'm supposed to come up with an idea for a foundation," Angelika explained, somewhat defensively. She, too, sometimes wondered about Kisha's attitude. She tended to go a bit far with her policy of keepin it real.

"I'm *just kidding*," Kisha protested, issuing a saccharine smile.

Angelika's scalp tingled. According to a clever piece she'd read somewhere—was it in *Talk of the Town?*—"just kidding" was "perhaps the most insincere phrase commonly uttered in polite company, usually meaning the exact opposite—*I'm not kidding at all.*" She deposited the last of the toys into the chest. Eleanor would have a fit if something was put away in the wrong place; that little girl was the true mistress of the household.

Angelika let the top slam, perhaps a bit too loudly. "Foundation ideas," she said, refocusing her little group. "What else do we have on the list?"

JamieLynn: "Water wells for African villages."

"I like that one," Angelika said, plopping down on the sectional.

"Except for the fact that *everybody* is doing something for Africa these days," Kisha said in a contrite voice, trying to contribute meaningfully. "You've got Madonna, Angelina and Brad, Paul Simon. The list goes on. I think I read something about Alyssa Milano being appointed some kind of UN special envoy to Africa."

"I heard about that," Angelika said.

"It was on ET," JamieLynn confirmed, ever on top of the Hollywood dirt. In practical terms, her network of peers were perhaps more powerful than the stars for which they worked.

Angelika: "What about all the invisible rays and stuff?"

"Rays and stuff?" JamieLynn ventured.

Kisha studied her nails.

"Microwaves. Telephone signals. Radar. Every different remote control and phone and Wi-Fi device is sending out waves or rays into the atmosphere, right? It's all around us everywhere, every day, passing though our bodies. I mean, doesn't that freak you out just a little bit? How can that be good for us?

"Like x-rays. Those aren't healthy. You have to wear that lead apron. Or when you drive by the cell phone towers and your car radio goes all *kaflooie*. Or people who live under those electric towers. They get cancer all the time. And people who shave their heads with electric razors. Some people think electromagnetic energy causes cancer. There have been studies, but nothing that pulls everything together."

"I think I *did* read something about that," JamieLynn said thoughtfully.

"What about cell phone cancer?" Angelika said. "My girlfriend from elementary school . . . her husband? He was some kind of medical supplies salesman. Always on his cell phone. Always his left ear. And then he ends up with these inoperable malignant tumors . . . on the left side of his brain. It was a nightmare. They tried to sue the company—Sprint or Verizon, one of the big providers, I can't remember which—but it never went anywhere. They couldn't prove anything."

Kisha: "Can you imagine the chaos if they did?"

"What should I write?" JamieLynn asked. "Cell phone cancer? Microwaves and stuff?"

"Write 'find the smoking cell phone!' " laughed Kisha.

JamieLynn started typing.

"Do *not* write that, JamieLynn!" Angelika ordered. The three women dissolved into laughter.

Angelika sat on a barstool in the pool house, scrolling through the backlog of e-mails on her phone.

The place was done in a beachcomber theme, with a fully stocked wet bar and faux thatched palapas. The flat screen TV on the wall had a series of smaller, picture-in-picture screens lining the bottom—security cams set at various locations around the property. Because the lot was terraced down the hill, from the Pacific Coast Highway to the ocean, part of the pool house was actually lower than the pool itself. High on the back wall, behind the bar, there was a large aquarium window, round and distorting like a fish-eye lens; through it you could watch the human swimmers romp. A prefab circular stairway provided access from poolside to this room at ground level. A sliding glass door opened onto the beach. The curtains were pulled.

A knuckle rap on glass: confident, rhythmic, upbeat.

Angelika checked the security screens. In one of them could be seen a black man with cornrows, wearing a motorcycle jacket. He cradled a full-faced helmet like a football in the crook of one arm.

She pressed a button and the curtains opened. The slider was not so easy. Sun and salt water had corroded the track.

Together they muscled open the door.

"May I help you, sir?" she asked cordially.

Chilly T. Neegrow issued a large, pearly, Ultrabright smile.

"I see you left your choppers at home," she said, delighted.

He stepped inside, muscled the slider shut. The curtains remained open.

"You parked in the public lot?"

"Stealth, baby. "

"And walked all this way in the sand?"

"One point two miles, according to my GPS." He pulled back the sleeve of the jacket to reveal a large watch equipped with a navigational system. It wasn't on the market yet; the manufacturer had sent it for him to test, hoping for an endorsement.

She pointed to his white Jordan sneakers and issued her mommy pout. "You got your Js all *sandy.*"

"I stand before you a humble man, in dirty kicks."

Laughing musically, she grabbed a handful of his jacket and pulled him toward her.

8

Going the Extra Mile

One point two miles north of Planet Angelika, Calvin Scott from *StarNews* parked his rented Chevy Malibu. The marine layer had descended like a thick damp blanket; emerging from the driver's seat he felt instantly cold and wet. He checked his work satchel one last time. The tools of the modern journo: Mini videocam, mini night vision cam, digital voice recorder, long-range listening device, cell phone. Also included were a notebook and a pen. He never used either; it just felt right to bring them along.

Scott locked the doors of the car and headed across the public lot, toward the Ducati Monster sitting vulnerably beneath a streetlamp. No mere mortal would abandon to the elements a motorcycle as fine as this. Rare and expensive, Italian made, its bulbous gas tank and sleek exposed tubular chassis brought to mind the muscular, found-art vehicles in the postapocalyptic movie classic *Mad Max*. The brand was popular among Hollywood cognoscenti, guys like Brad Pitt and George Clooney, who found the speed and maneuverability of two wheels, along with the anonymity of a full-face helmet, to be one answer to the problem of free passage around town. Chill was well known for his collection of custom, racing, and antique bikes. A special episode of *Cribs* had been devoted to his stable of high-performance machinery—housed in a real stable, a replica of an English barn he'd ordered built on the grounds of his Agoura Hills estate.

Drawing from the well of insider information gathered over the course of his time embedded within Chill's camp, Scott's initial news reports about the "assassination attempt" on the mogul—the first bits uploaded as bulletins to the *StarNews* website from a stall in the men's toilet at RAP Records—had beat to smithereens any and all competition. His footage from the crime scene went immediately into worldwide syndication.

Even so, the powers at *StarNews* were not pleased.

His employers had negotiated for nearly a year to obtain access to Chill's inner world. There were contracts, givebacks, caveats, promises—it was a huge *get* for the organization; a lot of resources had been marshalled. (And it was a huge get for Scott, whose main qualification turned out to be his availability; he wasn't exactly anyone's first choice.) But as it happened, right before the dustup with *Los Vatos* went down, Scott had gone AWOL from his post—he'd slipped out of Chill's office to go see his film agent, hoping to rekindle several projects he had in turnaround, one of the more vainglorious objectives in Hollywood.

Managing, meanwhile, to miss the real prize—what foreign correspondents call the Bang Bang Footage.

Not to mention the meat of the story: what really happened in Chill's office?

Scott hadn't visited the LA bureau since yesterday's shooting, but his immediate boss, his assigning editor, had been frosty on the phone. The editor in chief, back in New York, was quoted as being "hugely disappointed." And so up the line to the publisher, who'd labeled Scott's story a "dry hump" and asked someone to take a look at Scott's expense accounts. In a company that placed high value on teamwork (one way to get more from your employees and pay less), it was perceived that Scott had let everyone down—every employee of the entire publishing/broadcasting/entertainment conglomerate that owned *StarNews*. Had he not been their best source inside the Chill camp, irreplaceable at this point, Scott would probably be out on his ass.

Truly, no one was more disappointed about this turn of events than Scott himself.

Working in LA always presented a challenge. Twice divorced, he had the usual human frailties and financial needs. Like a junkie driving past an old hook spot, the minute he'd arrive in Tinseltown, his motor would begin to run, his teeth would gnash. Everywhere he looked he could see possibility: The houses! The cars! The food! The women! The umbrella deals! Once you trade a six-page magazine article for a seven-figure Hollywood paycheck, as he had some years earlier, you're forever doomed to feeling like you're working for minimum wage.

How else to explain his ridiculous compulsion to leave Chill's inner sanctum to go visit his agent? It's not like he had any new product to discuss; there was nothing saleable on the horizon (his Chill assignment was work-for-hire; he would own the rights to nothing). Nobody was going to lift a finger to hawk his backpack full of slightly used properties and lapsed options.

With the economy taking a dump, the screenwriters on strike, newspapers dying all across the nation, the value of the printed word itself seemingly teetering on the brink, this was not the time to fuck up a primo assignment. It was only by stroke of luck that he'd arrived back into the RAP offices just before the police had begun shutting the building down.

Humbled by the devastation wrought by his own hubris, determined to win himself back into the good graces of management (and perhaps to rediscover some modicum of self-respect), Scott had canceled a previously scheduled dinner with a reality show producer and made the forty-minute trek out the 101 Freeway to Chill's mansion. From his time spent with the mogul, he knew that Chill often enjoyed late-night rides on one of his motorcycles. "Clearing the seeds out the melon" is how he'd described it. A private road led from the motor stables to a gate at the back of the property. The landscaped concealment was appropriately ingenious, modeled after a secret gate in one of the Batman movies. Had Chill not taken him there to show it off, Scott would have never found it.

Now it was after midnight and he was standing in a public parking lot in Malibu next to Chill's beautiful Ducati, feeling reinforced . . . and lucky to be alive—tailing a racing-caliber motorcycle at high speeds on winding roads in a rental car, while not arousing suspicion, was not an accomplishment to be underrated.

In front of him stretched a public beach. Multimillion-dollar houses led away in either direction. He wished he hadn't left his Kangol cap in the car—for a moment he thought about retrieving it; he knew if he allowed himself to walk back and open the car door he might drive away. More than once before at similar crossroads, he'd lost his stomach for this kind of task.

Because the motorcycle was parked at the south end of the sand-swept asphalt, Scott elected to head south. Removing his Tod's brown suede loafers—they'd cost nearly four hundred bucks with shipping—he set off down the beach.

9

The Nurturing Elbow of the Sectional Sofa

Sulcov, lids heavy, melted into the nurturing elbow of the white leather sectional sofa that dominated his great room. Lakers postgame highlights played on Fox Sports West.

On the coffee table: One cardboard pizza box, lid agape, partially eaten crusts remaindered like cigarette butts. Two cans of Diet Coke, one crushed. A fifth of Knob Creek bourbon, the dusty gift box with garish stick-on ribbon discarded on the floor. One highball glass, greasy fingerprints, half full.

Tish's arrival was heralded by the rusty, horror-house squeal of the garage door opening, the frame bent by a contractor some years ago and never properly repaired. High heels click-clacked across the wood-plank floor. The cable box said 12:32.

She was dressed in a classic black Hervé Léger V-neck bandage dress and a vintage denim jacket, the collar flipped jauntily. She'd always had an eclectic, thrown-together sense of style—tonight she looked like someone who'd been out on a swank dinner date but decided at the last minute to dress down a notch by throwing on this old thing, found buried beneath some gift bags and yoga clothes in the cargo space of her Land Rover. Her hair was slicked back into a tight, sophisticated braid the way he liked—here and there a kinky wisp betrayed her perfectionist's eye.

"You're still up?" There was a distant, accusatory tone in her voice.

He indicated the box. "I brought us home a pizza for dinner." His own tone bespoke a lingering and bitterly unrequited eagerness to please someone who historically didn't really seem to want to be pleased.

"You're using the good crystal?"

He picked up his glass and took a slug. "I went down to Martini's. You didn't answer my call."

With business-like efficiency she removed her Blackberry from her Prada clutch and tapped out a four-number passcode.

"Since when do you have a password on your phone?"

A beat. "Since forever." Eyes still focused on the screen, thumb scrolling. "You don't have one?"

"Another thing I didn't know I needed."

"What if somebody gets hold of your contacts?"

Everything felt a little fuzzy. He didn't often drink. *Who would want my contacts?* "Could you show me how? Can you even do it on this shitty flip phone?" He held out his cell impotently in her direction.

She raised her blue eyes from her device and met his interrogatory with a look of utter . . . *something.* It was like she was staring straight at him but he wasn't there. Or she wasn't there. Like she'd suddenly vacated the conversation, retreated to a safe harbor behind her pleasant face to wait out a looming storm of unpleasantness.

From the moment he'd seen her at *NewsSource,* this fabulous leggy intern from USC everyone was talking about, Sulcov was dead meat.

Not much older than she, a former intern himself—the fabled one who'd actually landed a job at the end of his term—Sulcov had become her go-to guy in a crisis, that perfect work buddy you could always count on. Many an afternoon they'd made a therapeutic Starbucks run and dished endlessly about the other staffers. After he helped engineer her first feature assignment, they pulled an all-nighter together on the eve of her deadline; tenderly he'd inspected and polished each word and paragraph. Surely there'd been no sunrise in his life more invigorating and bittersweet than the one that morning, the first rays of humid light penetrating the window of her sublet near Columbus Circle.

Their newsroom friendship, despite any sparks or undertones, had been properly chaste, following the letter of human resource guidelines. And of course, the longer he knew her, the more beautiful and rare and marvelous she seemed—the more he wanted her fuck her brains out. As the days of summer wore on, he could think of little else. For her part, she seemed totally oblivious—of both her appeal and of his interest. Either that or she was playing him like a banjo. Or some combination of both, more likely—what man ever had a clue? He started to feel a little like the writer in *Breakfast at Tiffany's*. Many times during the torturous duration of their strange noncourtship he'd wondered: *does she think I'm gay?*

Now Tish held up her cell triumphantly, turned the glowing face in his direction. "See? 'Hubby. 6:37.' I guess I didn't hear it. We were having girls' night at Jill's."

"Goat cheese and prosciutto with basil," he chided, gesturing with the glass toward the pizza box. "Your *fave*."

She gave him her best cocktail party smile, a toothy display of warmth and engagement she could summon at will—something else that came to her naturally, like her devastating backhand. More and more lately you could find her in the society pages of the *LA Times* or *Flaunt* or *Los Angeles*. (On those rare occasions when he was pictured at her side, Sulcov always appeared deranged, his mouth akimbo, deformed by the consummation of some clever sentence or passed finger food at the momentous snap of the aperture.)

"I'm sure it was *yummie*," she said, a tone of voice usually reserved for Jake.

He drained his glass. "I always wonder what you girls have to babble about for so long. When I eat out with Bave, I'm home in, like, two hours, tops. That's *with* dessert and coffee."

"Jill always has the music blaring. The house is *totally* wired. There are monitors and speakers *every*where. Even in the *bathrooms*. Jake would love it. It's like you're in a club! You know how you can feel the base rumbling? It kind of made me sick to my stomach. I had to take a Dramamine."

"Subwoofers," Sulcov offered. "They can mess with your equilibrium."

On the last Saturday of her *NewsSource* internship, her Manhattan sojourn officially expired, her bags nearly all packed, Tish had finally agreed to an *official* date with her quote unquote best new friend in New York.

Sulcov chose a sunset cruise around Manhattan on the touristy Circle Line. Late August in the city was hot and rank; the boat proved the perfect respite, providing as it did its own breeze, its own bar, and its own colorfully ironic tableaux of hayseeds and Asians upon which to train their shared verbal acuity. Not to mention the perfect orange sunset, followed by a romantic full moon. Even nature seemed to be pulling for him.

Upon disembarking at Pier 83, drunk on two-for-one margaritas and now-or-never *joie de vivre*, she pulled him into a dark alley off West 42nd Street and took him hungrily.

At that moment, Sulcov's life changed.

Am I really inside this gorgeous creature?

He became a guy who could have the most coveted woman in the office against a grimy brick wall in a dark alley in the greatest city on earth.

A guy who could marry into a wealthy and well-connected African American family, father a biracial child, take a leave of absence from his respectably important job in journalism and move to Hollywood on a whim. A guy who could create and write an Emmy- and Golden Globe-winning show—albeit without proper credit. A guy who could build for himself a seemingly fairy-tale existence— cool castle, gorgeous queen, talented prince, copasetic lifestyle . . . complete with year-round blue sky, the sound of the waves to lull him to sleep at night.

And while the sex never again reached that pinnacle (or even came close, years of therapy notwithstanding), over time they'd settled into a comfortable and seemingly successful union.

In the same way that some people dance together wonderfully, Nathan and Letitia Harris Sulcov had a knack for simply *being* together. She was a great talker; he was a great listener—plus he never got tired of looking at her. Say what you might, it made him feel like a god to be married to such a head-turner (even as it reminded him every day of his own failure to turn *her* head).

Generally, they shared the same tastes and sensibilities; upon this friendly foundation they'd built a life. They each had gainful work to satisfy their individual souls; their co-ownership of Jake provided gravity and cement. That Nathan's particular variety of male ego wasn't the type threatened by his wife's financial hegemony was perhaps one of the reasons she eventually chose him—there were a lot of smooth operators and gold diggers out there; he was never very materialistic. Frankly, he was relieved *not* be the one in charge . . . or ultimately to be the one who had to be fiscally responsible.

At their wedding, Sulcov had noted to the gathering that his bride was a woman with whom he could happily share three meals a day and still look forward to the next breakfast.

And thus it went.

The years passed.

Friendly but tepid, workmanlike at times, it was a comfortable love, but not the storybook kind—a transient hug with a peck on the lips. Certainly it was not the marriage he'd envisioned when he got down on one knee.

About a year ago, Tish had helped found The Sisters, a group of young black women, most from family money, many native to Baldwin Hills. They aimed to be a junior league for African Americans, spreading good works and liberal influence. In addition there was the excitement of Barack Obama's historic run for the presidency—the women had a direct pipeline to potential First Sister Michelle Obama. With Obama in the White House, there was no telling where and how the group's considerable talents and resources might yet be needed.

Owing to her selection as founding chair, Tish lately had been gone frequently from the household, attending to all manner of fabulous and urgent affairs at all hours. When she was at home, she seemed distant and annoyed, preoccupied with her cell phone. Combined with the crisis of the writers' strike, it had been a particularly stressful time for the couple.

"The boy asleep?" she inquired.

"He's at Z's—there's been some bad news."

"On a school night?"

She walked over to the dining table and set down her clutch, stepped out of her shapely Brian Atwood pumps—the height adjustment to her stocking feet was always jarring, no matter how many times he witnessed it.

She let one hand linger on the polished wood surface, as if to ground herself. She'd never been comfortable with her son "hanging around those gangbangers"; for years she'd been waiting anxiously for her I-told-you-so moment to come.

Through the decades in the Southland, the *beaners* and the *miatas* had never been good at getting along. To some extent, the willingness of Latinos to work hard at menial jobs for chump change was an affront to the African American community's sense of cultural entitlement—descended from roots of kidnapping and enslavement, they figured they'd already paid their dues. The contempt ran openly in both directions in a state that was, by now, nearly 40 percent Latino and less than 10 percent black. Even as the Sulcovs exchanged their familiar pleasantries in their high-ceilinged great room—the money for which could be traced in part to the rents of uncountable illegals over the years who occupied her father's rental properties— the fate of Obama's campaign rested partially on the broad and long-suffering shoulders of the Latino vote . . . much of which was partial to Hillary Clinton at the moment.

"Remember when Jake was freaking out about the assassination attempt on Chill? It turns out the members of a rap group were responsible."

"What does this have to do with sleepovers on a school night?"

"Can you let me explain, please?"

"I really hope this hip-hop thing is just a phase with Jake-y. He keeps asking if he can download the *explicit* versions of songs. And

I'm just really opposed. All those *bitches* and *hos*. It's soooo misogynist. It's an affront to women. I just can't *allow* that in my home."

Sulcov didn't bother mentioning that he'd authorized Jake to use his debit card to buy whatever songs he wanted.

"So . . . the *assassination* attempt," he reminded her.

She rolled her eyes.

"I know! Can you believe the media is calling it that? A term usually reserved for heads of state. Remember Herb Denton at *NewsSource?* That time he—"

Her phone vibrated; her attention was drawn immediately to the screen. Tap tap tap. *Send*. "So what about Chilly T?"

"Oh my God!" Sulcov's eyes saucered. "Don't EVER call him that! The artist has evolved—"

"Into a shill for Target," she said flatly.

"Shillin n Chillin," he joked.

Another text. She looked at her phone. Tap tap tap. *Send*. "Is this gonna be a synopsis or a miniseries?"

His Joe Friday voice: "The perps were allegedly three members of a Mexican American rap group called *Los Vatos*."

"And?"

"*Los Vatos* is Sleeper's group."

"And Sleeper is?"

"Z's older brother?"

"Not the one who was killed a few years ago?"

"The second oldest. The one you used to say was the *handsome* one."

"With the widow's peak?"

"Yessss." *How can you not know this stuff?* "According to news reports, Sleeper and two of his Venice homeboys attacked Chill in his office with an automatic weapon."

"Oh my God!"

"All three were killed at the scene by Chill's bodyguards."

"*And Jake is sleeping over there?*"

"He's with his best friend who just lost his only remaining brother."

"What if there's another shooting? Won't there be . . . whatever you call it. Retribution?"

"*Payback?*"

Her voice rose in panic. "A drive-by shooting or *whateverthemotherfuck!* We need to get him out of there—at once!"

"He's fine. He's safe. Don't worry. The whole neighborhood is crawling with cops," he lied.

10

Is That a Mag in Your Pocket Or...

Detective Kenyatta Ducksworth pulled up in his black Crown Vic—has ever a variety of unmarked police vehicle been more obvious?—and parked in front of the entrance to the glass-and-steel, mixed-use high-rise that was crowned by RAP Records.

Despite the late hour, the curb lane was still cordoned off with yellow crime scene tape. A Mardi Gras atmosphere prevailed. The sidewalk, which itself constituted one tributary of the Hollywood Walk of Fame, was thronged with tourists and media; they in turn had attracted the usual multicell parasites—a fire eater, a David Blaine-inspired card sharp, an adorable homeless hippie girl, a one-armed vet. A legless man wearing leather pantaloons dragged himself from star to star, polishing the inlaid brass and scraping the chewing gum off marble. Joanne Dru. Fred Niblo. Bronco Billy Anderson . . . Once upon a time, they were household names.

Ducksworth nodded to the patrol officer on duty in the lobby and took the elevator to the top floor. Another officer was stationed outside RAP's suite of offices. Inside, the flat screen was black; there was trash scattered across the lobby. Several large sheets of plywood were sitting on the floor beside the reception desk, ready to be deployed on the broken windows. Ducksworth put a shoulder to the door of Chill's inner sanctum. As it opened the wind howled, stirring paper goods and dust.

Behind Chill's bulletproof desk, a thin man was worrying with something in the wall. He turned to face Ducksworth.

"So what's so important it couldn't wait till morning?" Ducksworth asked.

Colin Wee was the youngest forensic scientist on the staff. One half of his head was shaved. The hair on the other half was worn in a single pigtail. It gave him the look of a demented cheerleader.

A former Berkeley pre-med, Wee played bass in an electro/punk band called BrokenGlass HandJob. It was typical of him to get overly excited about a case; usually he'd wait until work hours to call. He checked his retro digital watch, the face of which was worn inward on his wrist. His central valley up-speak was rounded at the edges with the diphthongs of his Taiwanese immigrant parents, who owned a restaurant in Modesto. "The crime scene gets released back to the occupants at oh-seven hundred," he explained. "I wanted you to see this before I had to break it down."

"I thought you guys were all done in here." Ducksworth yawned. He'd been ready for bed when Wee called; only at the gym would he normally allow himself to be seen in sweatpants, lacking a shave. Fortunately, his Fairfax neighborhood was only minutes away.

"They authorized overtime. Even put a rush on ballistics."

"That's what happens when you're the entertainment at the mayor's inaugural ball." Ducksworth checked his large and fancy chronograph, another measure of the modern man—the size and cost of his watch. He'd promised himself a good night's sleep. Clearly that wasn't going to happen. "How long is this gonna take?"

"It'll be worth it, I promise."

In each bullet hole, Wee had placed something that appeared to be a standard writing implement—felt tip pens?

"Pen-*lights*," Wee corrected.

"Okay. Pen-*lights*. What's the deal?"

"The TEC-9 we recovered had a mag that holds thirty-two rounds. Actually, let me back up. What was used was not actually a TEC-9. The model was renamed TEC-DC9 in 1982, after it was first banned from production in this country."

"That's semi-auto, correct?"

"It can be converted to auto, but you have to do it yourself. There's no factory kit. Not many are converted. You find some now and then."

"Like this one, I take it. No way a semi-auto made this mess."

Idly, Wee twirled his ponytail around his finger. "Weapon of choice of Dylan Klebold," Wee said.

"The Columbine kid? I've seen plans for a TEC on the fuckin Internet. Build it yourself. It doesn't look complicated."

"This one was definitely store-bought."

"Did you trace it to anybody interesting?"

"I have no clue where it came from."

He was expecting a different answer. "No clue?"

"Personally, I don't think our *vatos* even *had* a TEC-DC9 when they walked into this room."

Ducksworth's brows knitted. *This freak is making no sense.*

Wee held up a finger—begging a moment of indulgence. He continued around the room, turning on, one by one, the laser pen-lights that were stuffed into the bullet holes, fiddling with each, making sure the angle of the pen matched the angle of the bullet's entry. Finally, he was done. He crossed to the door and doused the overheads.

The room went black. The city lights cast the two men in a faint ambient glow.

"Check it out!" Wee said triumphantly.

All of the laser beams were pointing to a single area in the corner of the room, ten feet north of the doorway.

"Wow," Ducksworth said, at once stumped and impressed. "So you're saying that someone standing in that corner sprayed the room with the TEC."

"Look at the pattern. Everybody knows the TEC is a hard gun to control. It's so short. It's hard to brace. That's basically why it never caught on for military use."

"Popular on the streets, though. Have you ever heard one? Sounds like a fucking mini-Gatling gun."

"I've read about instances where a mag gets emptied on a street corner and nobody even catches a bullet. See how the holes line up evenly across the wall? You never see that in a firefight. If you ask me, it looks more like somebody intentionally sprayed a line of bullets around the room. See what I mean?"

It did appear to be so.

Ducksworth: "All of the slugs recovered were from the TEC?"

"We recovered twenty-eight slugs—twenty-eight penlights. Twenty-nine if you count that one in the ceiling up there, a ricochet—it probably hit the desk and bounced. The last three rounds went out the windows with the glass. Two are unaccounted for. The third ended up in the brain of that poor lawyer dude across the street. "

"Ballistics confirmed?"

"We now have a *quadruple* homicide."

Ducksworth turned and looked out the broken window, across Vine Street. Damon Edwards, forty-six, a managing partner at McComb, Frankel, and Edwards, had been on the telephone, talking to a client. From where they were standing, they could see Edwards' twenty-eighth-story window. It was already boarded up.

"Talk about a bad day."

Removing an extra penlight from his breast pocket, Wee lit a path through the darkened room and switched on the overheads.

"What about the ballistics on the bodyguards?" Ducksworth asked.

"Between them, only *four* rounds were expended."

"Four?"

"Two bullets each," Wee confirmed. He pointed across the room to the space between the sofa and Chill's desk, where the bodies had been found. "Garcia—the body in the middle? Known as Sleeper? He gets tapped twice in the forehead. *Bang, bang.* The other two *Vatos* take one bullet each, also in the forehead."

"Four clean shots to the forehead?"

"Yup."

Ducksworth hummed appreciatively.

"And check *this* out: the slugs extracted from Garcia's brain came from two different guns.

"What do you get from that?"

"Seems more like target practice than a firefight."

"What do *you* think happened?"

Wee stood a moment, twirling his ponytail, gathering his thoughts. He was the baby of his family, the only son. His parents couldn't understand this detour into forensics; he was supposed to have become a doctor, achieve status, marry a suitable wife, support his parents in their dotage. His disobedience was anathema in his ancestor-worshipping society; his odd hairstyle was a family disgrace—his parents knew nothing of his black girlfriend or BrokenGlass HandJob, though he amused himself sometimes imagining himself translating the name into Mandarin. His three sisters, miserably married to older and diffident Taiwanese professionals, secretly cheered him on.

"Something happens, you know, something jumps off, and the *Vatos* make a move," Wee said, reconstructing. You could tell he loved his trade, a huge puzzle to solve, a game of wits. "And *boom*, both bodyguards act on instinct and open fire. According to the autopsy, the shots hit Garcia almost simultaneously. Otherwise, the bullets would have had different angles of entry."

"So you're saying, if one bullet hit him first, he'd be falling down—"

"Exactly. They had to have both fired at almost exactly the same time. And then, before anybody can make another move," he formed his thumbs and index fingers into two guns. "*Bang. Bang.* Each bodyguard takes out his mirror homeboy. Ballistics backs it up."

"What about the chrome 9 mm that was recovered?"

"It has Garcia's fingerprints only."

"But it was unloaded."

"Correct. They found the clip—"

"In his pants pocket, I know. I'm the one who found it."

"Ballistics said it hasn't been fired."

"Which leads me to my next big question: who comes to a rumble unloaded?"

"Is that a mag in your pocket or are you just happy to see me?" Wee said in a husky voice, doing Mae West.

"And for sure no fingerprints on the TEC?"

"Nothing useable. Usual smudgy wipe-down. None of the vics showed any signs of residue on their hands or clothes, either."

"No residue? On none of them?"

"Nope."

"No fuckin way."

"*Waa-aay*," Wee sang gleefully. "And take a look at those two bar chairs." He indicated a pair of barstools flanking Chill's desk.

"Supposedly the bodyguards were sitting in them when *Los Vatos* entered the office and commenced firing . . . *from the doorway.*"

"Correct. But look at the bullet holes behind each chair."

"Behind . . . and just above. If they'd been sitting there—"

"*Exactly.*"

"—they'd be toast."

"Not small targets, those guys."

"So while being sprayed with TEC fire but somehow avoiding getting hit, the two bodyguards managed to kill *three* guys with only *four* bullets."

Wee shrugged. "As they were jumping over the sofa?"

PART TWO

11

Learning Again How to Sleep in the Middle of the Bed

Swaddled in successive layers of Egyptian cotton, Scottish cashmere, Canadian goose down and New Zealand shearling, Angelika Collette greeted the new day—a cozy lump in the center of her huge new California king mattress.

The air in the room was damp and cool; the smell of him was still on her. She hugged an extra pillow. Bits and flashes of last night returned. It was nearly dawn when Chill had left. She'd been careful to lock the slider and close the curtain before making her way back upstairs to her bedroom. She tried to remember the last time she felt this way. So relaxed, so perfectly at ease.

So perfectly perfect.

After her separation from Christopher, it had taken some time to learn again how to sleep in the middle of the bed. He was a huge slab of a man, a weight lifter and a martial artist with a thick football player's neck, veins bulging everywhere. During their marriage, he'd insisted upon a heavily carved, circa-fourteenth-century, four-poster monstrosity—a family heirloom kept in storage for decades. It is a historical fact that people were smaller back then; even after a craftsman was hired at a dear price to re-engineer the frame, it still wasn't big enough for the two of them. If Christopher wasn't trying to smother her within his heavy embrace—his limbs carefully denuded and lotioned to a point of moist saturation—he was sprawled expansively, snoring (a deviated septum), taking up the most possible space, leaving her clinging to the tiny strip of territory at the very edge of her side. (The left side. The side she *hated, hated, hated* for every minute of their marriage.)

All of that was behind her now. She had a new bed all to herself (unless she desired otherwise), and pretty much a whole new existence, new parameters and new rules and new expectations for herself—a fresh surface on which to sketch. Or maybe her life was best viewed, at twenty-five, as more of an oil painting-in-progress, with parts of the canvas continually undergoing revision. The old colors were still there, beneath the new, contributing to the contours. They just didn't show anymore.

She floated on the surface of wakefulness like a woman on a large raft—a woman at the very center of her own large raft. As the minutes passed, as the earth turned imperceptibly, as Angelika breathed deeply and stretched and ruminated . . . the whole of the sun's burning yellow disk came to fill the center of the skylight's happy plastic bubble, which acted as a lens, projecting the solar energy downward, bathing the megastarlet in a shaft of honest-to-God golden light.

She stretched her arms and legs to the four corners of the bed, Leonardo's Vitruvian Woman—safe, warm, naked, and freshly rested in the soft expanse of the eight hundred–thread-count sheets. For a moment, she imagined herself to be a McDonald's apple pie, warm and crispy beneath the heat lamps. The notion of X-ing days off her calendar, of putting her own sanity before the increasing demands of so many others, was something else new in her life. In her self-directed readings, she'd recently come across an item about Andy Grove, the billionaire founder of chipmaker Intel. When asked to tell the most important thing he'd ever learned, he'd said, "How to say no."

When she read that quote, lights and buzzers and sirens went off.

Along with her other areas of interest, Angelika was a big reader of biographies; according to the inventory list in JamieLynn's office, there were twenty-seven boxes of books in the library of the new house yet to be unpacked. She'd made a study of successful women in history, particularly the tragic divas: Judy Garland, Marilyn Monroe, Whitney Houston, Liza Minnelli (Judy's daughter, go figure). From Josephine Baker to Britney Spears, one thing was pretty obvious to Angelika: none of those women had *ever* learned how to properly say no.

Swept into the whirlwind of career, commitment, and obligation, what they did instead was find ways to incapacitate themselves—to remove themselves incidentally from the game. They acted out with sex, with alcohol, with drugs. If you're too fucked up, you don't have to find the courage to say no—the dope says it for you. You can't sing when you're passed out in your dressing room. Or when you refuse do to your community service hours and end up in jail. Or when you make working so difficult that nobody wants to hire you anymore. As Missy liked to say, "Success is like standing in a field watching a sunset—it's the most beautiful time of day, but it's also the time of day when all the bugs come out."

City to city, hotel to hotel, interview to commercial shoot to concert venue to film location . . . you're flying along the tracks, you're harnessed in, you can't get off the ride, you're at the mercy of forces much larger than yourself. There's no clock or calendar. You're living in your own world, a place where everyone around you does anything you ask—your stable of enablers. Every time you look in the mirror, someone has changed your hairstyle and your makeup, has put you in a weird outfit. You think, *who is this person staring back at me?*

Unless *you* take control. Unless you learn how to say *no*. Unless you order your assistant to put a big X through an entire day on your calendar of events once in a while, a day to sleep late, to bum around, to eat some highly fattening foods. To take some time, as her spiritual adviser had advised, to acknowledge her blessings.

No matter what happened from now on, no matter what mishaps or missteps or misdeeds might occur—she'd been ready for the other shoe to drop since day one—Angelika could say unequivocally that she'd made a big success of her life. It's hard to describe how it feels to be so young and to have already accomplished your life's goals. On the one hand, it can be crushing—whatever do you do for an encore? But on the other hand, she had nothing more to prove to *anyone*. The fear was gone. The onus was off. Looking forward, she knew she could handle whatever came her way. Certainly she'd been through the worst of it.

She swam across the cold unoccupied territory of the sheets toward her night table (on the right side of the bed!) and touched a button on a remote control. The blackout curtains rose from a bank of windows, revealing the blue Pacific. She stacked her pillows, propped herself in a queenly position, powered up her Blackberry. Absently she watched a flock of pelicans flying south together in a perfect V formation.

12

Soweto South of Pico

Chill was kicked back in one of three Herman Miller Aeron chairs set side by side in front of the mixing console in the largest of three recording studios at RAP Records. His fingers were interlocked behind his head; the overhead spots lit up his hundred K smile and a good bit of the surrounding airspace. Nobody could tell he was wearing his spare grills, stored in the office safe.

On the other side of the thick, soundproof glass was a colorful new group called Artificial Intelligence. There were three of them— two were sixteen; the leader was eighteen. The eldest was front and center, standing behind a mic. The two younger boys occupied bar stools, one on either side. Each had his own mic, too.

The trio had met and formed at a school for homeless children, products of the late-century boomlet of crack babies born in the unfortunate region stretching roughly from Pico Boulevard to Long Beach (an area known by some residents as Soweto South of Pico). Their expression of style suggested the mélange of cultures encountered as they'd made their way through the opaque intestines of California's child welfare system—lollipop afros with bleached blond chunks, Goth facial piercings, labyrinthine tribal tattoos, ultra-skinny jeans, Vans skater shoes.

"You *hate* this record," protested the eldest. His body language suggested his immediate desire to launch himself through this plate glass cage and attack his tormentor.

Chill leaned forward and pressed a button, spoke into a telescoping mic. The lighting and his model-quality bone structure combined to give him a spectral appearance. "I do not hate this record," Chill said. The word *record* in this case was a hip-hop synonym for *song*, as in: this will be the first record on the album. "It just needs more *clarity.*"

The younger boy on the stool to the right had a third eye tattooed in the middle of his forehead. He leaned close to the mic. "More *clarrriTEEEEE,*" he repeated, a mocking tone enhanced by the reverb.

Ever mindful of his mission statement—available on his website—which included the goal of "achieving separation from the hatred that leads to terrestrial torment," Chill ignored the disrespectful little shithead's provocation. He'd seen a lot of hard cases, beginning with himself—an All-County prep school wide receiver arrested just before prom his junior year for being part of a conspiracy to sell crack cocaine. He understood how it works: out of the wildness and sociopathology comes the drive and creativity. Given ten hours in a room with a Mac computer these kids could hatch at least fifteen new ideas for records. It was Chill's job to pick the best of the little fliers and guide them in for landings . . . hopefully onto the tarmac of Billboard's Top Ten.

"I love where you going wit this record," Chill explained. He lit up a blunt of Abusive, long and skinny like himself. "But your sound all dirty. It like you mumblin. Like you don't believe what you sayin and can't even remember the words. I got no sense of your *commitment.*"

The eldest continued to glare homicidally.

"Coooooomit-MENTTTTTTT," echoed third eye.

Chill took another hit . . . held it for a long count . . . exhaled a thick plume.

The smoke filtered upward, drawn toward an industrial air vent strapped to a beam running along the exposed ceiling. His scalp tingled at the hairline, a pleasant minirush.

Hours earlier, as dawn was breaking, he'd left Angelika's place and trudged back to the parking lot to retrieve his motorcycle, seemingly unobserved. The marine layer was thick, the air foggy and wet on his face; the sensation was like walking through a cloud. He was barefoot; the beach was deserted. The sand was full of puddles. He may have taken a few moments to recreate the Gene Kelly dance solo from *Singing in the Rain.*

Reaching the Ducati, he'd zipped up his leather jacket, retied his ruined white J's, and blasted south on the PCH, then east along Sunset Boulevard. Leaning low around the serpentine curves, the needle pushed one hundred miles per hour. He carved an edge between grace and catastrophe, that place he fancied he liked to live.

By the time he arrived at work, he felt larger than life . . . supercharged . . . indestructible.

The way he felt when he came off stage: possessed for the moment by the certain knowledge that no task could elude him, no goal could possibly go unrealized, no prize could not be his.

He pushed the button on the private elevator in the basement, threw a James Brown triple spin...

The doors slid open.

He caught a peep of himself in the smoky mirror at the back of the car—this gangly mofo with an Ultrabrite smile lighting his entire face.

Nigga, you in love with a white girl.

Now, in the studio, the smell of her was still with him, a pastiche of fresh and sweet and deliciously pungent, intermingling in his immediate atmosphere with the aromas of his Chilly T. brand cologne, Abusive Kush; tobacco leaf rolling papers; and a Six Dollar Burger from Carl's Jr, which was sitting at the moment in its greasy wrapper just to the left of him, lunch for the Japanese sound technician—his delicate doll hands flitting across the soundboard like a pair of water bugs across a still pond, making minute adjustments to the mix.

"I think we need to go back to usin our old shit." This was the third boy, the one on the left. Instead of tears tattooed in a trail beneath his eye—a gangland accounting of human kills—he had a heart, a star, a crescent moon, and a four-leaf clover, homage to his favorite cereal. He raised his hand to his mouth and commenced biting his pinkie fingernail. Across his knuckles he had tattooed the letters MOMS.

"What wrong with all the *new* shit y'all bought?" Chill asked.

"I don't know. Maybe it *too* fancy." He bowed his head. "The sound come out wack."

Chill sighed into the mic; amplified, the gust of his frustration registered inside the booth like God's own tired breath. "It ain't *wack*. Okay? None of this shit wack. It just *unfinished*. It *unrealized*. You just need to bring the sizzle, youngin. This is what they mean by *workin it out*. The operative word is *work*. It's like Kobe, you know? You gotta get out there every day and make a thousand baskets."

The boy at the center: "*You* think it wack."

Chill took another long hit off his blunt. He'd personally helped these kids use their advance to buy a condo. For the first time in their lives, each of the boys had his own bedroom. By daybreak of their inaugural night in the place, all three had dragged their pillows and blankets into the living room to sleep together on the plush carpet floor. At present, the living room still served as a dorm with three beds. They used their bedrooms as personal playrooms. Each had a digital lock on his door. (Everybody kept losing their keys; the locksmith bills had been a fortune).

"It's one thing to have a big hit record," Chill said. "It's another thing to create a musical voice that can last and grow. I'm trying to help you fellas find your sound. I was once where you are now. If you do this right, in thirty years from now you'll *still* be getting paid."

He clapped his hands, a coach rallying his basketball players. "Let's try it again from the top. Stay in the pocket, fellas. Be true to yourself. Let's nail this shit and move on. You feel me?"

They all three looked at him dumbly, a collective institutional stare, sad orphan toddlers in a roomful of cribs. There is no telling what they were thinking.

Third eye leaned forward into his spit screen. "You feeeeeeel MEEEEEE?"

13

An Outpost on the Frontier of the Inevitable

It was nearly noon when Sulcov pushed through the revolving door at Casa Manana.

From the street, the building appeared to be similar to the other lux accommodations lining the Wilshire canyon, convenient to shopping in Westwood and also to the UCLA campus, where his father, Marv Sulcov, enjoyed taking his adult extension classes—this semester it was music appreciation. There were liveried doormen and valet parking attendants; you could tip them to carry your groceries, to change a light bulb, or to perform other domestic chores as needed. The higher floors were zoned for condos; the views were spectacular. The lower levels housed assisted living, where aesthetics played a lesser role. Just above the lobby, on the mezzanine, was a small critical care unit, linked by its own set of elevators to a basement sally port so as not to upset the more able-bodied residents— you'd be there soon enough and didn't need reminding. Included with the package was a membership at a health club around the corner; at seventy-nine, Marv still made it his business to work out three times a week.

Spotting his father in his usual small circle of resident *compadres*, Sulcov sidled up and said his hellos.

To be a visiting child aboard the good ship Casa Manana was to be *everyone's* visiting child—all at once the minicaucus of three seniors turned their complete attention toward him, faces aglow. Everyone in the building knew that Marv Sulcov's son was responsible for the hit series *High Tolerance*. Everyone in the building had connections to show biz; being somehow associated with the latest megahit has always been the coin of the realm. Before the strike, there were *HT* viewing parties every Tuesday night at nine in the condo's screening room; same as the rest of America, the residents had over the years taken a certain ownership of the characters. To say that Sulcov himself was a celebrity at Casa Manana was not taking it too far. The simple fact of his regular weekly visits didn't hurt, either.

"You look a little thin," offered Leon, his dad's closest pal. The old man threw a faux left cross, connecting gently with Sulcov's chin.

In his day Leon had been one of the original Muscle Beach bodybuilders; at seventy-seven he was still in amazing shape, deep-tanned to a leathery color with a receding but carefully tended George Hamilton pompadour. Three years ago, Sulcov didn't even know this guy, and neither did Marv. Now the two old roosters did everything together. Scarce as males were hereabouts, their bromance was much celebrated around the condo by the flock of resident hens. As you would imagine, neither man went wanting for a home-cooked meal. Leon kept a calendar. Marv always complained about the quality of the various widows' cuisine—a New York food snob to the core.

Sulcov reached out and playfully grabbed Leon's biceps, smooth and solid as a river stone. "Not skinny. Just lean. I've been working out with a trainer, trying to catch up to you, big guy."

The old man patted the back of Sulcov's warm hand as it rested for an extra count on his arm muscle. He'd never gotten around to having children—too busy playing the field. Except for Marv and the other residents, he was truly alone in the world. "Any word on the strike?"

"Just keeps dragging on," Sulcov sighed.

"Someday those studios will learn," Leon said, wagging a crooked finger. "You can't make movies without people—"

"—and people gotta eat," Sulcov said, wagging his own finger, jumping in to finish the sentiment . . . they'd had the exact same exchange every Wednesday for the past three months, in almost the exact same spot on the shiny marble floor.

Leon was a retired union man himself, a camera operator by trade. He'd lived through several different Hollywood strikes; the first and most memorable to him was remembered as Black Friday—October 5, 1945. He was fifteen at the time, living with his parents in Toluca Lake, which would later become famous as the home of the comedian Bob Hope. A melee broke out between scabs and striking set designers at the Warner Bros.' studio in nearby Burbank. He and his neighborhood friends peddled over on their bikes to catch the action. The striking designers wore matching outfits, complete with white helmets. They were no equal to the studio's thugs. Police and firefighters were eventually summoned—high-powered water hoses were deployed.

"Well they need to hurry up and make a deal, already!" This was Edith. She lived down the hall from Marv on the twenty-seventh floor. The joints of her fingers were twisted and swollen. It looked painful.

"Can you just tell us what happens to Jennifer Morrow?" the old lady pleaded, asking about her favorite member of the ensemble cast, a hard-nosed investigator from humble Queens roots, last seen awaiting a rendezvous with a Taliban operative. She smiled coquettishly. The way she stood, one foot forward like a fashion model, you could tell she'd been a looker in her day. "We won't tell anyone! It's killing me: how could you just *leave* her there, stranded in the desert?"

Sulcov offered an overlarge smile. It was always amazing to him that these characters he'd created were actually alive in people's minds.

"If he tells you he has to kill you," Leon joked. He elbowed her gently in the side.

"I just loved that episode when Kirk Douglas guest starred," Edith said. "You know my late husband, Lou—may he rest in peace—he used to represent Kirk. What a man. Such a *mensch*. And his wives. Diana and then Anne. Just lovely, *lovely* gals."

Leon: "What I want to know is, when are you going to have that Angelika bird back on the show? That episode was on reruns the other night. *Yowza!* You never said—did you ever get to actually meet *her?*"

Sulcov shrugged. "I wrote that script, so yeah, I got to meet her."

In Hollywood, to paraphrase the great journalist Tom Wolfe, you're either on the set or off the set. Either you're one of the people who makes the magic happen or you're one of the ones who watches and fawns. To admit being impressed by meeting a star . . . oh no, never cool, *no bueno.*

Not only had he met Angelika, he had sat in her trailer with her, alone, for more than four hours, going over the substantial changes to her lines that her people had requested through the highest studio channels.

Lounging on the plush settee in her top-of-the-line Star Carriage mobile dressing room, Angelika had been disarmingly sweet. Just charming and solicitous and real and . . . unbelievably, captivatingly, stupifyingly *gorgeous.*

That he'd chosen to share with his wife the bit about rehearsing the makeout scene with the toned and beautiful superstarlet . . . Well, that was another story, the moral of which might have been: some things between spouses are best left unshared.

Edith to Sulcov, her painted-on eyebrows knitted with concern: "Your eyes look bloodshot, dear. Are you sick?"

"Smokin that Mary Jane?" Leon joshed. "When are you gonna bring *me* some? We could round up a coupla chicks and have us a real tea party! What do you say, Edith? Wanna blow some grass?"

"Allergies," Sulcov said, soberly and definitively. "Itchy eyes. This is the season for tree pollen."

"Tree pollen?" For the first time since his son had joined the group, Marv Sulcov spoke.

He was smaller and more crooked than his only child, wearing oversize aviator-frame glasses and an expensive toupee.

"Yes, Dad. Same as every year."

Marv's voice assumed a concerned professional tone. "Stop by my office later and I'll write you a prescription for Dimetapp."

Stop by his office? "I'm taking generic Zyrtec, Dad," Sulcov assured him. "It's over the counter now, remember?"

"Every spring in Carol Gardens, the streets would be covered with yellow tree pollen," Marv told the assembled. "My office would be full of sneezing women. I kept samples of Dimetapp in a candy bowl in the waiting room."

Until he moved to LA, Marv Sulcov had lived his entire life in Brooklyn. The son of an immigrant tailor from Lithuania, he himself was forty when Nathan was born. Judy Lewinsky had been his receptionist, one in a long series of fetching young office employees who fueled a lifetime of domestic drama. Even as a child, Sulcov somehow understood that his father was an addict whose drug of choice was women. The marriage was Marv's first and last attempt at a legal domestic arrangement.

Following the divorce, young Sulcov had bounced back and forth between his parents. His mother eventually remarried. The man was closer to her age, a widower with three children. Practically overnight, Sulcov became the second youngest of four. Raised as an only child on a steady diet of worshipful unconditional love, he had no taste or facility for the rituals of sibling rivalry—the requisite jostling, jockeying, and one-upmanship that marks the social politics of every brood. In the past, with Marv frequently off delivering babies or working late or courting other women, Sulcov and his mother had been exceptionally close. That he had to share her now with these strangers seemed unfair—and she actually seemed to favor them. They said it was *his* family too, but he was the only one with a different last name.

When he was living with his father, on the other hand, he felt like a burden, another responsibility to be shouldered by a man who was already overworked—and wasn't shy about saying so, big important baby doctor that he was. Considering Marv's unpredictable schedule, Sulcov spent a lot of time alone in the two-bedroom apartment, or down in the lobby, hanging out with the various doormen. The old pug who worked the evening shift for many years was Sulcov's favorite. They'd order delivery, share dinner. A couple of times they'd taken in a Knicks game at the Garden. Long dead now, his name was Jake.

Not counting a cruise to the Caribbean and a pair of trips to visit transplanted cronies in Florida ("Too many goddamn old people!"), Marv had never been much of a traveler. As could be expected, there'd been a lot of hemming and hawing before he finally consented to move to a place where he "didn't know a soul."

The spacious lobby of Casa Manana was crowded at the moment with seniors and their visitors, arrayed in small groups. Almost all the residents were sporting their distinctive Wednesday Walking Club T-shirts—purple and black with their first names on the back. Seeing everyone in their uniforms, Sulcov couldn't help but think of Jake's early days in rec league sports, where the most important element was by far the personalized uniform.

"So how was the walk today?" Sulcov asked, putting the chatter back on track.

"It was a little windy, " Edith said.

"We were bucking the breeze going, but we got a nice little rear-end push on the way back," Leon agreed.

Edith giggled. "Is *that* what that was."

"You mean you thought that rear-end push was me?" Leon deadpanned.

Edith swatted the air in his direction. Everybody laughed except for Marv. He seemed agitated.

"What's up, big guy?" Leon patted his friend's shoulder reassuringly.

"Who the hell is this tall man?" Marv indicated his son.

Sulcov searched his father's wrinkled face, looking for a sign that he was kibitzing. But all he saw was fear and confusion.

Leon and Edith exchanged glances.

"Dad? It's me, Nate. *Nathan.* You don't know who I am?"

Indignant: "Of course I know who you are. *Jesus H. Christ.*"

Leon put a calming arm around his buddy. "He gets a little forgetful sometimes, don't you pal?"

Sulcov's heart thumped against his breastbone. *Holy fucking shit!* "How long . . ." he sputtered. "Why didn't anybody tell me?"

"We didn't want to worry you," Edith offered.

"It's just a little forgetfulness," Leon said.

"A senior moment," Edith chuckled nervously, fingering her strand of pearls with her small, twisted hand.

"Is it time for lunch yet?" Marv asked.

"Yes, Dad. It's time for lunch," Sulcov said, putting an arm around the old man's shoulders. With Leon still embracing Marv from the other side, it looked like they were posing for a picture, an awkward trio with forced smiles.

"It's Reuben Wednesday," Edith enthused.

"What kind of Reuben has *lettuce*?" Marv grumbled.

"You *love* Reubens," Sulcov reminded him.

"A real Reuben has sauerkraut."

Leon: "You know we can't give sauerkraut to all these old *farts*, Dr. Sulcov."

14

What They Say About White Women

"Take 38," Chill said, speaking into the projecting microphone at the studio console, making a note on a paper log with a yellow No. 2 pencil, an action that seemed entirely out of place in the super high-tech environment of the studio.

The track rolled. Chill gave the "go" sign with his finger and the lost boys of Artificial Intelligence began to spit their off-kilter rhymes. The 808 thumped like a beating heart; the snare and the old school horns worked the hook. Chill's head began to bob. He kicked back in his Aeron chair, relit his blunt. Smoke curled upward. "Now that's the shit, eh Hiro?" he said to the Japanese engineer.

"You were pretty hard on them."

This was Calvin Scott from *StarNews*. He was occupying the third Aeron chair at the console, the one on the far right. He needed a shave. Clearly he hadn't slept. He had his digital recorder in hand, aiming it gamely at Chill.

The mogul's eyes fixed upon the tiny red light that indicated record mode. *How much longer is this asshole gonna follow me around?* He raised his gaze to meet the journalist's.

"It what they understand," Chill said, speaking loudly over the music. "The alpha dog gotta growl, you know what I'm sayin?"

Scott made a face. He waved his recorder in the air, indicating the decibel level in the room. "Would you mind muting the sound for a bit? It's blowing out my audio."

Chill glared at him, a ship captain who'd just been informed of a mutiny. He motioned for Hiro to switch over to headphones.

The studio became instantly, eerily silent. Inside the booth, the members of Artificial Intelligence seemed to be engaged in an elaborate pantomime.

"A lot of people say that's what's *wrong* with hip-hop—the whole music business in general," Scott said, playing devil's advocate. "They say it's too thuggish, that it mirrors the criminal ways of the street. Are we sending the wrong message to American youth?"

"We do business like we growed up with," Chill said. "For a black man, the streets is business school. It's fuckin Wharton and Harvard and Yale all rolled into one. It like Wall Street, only you playin for you money *and* you life. You feel me? "

"I feel you," Scott said. Coming from his thin, lunch meat–colored lips, the words sounded undercooked.

"Back in the day, my set specialized in what you might call *hostile takeovers*. We'd find a spot where the crack business was poppin. Then we'd put together a crew and go in there and start sellin across the street."

"Like Blockbuster."

"E-zactly. We didn't care who the fuck was sellin there already. We'd *take* the motherfucker like Hamburger Hill. We'd wreck shit on that corner. We'd tag every bus bench and blank wall in the hood with insults about the other gang and they mothers. We'd sell a twenty-dollar rock for fifteen. Fives for two dollars. We had this group of fighters—we called them the gladiators. We'd drive up in three SUVs and let them go to war. These was big motherfuckers, ex-football stars and ex-cons and whatnot. Guys who just *loved to dance*, you know what I'm sayin? Blood was spilled. Heads was busted with baseball bats. You ever hear the sound of a melon cracking? It like, *thunk.*

Brains explodin all over the damn place. You probably don't know this, but brains don't *never* come outta you clothes. You just gotta throw that shit away when you get brains on it, yo."

"That's *brutal*."

"That ain't shit compared to the music business. Once I was into the rap game, I swear I couldn't see a whole lot of difference between the way business was done in legit circles and the way it done on the street. Look at Eazy E and Suge Knight. Look at Tupac and Biggie. You say we thugs, and maybe we is. But look at all these white motherfuckers in they business suits. White-collar criminals. Wall Street hustlers. Hollywood producers and studio heads and union motherfuckers. CEOs and CFOs and all the initials. The mo legit they is, the worse they are. *They* the diabolical ones. They fuckin with *e'erybody* money. They fuckin folks *globally*."

He took another hit and exhaled. "Music exactly like slingin dope. It the same, my brother. Same same. You got a product that everybody want to carry cause they know there's a market. They all looking to get a piece of the action anyway they can. Niggas lie, steal, rob, even kill to get into the music business. I can't think of better training than sellin dope on a street corner in broad daylight. One way or the other, you gotta keep your pimp hand strong to survive."

Scott eyeballed him for a beat. "You went to a ritzy prep school, right?"

Chill flashed his replacement grills, which were plenty sparkly but lacked the vampire incisors. "Class vice president."

"So what makes you so disaffected? I know where you lived was bad and all, but you certainly had every advantage. Manhattan Beach Country Day—right?"

"Go Gulls!"

"What kind of experience was that?"

"Eye-opening."

"What was so eye-opening?"

"Let's just say that before I went there, I'd never even *met* a white person. In LB, the doctors at the clinic was Indian or Asian or some shit; they never even let no white doctors work on us welfare cases, you know what I'm sayin? I lived in this whole black world. Black and Mexican. And the Koreans and the A-rabs who owned all the stores. The only white people I knew was the ones on television. Motherfuckin Fonzie and Richie and whoever. They were my only experience with Caucasians.

"Before you got to Country Day."

"Right. And then, after I got to Country Day, I was like, 'Holy shit, what all these fuckin forks doing on the table?' "

"You were a stranger in a strange land."

"A motherfuckin *astronaut*."

"You didn't make friends? Wasn't vice president an elected position? School elections are usually based on popularity in my experience."

"I was everybody's friend, my brother. I was like this cool toy everybody wanted a piece of—like in kindergarten when the class gets a guinea pig and all the students take turns bringing it home for the weekend or whatnot. These little white punks would invite me home after school, and they parents would be falling all over theyselves to show a little black kid from the ghetto just how open-minded and understanding they could be.

"I remember the first time I had Pepperidge Farm cookies. A tall glass of cold milk and plate full of fuckin Pepperidge Farm Milanos— oh my *motherfuckin God*. I thought I done died and gone to heaven. Do you know what it's like to be a kid raised on those two-for-a-dollar packages of imitation Oreos they sell in the Korean market and then you take a bite outta your first Pepperidge Farm? My mouth is watering right now just remembering, I shit you not. It like your first hit of crack. It's like getting your cherry popped. It fuckin *monumental*. It makes you question everything. You're like, *what the fuck else have I been missing?* From that moment on, you don't trust anything ever again, you feel me? Cause you know now that life has been holding out on you."

"But they were just trying to be nice, weren't they?" Scott asked.

"Noble. Charitable. Call it what you will. And you *benefited*. You got a scholarship, a ticket out. That's a big thing for somebody, isn't it? Why bite the hand that feeds you?"

"The way I see it, white people have an attitude of entitlement. They expect things to come they way, go they way, or get out of they way—it hard for them to accept the cold facts when they don't add up to the bottom line they have in mind. I mean, check it out: It ain't their fault, right? It's they environment. Caucasians are born thinking certain powers and privileges come with the territory. It like having a chip on your shoulder, only it's not a chip, it's a halo. It's being told, from the first moment you draw breath, that you're more special and select and choice than anybody else. You just naturally take that shit to heart. That's what comes from being society's top dog for so long. You just accept things as they are. You think you *owed* what you have."

"Obviously you have a lot of white fans," Scott said. "But you seem to have some strong feelings about white people in general. Would you ever date a white woman?"

"I had my one or two," Chill snickered.

"I guess I'm asking this in the context of Barack Obama's run for the presidency. Here's a biracial man, the product of a mixed union. I guess the question is, what do you think of interracial relationships? Would you marry a white woman?"

Chill flashed his hundred K smile. "I had this uncle, Uncle Ernie his name. He was like the Richard Pryor of Long Beach—funny as shit. He had a routine for everything. At family get-togethers, all the men would gather in the backyard of my gram-momma's house, drinkin they gin and juice. Give you a party and Ernie was *always* the center of things."

"Was Uncle Ernie married to a white woman?"

"Nah, man. But he used to did this whole routine on white girls. Shit was *funny*. I remember being little and cracking up. He be like, 'You know what they say about white women: *you can't bring em home to momma, but you can turn em out for twice the price.*' "

Scott looked aghast. "You're saying that white women are only good as whores?"

Chill laughed, took another hit of Abusive. "Nah, man. That's some old-school shit right there. My Uncle Ernie usta say that."

"What was he—a pimp?"

"He usta tell me, 'You *practice* on the white girls, but you *marry* the sista.'"

There was a disturbance behind them; the double door banged open. Both men swiveled around to see TBone entering. Chill's first lieutenant looked a little wild-eyed. He trotted over importantly and whispered something to Chill.

Chill to Scott: "Can I meet you out in the reception area? I got something to deal with right quick."

Scott made a pitiful face, meaning to protest. Surely after all this time he'd earned access to this important, behind-the-scenes development—whatever it was.

TBone nodded toward the door. "He'll catch you in the waiting room, *StarNews*."

The journalist backpedaled casually toward the exit. "Can you say how long you might be?"

Chill said something inaudible. TBone cracked up.

15

Her Personal Artifacts

Angelika opened the drawer of her bedside table and removed a cigar box, a precious piece of hobby-craft carefully collaged and lovingly varnished, bringing to mind one of those wildly decorated cargo trucks in India—all the surfaces painted and plastered with found art, some of it three dimensional, all of it reflective of the inner workings of her young heart: Scissored-out headlines and bits of text (*La Vida Loca; Just Do It; Remember your first rush; Say Goodbye to Unwanted Intrusions*). The original "Working Actress" button from the visor of the Delta 88. Calligraphed quotations (Jane Austen, Jimmy Carter, Mahatma Gandhi, Cher). Colorful pictures (Ganesh, a one-eyed alien, Bob Marley, Julia Child, a sunset on the North Shore of O'ahu).

She opened the top to reveal her trove of paraphernalia. She thought of it as a collection of personal artifacts; each piece had a story, marked a milestone. A purple glass one-hitter, a gift from *Friends* actor David Schwimmer. A pipe in the shape of a yellow taxi from her first trip to Manhattan. A mini-Coke bottle bong from her first trip to Amsterdam. A souvenir from one of her concerts in Tokyo—a Bic-variety lighter decorated with her own image (during her platinum blonde period) and the words "Number One Super Star Girl." A penis-shaped bronze butane lighter, a gift from Kisha. A lighter that resembled a Louis Vuitton purse, a gift from JamieLynn.

Angelika was fifteen when she first smoked weed. It was on the set of *Friends*, after shooting had wrapped for the day, with a group of younger grips and assistants; in time they would dub their little outlaw clique the Friends of Friends. (She might have been cast as Chandler's baby sister, but the precocious Goth act she'd auditioned with had turned out to be a potent man-magnet; there would be many firsts that season.) The cigar box itself had been a gift from the rapper Snoop Dogg. They'd got to talking at a VMA after-party; the next day, the antique wooden Cohiba box had been delivered to her house.

(Missy, hackles raised: "Why would someone send someone an *empty* cigar box?")

Angelika removed from the box a pack of orange Zig Zag rolling papers, a small pair of sewing shears, and a plastic tray decorated with a marijuana leaf. Then she retrieved a small canister, the top carrying the wonderfully ironic logo of Malibu Green's Farmacy—two smoking joints crossed like bones beneath a stoned-out-looking smiley face. Inside, a thumb-sized bud of Abusive Kush Private Reserve.

Yes, she was on the list, too.

Placing the tray on top of the cigar box, holding the bud carefully by the stem, she set to work with the scissors.

Her brow furrowed; tiny clippings rained down, brown and beige and green flakes, all of it dusted with crystalline THC, tetrahydrocannabinol, the main psychoactive ingredient in marijuana. When the pile grew to her liking, she used the cardboard package from the rolling papers like as a whisk broom to sweep the weed off the edge of the tray, into a sheet of rolling paper.

That she was not the most accomplished joint roller was well known within the very small group of people who were privy to her smoking. Kisha called them "crack-ho" joints because they were skinny on the ends with a big pregnant bulge in the middle. "Like a snake that just ate," is how Chill put it the first time she'd twisted one up for him. The coincidence of their slots on the Abusive list had served to bring them closer, an unexpected communality that led to the discovery of many more.

This time, following her new man's advice—put more weed on the ends than in the middle; begin rolling at the center and move outward—Angelika crafted for herself a nearly perfect little cigarillo, which she stored for a moment behind her ear, as Missy's third (and so-far final) ex-husband liked to do, the owner of the Delta 88. Fishing inside the cigar box again, she traded the vial and the papers for a clever portable ashtray with a screw top that someone else had given her, she couldn't remember who. She lit up with the Japanese Angelika lighter.

The sky through the windows reminded her of the opening credits of *The Simpsons*, cartoon blue with puffy white clouds. The ocean pounded; each rhythmic crash shook the foundation of the house—an endless series of detonations followed by intense, morning-after silence. In her short time living here she'd been fascinated by the way a powerful noise could create a sense of quiet, the same way the vibrant colors of the rainbow could be mixed together to create black. She loved this new place more intensely every day; she was already dreading her upcoming move to England to shoot her next film—a period piece her advisers believed would help position her as a serious actress (whose first Oscar was not a fluke).

Even though she loved the abandoned physicality of singing and dancing—once you learned the techniques, the words, the steps, it was all about throwing yourself into the performance, about letting go and *bringing* it—the actual lifestyle was grueling. Rehearsals, workouts, injuries, travel. The late nights in the studios with all those musicians, none of whom were exactly pillars of healthy living.

Acting was different—a little easier on your body, infinitely more cerebral. Career-wise, you could last longer as an actress. You might see a chanteuse like Eartha Kitt performing late in life, but what happens to a pop singer/dancer? How many people can muster Tina Turner–type energy late into their careers? Already Madonna was turning into a cartoon. Britney looked fat and trashy in her spangles. The absence of good scripts (and good parts) for older women notwithstanding, actresses could work late into life. There were lots of examples—Jessica Tandy, Ruby Dee, Judi Dench, Meryl Streep. She'd made a study of the successful ones, too.

As everyone knew, the path to respect and longevity in acting passed through the period drama. All great actresses had to put in time wearing corsets and wigs. All great actresses had to do a convincing English accent. (Just as they had to do a role in which they gained weight and looked ugly, the ultimate Hollywood sacrifice. Her people were searching for such a part, too.) Like it or not, she would go to dreary England and shoot *Lancelot and Guinevere*, a dramatic remake of the musical *Camelot*. She always did what she had to do, and then she did a little more. ("You gotta go the extra twenty-five feet," Missy liked to chirp.) Angelika always went two miles.

She took another hit and exhaled. Her heart beat faster, her thoughts felt light and agile. Her tummy rumbled; her thoughts turned to breakfast.

Maybe I should order up some pancakes?

With real maple syrup?

When's the last time you had REAL syrup?

With real butter?

Why the hell not? Live a little.

She felt the phone vibrating against her thigh, beneath the covers where she'd dropped it.

16

Without Fear of Reprisal

The bell sounded day's end at Santa Monica Prep. Doors flung open; a flood tide of teens and preteens raged down the concrete stairways of the two-story, stucco-and-stone building that served as the middle school, making good their escape, at least until morning.

A blend of landmark structures and expensively harmonious new ones, Prep was arranged in the manner of a college campus, five acres of prime real estate on the southeastern fringe of Santa Monica, servicing students from preschool through grade twelve.

As with many schools in warm climates, there were no hallways. Classroom doors opened into the sunlight; the rows of metal lockers were exposed to the elements. An outside proscenium was used for student gatherings (there was also a theater complex, endowed by another famous alum). Landscaped with red bougainvillea and purple-flowered jacaranda trees, surrounded by a high chain-link fence that kept out the harsher realities, the place had the feeling of a dollhouse—everything perfectly in place, open and easily observed.

Enveloped within the kinetic flock of his friends, Jake Sulcov's cappuccino-with-cinnamon-colored face wore a look of joyful animation. His shiny black Lebron James signature shorts hung down to mid shin, the red piping a match to the red laces on his black Jordan high-tops. An extra-long white tee shirt from Sleeper's drawer completed the ensemble. His Jewfro had been rendered the night before by Z's sister into neat cornrows.

Jake proceeded along the sidewalk employing his usual baller's strut—simultaneously texting, goof-balling with pals, flirting with girls, fist bumping worshipful sixth graders. Like Jake, most of the students at Prep were the sons and daughters of wealthy but not particularly lauded parents, the great silent majority of upper-crust LA, the minions who lived *next door* to the stars. The children had about them a grown-up air of sophisticated ease and entitlement; they appeared carefree and comfortable in their own skins, and in their designer sneaks and Ugg boots, the girls' expensively tended hair unfettered in the westside breeze.

He spotted Z standing in the usual location—a shade-dappled corner near the library, ensconced within his own affinity group, the faces distinctly darker than Jake's sun-kissed crew. A collection of scholarship students—athletes, musicians, debaters, and academics—they'd earned their way into Prep by dint of talent, hard work, and the strange good fortune of having been born disadvantaged. Most of these kids had long ago surpassed the abilities of their parents; among them they shared the sobering responsibility of having to navigate their own way through these deep and unfamiliar waters. There was a vibe of professionalism among them, an air of maturity. Prep was a way out, their first stop on a voyage to a different world, a different way of life, one they'd only just begun to even understand.

Peeling off from his own flock, Jake alighted within Z's—setting off a series of hugs, handshakes, cheek kisses, and other well-practiced rituals of greeting. As a biracial kid and a bona fide hooper, Jake was welcomed into this circle. As a rich kid, he was held somewhat apart. He often struggled with that; he couldn't help the good fortune of his own birth. He often felt he had to prove himself. Sometimes he tried too hard.

The microclimate around Z was subdued. He was a good-look-ing boy, large in scale yet still unformed; baby fat with a dark pubes-cent 'stache. His hair was buzzed short and lined up and faded. The widow's peak he shared with Sleeper lent him a roguish air. A pair of Latinas with mournful eyes and thick makeup stood at either elbow, dark clouds huddled against the mountain of his brooding presence. One girl held a tin of home-baked cookies.

Achieving proximity at last, Jake and Z commenced the se-quence of hand movements—palm pats, fist bumps, finger grabs and so forth—that constituted their personalized greeting. Jake grabbed a chocolate chip cookie and took a bite. "Did you hear from your Moms?"

"I think the funerals are gonna be on Monday—my phone died while I was talking to her." Z pulled his dead cell out of the pocket of his 4XL Under Armour-brand shorts and glared at it.

Jake eyeballed his own phone. Because he'd thought to turn it off last night, he still had one power bar left. "So what do you think?"

"About what?"

Jake helped himself to two more cookies and pulled Z off to the side, away from the girls and everybody. "About going to see the *po po*. About lettin em know what *up*." He handed one of the cookies to his pal.

"The police?" Z's ever-bright smile faded. "I don't know, dude. Sleeper always says if you call the cops on somebody, there's a good a chance they'll end up taking *you* to jail, too."

"We ain't did nothin wrong," Jake insisted, his Venice slang ac-commodating the urgency of the moment.

"Dude, we got *practice*."

"Newsflash: We do *not* have practice. The JV and Varsity have away games. We have no coach."

"The cops are never gonna listen to us. We have no *evidence*. All we have is *hearsay*." They'd both taken Criminal Justice as an elective last fall.

"Right now Sleeper and them are going down in history as these losers who tried to put a hit on a famous rap mogul."

"It just isn't fair," Z said. He popped the entire cookie into his mouth. The chocolate chips were still gooey. He felt the same way inside.

"I'll bet you one hundred bucks right now that Sleeper's piece wasn't even *loaded*," Jake said.

"That's a no-brainer."

"Remember when he caught us smoking behind the garage?"

"We were what, like ten?"

"And he pulls out that big-ass chrome-plated Beretta 9 from beneath his shirt."

"I about *pissed* my pants."

"I was like, '*Whatthefuck?*' "

"And then he shows us how he always carries the clip separate, in his left hand pocket."

Jake made his voice singsongy like Sleeper's: " 'Because sometime you need the gat—' "

" '—and sometime you need the bullets,' " Z said.

"I have *never* smoked a cigarette again, dude," Jake said.

"No fuckin *way*." Z reached out and took Jake's offered hand in a lingering soul shake, which evolved into a straight shake, which gave way to a fist bump and then a finger snap.

"How many times did he catch us doin shit?" Jake asked.

"It was like he had fuckin X ray vision."

"Like he had a fuckin *satellite* watching our every move."

Jake's phone vibrated. He drew the device from the holster clipped to the elastic waistband of his shorts, riding low on his hips. He read the text; his thumbs pistoned over the keyboard.

Z checked his own cell, forgetting momentarily that it was dead. "*Dude!*" he said to no one in particular. "I gotta charge my phone."

Jake holstered his phone, returned his attention to real time, the conversation at hand. "What gets me is the TEC-9."

"I know! If Sleeper and them had a TEC, *somebody* in the neighborhood woulda known," Z said conclusively. "Everybody's like, 'Huh?' It must have been a plant."

"Where did he even *get* a TEC? And why would he take it to a meeting?"

"And what about motive? "

"Exactly. What possible reason could Sleeper and them have to start some shit? They were going in to sign a deal, right?"

"It makes no sense," Z said again. He looked like he was about to cry.

"I say we go for it, *homes.*" Jake's face wore the look of determination he usually reserved for crunch time—the game on the line, the seconds ticking down, the ball bouncing confidently between the hardwood floor and his strong, calloused fingers, hands much older than his age.

Z fingered his peach fuzz moustache. He'd signed a zero-tolerance contract with Prep. His scholarship was *revocable.* A kid in his position wasn't allowed mistakes. He'd run too many wind sprints to throw it away now. A skeptical tone: "Go for what, *exactly?*"

"We explain to the police in a reasonable manner what really went down. It's the rule of law, right? That's how this whole—" he made quotation marks in the air with his fingers—" 'criminal justice system' is supposed to work, right? It's not just a course in school. It's the way our legal system runs."

"Well we all know that the system runs smoother in some neighborhoods than others," Z said. You could hear the personal history—the standing in line for government cheese, the long waits at clinics for health and dental care, the funerals of friends and relatives, the family trips by bus to visit his father and later Sleeper in various prisons. All those bar mitzvahs Z had attended so far this year? Don't think he never did the math: *my family could live for two years on the cost of this frickin party.*

"Either we down or we ain't," Jake said, invoking the creed of the hood.

Since they were six, Jake had been feeding the ball to Z down low for the easy basket. Since they were six, Jake and his family had been opening Z's eyes to the vast world beyond the borders of insular Venice. He hadn't gotten this far without trusting his friend. "What if I say yes?" Z asked.

"We go see the detective who is working the case," Jake said. "We act as *confidential* informants."

"Dude, you've been watching too much *Law and Order.*"

"That's what Ms. Ohnstad taught us, remember?" From memory, he recited: " 'any person has the right to come forward and give testimony—' "

"—without fear of reprisal.' " Z finished the sentence. They'd studied together for the Crim Jus final. He shook his head in resignation. "Do we gotta go *all the way* downtown to police headquarters?"

"The shooting was at Sunset and Vine; the case is being handled out of the Hollywood Station. It's on Wilcox between Sunset and Santa Monica. It's pretty close to the wax museum and Ripley's and all that."

"Near the Chinese movie theater?" Z brightened. He'd been getting around the city himself since his mother had enrolled him in a magnet elementary school across town. "We can just walk over to Santa Monica and catch the No. 7. It'll take us right past Wilcox."

"The bus?" Jake looked at his friend like he was crazy. "I'll just call my dad's car service."

He whipped out his cell phone and scrolled down his list of contacts.

When he came to the entry labeled "dad$limo," he pressed talk.

17

Pencils Down, People

As he had nearly every day since the strike began, Sulcov allowed his eyes to drift from the sign-in sheet to the several boxes of Krispy Kreme doughnuts provided by an anonymous union sympathizer.

One doughnut, he told himself. *What could it hurt?*

But you just ate lunch.

Look at those crullers! Look at those chocolate-glazed! I swear I could eat a whole box.

Each one has a zillion calories.

Come on. Why else do you work out six times a week?

You work out five times a week, sometimes four. And you always cheat on your sit-ups and pull-ups . . .

Near the doughnuts was a pile of red, black and white placards: WGA ON STRIKE. The handles were made of wood, about the thickness of the stirring wands given out free at paint stores. He sorted through the pile, looking for one with a *sandpapered* handle—in the early going, the rank and file had complained about splinters. As strike captain, he'd been called into headquarters to spend two hours sandpapering handles for the faithful.

The picket line stretched along an east-west axis on the wide sidewalk in front of the Pico Boulevard entrance of 20th Century Fox Studios—a huge billboard of the Simpsons cartoon family presided over all. A pair of orange traffic cones, set two hundred feet apart, marked the eastern- and western-most points of the picket line, which was not actually a line at all but rather more of a picket *oval*. Moving in a counter-clockwise direction, wheeling around the cones at either end, the strikers reminded Sulcov of film looping endlessly around a pair of sprockets, so many frames of human celluloid.

According to union bylaws, each member was required to picket a minimum of four hours a day, four times a week—a considerable amount of time and mileage, it turned out, requiring a different set of muscles than his usual basketball and core training. Sulcov's calves complained for the first two weeks. After that, his feet started to break down. He tried all different combinations of shoes and socks, Band-Aids, athletic tape, moleskin, insoles. Clearly, as a writer, he was best suited to sitting.

Because he'd come to television as a second career, and because he preferred his own pool house/office to his desk at the show's sterile facility near Melrose Avenue . . . because he was the type of guy who shopped at Gap Online instead of Fred Siegel, settled for a 3-Series Bimmer, and begged off "boys' trips" to Las Vegas in favor of attending basketball tournaments with his son . . . Sulcov tended to be the outcast on the quirky, award-winning, seven-person writing staff at *High Tolerance*. His appointment as strike captain was indicative of his status, an honor on the order of fire drill monitor, last one out of the burning building.

Surprisingly, he found himself enjoying his new duties. Not only did it give him something useful to do (keeping tabs on the hours put in by the other writers, passing along e-mail notifications, etc.); it also evoked in him the spirit of his paternal grandfather, a minor New York writer, union activist, and staunch Bolshevik who supported himself by taking in tailoring.

Where Pop-pop Sulcov wrote so eloquently (in his third language) of the brotherhood in hardship and common cause, his grandson's experience with labor action was quite a bit different. Despite the friendly banter at meetings, the office doorway bull sessions, the occasional parties and get-togethers, everyone on the staff kind of hated everyone else. Like siblings, they vied for the affections of their daddy, the show runner Zondo. And like siblings, they loved and relied upon each other even as they resented each other bitterly ... all of which made for a toxic yet highly charged atmosphere that often gave birth to memorable television—a formula repeated in workplaces all across this wonderfully dysfunctional town.

Sulcov's standing with his fellows was further complicated by his relationship with Zondo. Everyone at HT knew the backstory: Zondo had been an economics major. He'd never even set foot into a newsroom. He'd derived the idea from Sulcov's fascinating and sometimes hilarious barroom anecdotes about working as editorial assistant to *NewsSource*'s award-winning investigative team. Everyone knew Sulcov had written the pilot. And everyone knew Sulcov had been maneuvered out of his co-creator credit—and that he'd declined to sue, as many an agent had advised, even as Zondo was being swept into the ranks of A-list Hollywood royalty. In an odd way, this failure to stand up for himself had made Sulcov bulletproof ... the kind where slugs pass through you instead of bouncing off.

Which was fine with Sulcov. He was making five hundred grand a year writing a few one-hour teleplays. His wife had plenty of money. He was happily engaged doing a job he loved, living a life he loved, getting to spend a lot of time with his family. He didn't care about celebrity—was that a flaw?

"Hey, Sully! What's up?"

Sulcov turned around in his place at the sign-in table to greet his oldest local pal, Superior Court Judge Kenneth Lee Baverman.

He was nearly a foot shorter than Sulcov but weighed about the same. The two greeted one another as men did in the year 2008, a soul shake that morphed into a manly half-hug/back slap ... culminating in a brotherly kiss, planted in the awkward region between ear and neck, so as not to appear gay—even so, many times over the years they'd been mistaken for a couple.

"I can't believe you really came," Sulcov said, with the fervor of Robinson Crusoe greeting Friday.

Without hesitation, Bave reached for a glazed chocolate doughnut and took a huge bite. "This is amazing!" he enthused with his mouth full.

Except for those times when he was feeling extremely down, Ken Baverman was relentlessly upbeat, always looking for a silver lining. A loyal Sulcov booster, he was quick with a pat on the back, something people don't give or get enough anymore. Bave had also attended Columbia undergrad, a history major who'd gone on to law school at UCLA. (Did anyone ever return east? From what Sulcov could tell, only disgruntled writers looking for op-ed material.)

Bave lived with his wife and three daughters in Santa Monica. Sulcov truly loved him—a fond, loyal, and sometimes annoying dude who was always there in the clutch. Bave would say the same.

"You don't have to do this, you know. Showing up is enough to get your ticket punched."

"What are you talking about? I'm totally *psyched*." Bave wiped chocolate from his lips with the back of his hand. "Isn't that Sally Field over there?"

Sulcov handed him a napkin. "Botoxed to within an inch of her life."

Bave appraised the aging but still vital actress from a distance, meanwhile wiping his face. "I used to love her when she was the flying nun."

"Just so you know," Sulcov said, handing him a picket sign with a sandpapered handle, "we're about to walk about six miles in three hours. There are two half-hour breaks. You are free to leave at any time, okay?"

Baverman tested the weight of the sign, twirled it around joyfully, a flag girl in a marching band. "Are you sure I'm legally authorized to carry this?"

"Why not?"

"Because I'm not in the union?"

"Look around. Obviously, the WGA will take anyone."

In contrast to the gorgeous human specimens for whom they wrote scripts, a gathering of television scribes resembled a collection of misfit toys—think *Toy Story* reinterpreted by Larry David, television's prickly iconoclast. Slew feet, frizzy hair, stomach rolls, receding chins, bald spots. One guy pulled a roller bag behind him. You got the sense that he was homeless—or trying to sell a bunch of scripts? He muttered to himself as he perambulated.

Like two kids jumping into game of double Dutch, Sully and Bave found a break in the loop and merged. They trudged along silently, seriously, falling into the shambling rhythm of the others.

Though writing for TV could be extremely lucrative for some, the average screenwriter made about $62,000 a year, according to WGA statistics. Tinseltown wisdom said career expectancy for a TV writer was five years—the same as an NFL football player. Shows came and went; writers were constantly being hired and fired. Between jobs, they were always faced with the cruelest question: *will I ever work again?* Many writers survived lean times on their residuals—payments for episode reruns—and also on residual payments for video and DVD sales. Many more had to find . . . jobs.

The last time the WGA struck, in 1988, the writers were out for twenty-one weeks and six days. Estimates quoted in the *Times* valued the losses to the entertainment industry and the general economy of Los Angeles at $1.5 billion. The main issue in '88 was the home video market. At the time, VCR machines were a new product; VHS and Betamax tapes were expensive to produce. Video movies started out selling in the range of $40 to $100 per tape. Based on those numbers, the WGA accepted a residuals formula in which a writer would receive only 0.3 percent of the first million dollars of reportable gross. As manufacturing costs for videos dropped (and were then replaced by even-cheaper-to-produce DVDs), the home video market took off. By 2004 it was reported in the *New York Times* that sales of DVDs, *in the first four months of the year*, had reached $4.8 billion, versus $1.78 billion at the box office.

This time around, as contract talks began, the writers had taken a harder position. They felt they were entitled to a little more of a percentage. Without writers, after all, what would you have? Even talk shows had writers. Even *game* shows needed scripts. Every show that ever aired began with a writer staring down a blank screen.

Looming larger was the issue of "new media," which allowed for instant delivery and sales of shows and movies through websites, streaming video, smartphone programming, and other marketplaces. Even in 2008, nobody had any idea how big that would become. The WGA leadership was determined not to be screwed again.

And so it was, on November 5, 2007, with the bargaining stalled, that Sulcov and his fellow cardholders followed their leadership's wishes and voted to strike.

"Pencils down, people," wrote one prominent screenwriter in his blog.

Now it was the second week in January 2008. The bitch queens and militants weren't feeling quite so pleased with themselves anymore.

And there was no end in sight.

Passing motorists along Pico Boulevard blared horns and cheered in solidarity. For the most part, public sympathy seemed to favor the writers; on one occasion they'd been bombarded with water balloons. From the somewhat biased coverage in the media, one thing about the strike was abundantly clear: the people in TV land missed their television; the electronic hearth around which the family traditionally gathered had turned cold. Production on all shows had halted midseason. There was little or nothing in the can, cliffhangers in every plot. Half a season of *Desperate Housewives?* Half a season of *Lost?* What happened to Jack? Who the hell is this Jacob guy? The reruns offered as pacification by the networks just made everything worse.

Sulcov and Baverman *schlumped* along the strike oval with the rest, a scene playing out identically at studios all across town and in New York. Sulcov was glad to have someone to talk to. Most of his cohorts from *High Tolerance* lived across town in Silver Lake or Echo Park. The rules allowed you to picket at any strike location that was convenient, as long as you put in your required hours. Given that he'd only worked for the one show, he didn't really know any other writers in town, had no network of friends. Usually he'd walk his shift alone—he did his own time, as they always said in the prison movies; now he knew what that meant—accompanied only by his lively and anxious internal monologue. You would think he'd have met some new people, but writers tend to stay to themselves. Nobody made any effort to be social. You just showed up and walked. As they'd learned to do on sets, everybody kept their eyes averted, lest they cross a controversial sight line.

"So what's up with the Campfire Girls?" Sulcov asked, referencing his friend's estrogen-drenched home environment.

"They tell me we're getting a new dog," the esteemed judge reported morosely. All day long, his voice carried the rule of law. At home, things were distinctly different. On average the friends met once a week, usually for a vigorous walk along the Strand. They both had personal trainers. Neither really needed the exercise. "Cheaper than therapy," Bave would say whenever it was his turn to pick up the tab for their postexercise brunch.

"You don't have enough dogs already?"

"Hannah wants some little rat-dog. A miniature Chihuahua." He pointed discreetly to a striker across the oval. Her floppy sun hat was tied onto her head with an Hermès scarf. "See? She's carrying one in her shoulder bag."

"Like the Taco Bell dog."

"Exactly."

"Beats another Great Dane."

"Or another *baby*."

"*Dude.* You're not still trying for a boy, are you? Come *on*. It's outta your hands. Obviously you're shooting Xs."

"It's been IN my hand *way too much* lately," Bave joked. "In the navy they call it whiteout. It's what happens when you're at sea for long periods. All the seminal fluids back up into your system until you go blind."

"Not a diagnosis I'm familiar with," Sulcov confessed, "but a universal condition, nonetheless."

"True dat," Bave offered. From the side pocket of his cargo shorts he fished a tin of Altoids. Sulcov took one. Bave took three, popped them simultaneously.

"A fling would be too risky," Sulcov said.

"And too much work. Can you see dealing with a *second* female and her *mishigas*? *Way* too many variables. Too much to go wrong."

"Secrets and lies. Weighty moral baggage."

"A standing appointment with a high-priced hooker?"

"That could get expensive."

"A lower-priced hooker?"

"Zoftig with a few pimples on her ass."

"As your lawyer I'd advise you to stay off Sunset Boulevard," Bave laughed. "Remember Hugh Grant."

"Remember *Divine Brown*."

"At least she was a *she*. Was it Eddie Murphy who picked up the transvestite?"

"Remember *I Dream of Jeannie?*" Sulcov asked, recalling the old TV show. "Female companionship in a bottle, on demand. That would work for me."

"Something else you could make a fortune bottling."

"Something else you could rub."

Feeling commiserated, the two men flowed along in companionable silence. As the strikers rounded the orange cones at either end, walking two by two, the person in the outside lane (Bave) had to walk a little faster to keep up with person on the inside (Sulcov), giving the momentary impression of a little brother struggling to keep up.

"I think we need a whole new construct," Sulcov said, resting his strike sign thoughtfully on his shoulder as he walked. "Why does sex have to be something that's under marital jurisdiction in the first place?"

"Because marriage was created to legitimize sex? And of course to legitimize the by-product of sex, which is children."

"It's also another attempt by government and religion to legislate morality and social behavior."

"A fairly effective attempt, I'd say."

"What if we saw sex as something other than mushy and mystical. What if we see it as *just another bodily function.* Just as a man needs to cleanse his bowels, he needs to cleanse his reproductive system. Am I wrong? The pipes must be cleaned. Otherwise I feel . . . uncomfortable. Don't you?"

"The pipes *must* be cleaned," Baverman intoned. He banged an imaginary gavel with his free hand.

"I mean, she has no say over how many times a day I elect to take a dump, right? She doesn't care whether I use the toilet at home or at the studio or even at some seedy gas station near the airport. Ditto pissing. I can piss all I want, wherever I want. I have fuckin *carte blanche* to take a piss. I could walk across the street to that country club right now and piss on a tree if I so desired."

Baverman reached up, patted his friend's shoulder. "That's right. You're a big boy now. You can go wee-wee whenever you want."

"But under the modern, feminist, politically correct construct of marriage, the female is in charge of my ejaculation. Her orifice. Her prerogative."

"As opposed to most of recorded history, when women had no free will and were treated like chattel."

"Clearly the system was designed so men could have sex whenever they wanted."

"Technically," the judge reasoned, "I don't think the marriage contract prohibits a moderate amount of self-pleasuring. In that way, you could say your ejaculations *are indeed* your own provenance. It's the method of ejaculation that's at issue here, I think. "

"I don't know about you, but I've run out of mental imagery. And porn viewing in some liberal feminist-occupied households is strictly *verboten.*"

"One's greatest hits do tend to lose their luster with use."

"*Over*use."

"What about your Angelika encounter?"

"For the zillionth time, *nothing* happened!"

Sotto voce: "You *kissed* Angelika Collette. She gave you *tongue,* correct?"

"We were rehearsing a scene."

"Did it say 'tongue' in the script? Did it say 'lingering kiss'?"

"You know *actresses*," Sulcov whispered, leaning down to speak into Bave's ear. "It meant nothing to her. She probably just got carried away. Lost in her role and all that. She probably wouldn't even recognize me again if she tripped over me."

"Sounds like you've spent a little time considering the possibility . . . "

Horns honked. Left right left. The sun made its way westward. Across the street at the Hillcrest Country Club, you could see foursomes playing through, no doubt some of them studio brass enjoying their unofficial paid vacation.

"What we need is some kind of co-op," Sulcov said at last. "You could have one in every town. Hell, you could go micro and have one in every *neighborhood*. If you need sex, you go there. No muss, no fuss, no conversation. Everyone could be licensed and inspected. Hell, it could be taxed and regulated, like alcohol. Or like marijuana. A sex *collective*, members only. And 8.25 percent of every transaction would go to the state of California."

"We'd be out of this financial crisis in no time," Bave laughed.

18

Pretty Much All of Them

Angelika, secreted away in her bedroom on an Xed-off afternoon, cell phone to ear.

"Hello, Missy." She hadn't called her "Mom" in a decade, since she'd started paying all the bills.

In the living room of the Century City condo Angelika had bought after *Skag*, Missy Collette was sitting in her favorite chair. As she spoke into her portable phone, she looked northwest from her sixteenth-story window, toward the direction of Malibu, where the ocean was shimmering in the afternoon sun. She imagined her daughter as a speck on the shoreline; she wondered when she'd be invited again to the new house. "Is everything okay?" she asked obliquely.

"Why wouldn't everything be okay?"

"I don't know? I was just wondering. You know. With all the *news* and all?"

The starlet laughed. "You mean all that 'new boyfriend' talk? Oh my God! I know. You should have been at the photo shoot yesterday. There was like, a *stampede* of paparazzi. I could hardly get to the car. Kisha had to—"

"Angelika?"

"Let's get together for dinner this weekend. You can come out to the house and we'll—"

"*Angelika.*"

The starlet held her cell phone at arms length. She made a crazy face, pantomimed throwing the damn thing across the room.

"Hello? Hello?"

"I'm here, Missy. What is it?"

"I don't know how to say this."

Annoyed: "Say *what*?"

"Have you turned on your TV today?"

Alarmed: "Was there another terrorist attack?"

Silence.

"Hello? Did something happen? Are you sick? Can you please stop beating around the bush, Missy?"

"Just turn on the TV.

"The TV?"

"And then call me back—if you want to, that is."

"What channel?"

"Pretty much all of them."

19

Ready To Go Home, Boys?

Detective Kenyatta Ducksworth escorted his new pals, Jake and Z, down the hallway from the homicide squad room back toward the intake lobby of the Hollywood Community Police Station and Jail. Better known as Hollywood Station, it was a designated historic landmark, the site of many a celebrity perp walk over the decades. The boys cradled their complimentary sodas; their fingers still carried the orange residue of vending machine Cheetos.

It turned out Ducksworth was still a weekend baller himself. The former prep-school scholarship athlete received the boys with respect—as a rule, old jocks are suckers for coltish youngbloods, reminders of their own glories past. While nothing the boys told him had been directly useful, they confirmed Ducksworth's (and Wee's) suspicions: the origin of the TEC was dubious; something major in the working version of the reconstruction of this crime was missing or incorrect. In his experience, there was a certain logicality to truth. Simple as it sounds, when people's stories don't add up, when it doesn't seem plausible that one thing or another happened in a certain way, chances are pretty good it didn't.

Which was usually okay—that's what made his job challenging and fulfilling; that's why he'd become a cop; that's what the Los Angeles Police Department was paying him for. To gather information and evidence, play hunches, hunt down inconsistencies, draw conclusions, bring the right people to justice.

This case was anything but usual. A career-maker or breaker. A sociopolitical minefield. A billionaire black rap mogul's office shot up with a banned automatic weapon. Three dead Hispanic gang bangers/rappers. One dead white lawyer. No useable fingerprints. And a Hispanic mayor, the first in 130 years, and a population growing more Hispanic by the day—one of every two babies born in the U.S. during the year 2007 had been Hispanic.

It was no secret that Chill and the mayor were close. Anytime his honor beckoned, the rapper was there with his hundred K smile, a potent symbol to bolster the tenuous solidarity between LA's historic underclasses, the beaners and the *miatas*. Usually the flare-ups were confined to the various hoods. Los V-13s vs. Shoreline Crips. MS vs. Grape Street. Turf battles, drive-bys, kneecappings, summary executions—it was business as usual in the neighborhoods, as much a part of the natural ebb and flow as the cycles of the tides. As long as the violence stayed localized, the rest of the city could carry on unconcerned.

This time, tragedy had struck the center of the center, just steps from the historic intersection of Hollywood and Vine. A taxpayer had been killed by a stray bullet in his plush corner office in a newly renovated building. The message: nobody is safe from random violence. (The subcontext: the Land of Dreams isn't so perfect as advertised.)

Add to the mix a viewing public, deprived of entertainment by the writers' strike, especially hungry for a fresh storyline. . . . Expensive airtime lacking content (and sponsors). . . . A corps of journalists and paparazzi unaffected by the WGA strike (working at a comparative pittance). . . . And great video and music (short segments of which could be aired for free).

Given the emergent facts in the case—a contract waiting to be signed, a million-dollar check waiting to be issued—it was also becoming clear to the public that some vital piece of the story was thus far unreported. There was a mystery afoot, the best kind of entertainment, good for the viewer, great for the purveyor, stay tuned as details develop. The journos were already fanning the flames, working the corners, putting an ugly edge on Angelinos' long-suppressed tensions. Reporters were starting to ask: Was this shooting just another example of gang-style, hip-hop industry thuggery? Or was it something more?

Perhaps a racial slur been had been uttered.

Perhaps what we had here was . . .

A federal hate crime?

Ducksworth could feel it on the back of his neck—the hot breath of the pasty and long-suffering lawyer/bureaucrats in the U.S. Attorney's Office in Washington, DC, eagerly packing their bags for an extended stay in La La Land.

In less than an hour Ducksworth had a meeting downtown with his lieutenant and his captain in the deputy mayor's office to discuss his findings. The deputy mayor's office! The last time he'd been to City Hall was eight years earlier, in his brand new blue uniform and shiny-billed cap, for his swearing-in ceremony. Nobody down there was going to like what he had to say. There was a reason they'd pushed through ballistics and authorized overtime—notwithstanding the backlog of thousands of rape kits being stored in giant refrigeration containers downtown, waiting to be processed for DNA, according to the *LA Times*. The mayor wanted this case to go away as quickly as possible. (Even as the media worked to keep it alive for as long as possible.)

Ducksworth slapped a pressure plate on the wall and a pair of industrial doors swept open.

The spartan lobby of Hollywood Station was crowded with anxious people awaiting word about the friend/loved one/relative who'd been sucked into the legal system through this squat brick portal of justice, located just ten blocks southwest of the intersection of Hollywood and Vine. Perhaps no other precinct in the world could boast such eclectic responsibilities—its boundaries stretched from the HOLLYWOOD sign, to the hip Melrose Avenue shopping district, to the breathtaking views of Mulholland Drive, to the quirky Jewish/ Ethiopian Fairfax District where Ducksworth himself lived and where he never, ever lacked for something good to eat or wear.

From the sergeant's desk, typically elevated, a line of petty inquirers stretched out the front door. Rows of egg-shaped plastic chairs occupied most of the remaining square footage of the lobby. An Asian man in a conical hat ate from a container with chopsticks. Two Arab men held their heads in close confab, worry beads in their hands. A twenty-something in a sharp business suit worked two Blackberries simultaneously. A stringy white girl with missing teeth fed a baby its bottle. Outside, a couple of Japanese tourists shot video—the gritty precinct had been the inspiration for a popular novel by the former cop Joseph Wambaugh, adding additional fairy dust to the site.

Oblivious to the sideshow, Ducksworth faced the boys, a three-man huddle.

"So you're gonna e-mail me and let me know what time your next game is, correct?"

"It's Saturday at 1:30 at Prep, " Z said authoritatively. This Ducksworth guy was cool. Not that Z wanted to be a cop, but he could see—in Ducksworth's exquisitely tailored suit, his expensive watch, his spit-shined shoes, his ability to fluidly switch from street talk to the King's English as the situation dictated—actual proof that getting out was possible for a kid like him, no matter where he might have begun.

"We have your card," Jake said. He held it up like a prize—the gold-embossed shield gave it the look and feel of something valuable. This whole expedition had been his idea; right now he was feeling pretty good about himself.

"Lemme know if you hear anything else you might think is useful."

"You got it," Jake said.

"No problem," said Z.

And then a voice from behind, a nasal sing-song:

"You ready to go home, boys?"

It was Big Gato. He'd been picked up hours earlier for questioning. As luck would have it, he'd been leaving the station house just as the boys arrived in their hired town car.

Ducksworth: "I'm guessing you know these superstars, Mr. Fernandez."

"Since they was knee-high," Big Gato said, his grin too wide. He had a gold front tooth on the top but was missing an incisor. He pointed his cell phone in Z's direction. "I told his *abuela* I'd get him home safe," he told the detective.

"We have practice," Jake croaked, trying to sound nonchalant.

20

Two Trained Athletes, Bodies Glistening

Angelika padded into the kitchen wearing a T-shirt and men's boxers, her hair in disarray.

The cook twirled around to the sink and started in furiously scrubbing.

JamieLynn's office was off the pantry, the majordomo's lair. From here she ran Team Angelika. She was sitting in a desk chair in front of twin computer monitors—both displayed a digital quilt of screaming websites: Perez Hilton, Gawker, TMZ, CNN, Fox, E! News, US magazine ... the pantheon of gossips and muckrakers. On the wall was a large TV monitor. Similar to the one in the pool house, you could view up to six screens at once. All of them were playing different portions of the same video.

"Click on CNN," Angelika commanded.

The large screen was instantly filled with a single image.

The footage had been shot from the vantage point of the beach, through the sliding glass door of the pool house. Living in the moment—which is what this thing with Chill was supposed to be about after the brutal readjustments of her very public divorce—Angelika had forgotten to close the curtain. A diaphanous orange and white polka dot print specially designed to allow light while also providing privacy, it had been added by her team as part of their remodel/security retrofit of the house before she'd been cleared to move in.

As it happened, the couple had ended up together on a goat-hair rug (an oval field of pink tendrils that came with its own rake), beside a smoked glass boomerang coffee table. Almost directly above them was the spotlight of a trendy Castiglioni Arco lamp. The video was clear and well lighted enough to require digital censoring.

The starlet was on top, her head reared back, her eyes closed, riding the hip-hop mogul with abandon—two trained athletes, their bodies like glistening anatomical models, every sinew and muscle wonderfully sculpted and defined.

And at the bottom right of the screen, the *StarNewsNetwork* logo.

21

Big Gato's Baby Blue Metalflake Impala

Admonished to ditch their sodas . . . and to wipe all the Cheetos dust from their greasy fuckin fingers . . . and to remember what happens to cheese-eaters and rats, in case they might have forgotten . . . the boys tumbled into Big Gato's baby blue metalflake Impala convertible.

It was a cherry of a car, fully chromed-out, circa 1963, the exact model driven by the rapper/movie producer Ice Cube in the seminal gang movie *Boyz N the Hood.* The interior was white leather tuck-and-roll with baby blue metalflake accents. Connected at six o'clock to the oversize steering wheel was an antique-quality brass-and-wood necker knob, developed during the late fifties to make it easier to drive with one hand while using the other to attend to your date.

Big Gato had bought the car during his salad days as a midlevel heroin dealer, just as crack was beginning to show up on the corners. He loved the car fiercely; he'd even killed for it (still an unsolved case). Besides his three children by two different *heinas*, the Impala was all he had left to show for his years of hustling—the shadow economy paid no pensions. During Big Gato's prison stay, the car had been ga-rage-kept at his *abula's* place, lovingly cared for by his protégé, Lil

Gato, who never once broke his pledge not to drive it, knowing well that the news would reach Biggie within the hour if he ever did.

Joining Big and Lil Gato and Jake and Z in the Impala were two other *vatos* from Lil Gato's *cliqua*. The six passengers were arranged shoulder to shoulder along the two bench seats, which were protected from spillage and other destructive elements by a set of custom vinyl slipcovers. Jake rode up front, sandwiched between the two Gatos. Despite his size, Z was similarly situated in the back. Even with the top down, the car reeked of pomade, cigarettes, beer, and marijuana. Jake worried a contact high might taint their urine samples; the private school league collected pee before the season and then again before the playoffs.

Uppermost in Z's mind was the possibility that Big Gato would do something stupid on the way home, just to fuck with him. People in the neighborhood were always quick to take credit for his success; he was always introduced as this big basketball star, someone who was going places for the glory of the hood. And yet those same people who touted him were always tempting and taunting him too, with drugs and money and crime, angling to include him in their nefarious activities, to make him their baby daddy, to drag him down to their level, where nobody tried hard at anything and nothing ever changed. "You have to be the big man God made you," his mother always said. At times, no task in the world seemed more difficult.

Big Gato pulled the Impala into the sparse traffic on Wilcox and headed north on the quiet four-lane street.

Instantly, both boys shared the same alarming thought:

We're going the wrong direction.

A few blocks farther, the Impala pulled to a stop at a red light. The twin exhausts purred; the smell of gasoline filtered upward through the deep pile carpeting. The spiffy new crosswalk signs flashed and beeped, gave orders in a calm Orwellian voice: *please walk.* A stream of tourists hustled across, dressed in their various unintended costumes of origin, each one gawking at the Impala and its occupants—Could it be? The Hollywood moment they'd been hoping for? It did appear the Impala and its occupants had driven straight off the lot at Central Casting.

Big Gato flipped a switch and the pristine convertible top clambered up and over with a stressed-sounding mechanical whine. Z had to scooch down to accommodate. The dark-tinted windows closed with a final rubber *thunk*.

The light changed and Big Gato turned right onto Hollywood Boulevard, heading east in the right-hand lane. The buildings were tall, creating a canyon effect. The sky above was a pure cloudless blue. The traffic was moderately heavy, building toward the rush-hour crescendo.

Jake watched the storefronts lining the south side of the street. Hollywood Smoke Shop, Hollywood Lingerie, Hollywood Souvenirs, Hollywood Wigs, Wig Masters. Playmates, Foreplay, and Temptation, the latter two featuring the same stock, lurid rayon crotchless panties and see-though baby-doll nighties, the manikins fetchingly constructed to include erect nipples. Checks Cashed Here. Popeye's Chicken and Biscuits. Hollywood Pizza. Hollywood Kabobs. Psychic Readings. The L Ron Hubbard Life Exhibition. Hollywood Tattoo. Taboo Smoke Shop. Hollywood Cabaret: *Girls Girls Girls*. Cheech and Chong's Bongs.

Had he been older, Jake might have wondered about the particular mix of businesses that had grown up along the Walk of Fame. Maybe the message was this: boiled down to its essential elements, American celebrity is equal parts desire, illusion, willful hedonistic pursuit . . . and junk food?

Inside the car, the air was becoming hot and difficult to breathe. Jake could feel his heart beating inside his temples. He was pretty sure there was deadly CO_2 present in the immediate atmosphere—he was positive somebody had cut a fart. As his dad would sometimes say, it smelled like "something had crawled up someone's asshole and died."

Jake did not like being in stuffy places. He liked fresh air. At home he always slept with a window open in his room—every night before bed, Sulcov adjusted it ritualistically to a certain position, depending upon the season and the outside temperature. Being in a closed, moving compartment often gave him motion sickness; he was starting to feel a little queasy, like he might have to puke. Whenever he was traveling somewhere he always took Dramamine. He wished he had one now—the child's dosage was chewable and orange-flavored—washed down with orange juice, the kind from Starbucks in the airport was his favorite. He took a deep breath through his nose the way his dad always told him to do when he felt sick. He exhaled through his mouth, quietly, so as not to bring any attention to himself. For once in his life, he tried to be as small as he could possibly be.

Big Gato reached across Jake's body and poked on the CD player. *Los Vatos'* demo album—*Da Me Su Girlfriend*—blasted from all eight speakers.

The OG clicked through the playlist until he found the track he was seeking, a remix of a controversial hit by the seminal West Coast rappers, Niggaz Wit Attitudes, called "Fuck tha Police." The *Los Vatos* remix was entitled "Chinga La Policia." A catchy mélange of mariachi brass had been added to the thumping, old-school, hip-hop beat. The homies on the record rapped in the Spanglish patois common to the Venice hood.

The Impala made a right on red at the corner of Vine Street and headed south. The sidewalks were typically thronged—tourists, locals, homeless panhandlers and sidewalk vendors, cops on bicycles, workers on lunch break from their jobs in the surrounding stores and tall buildings . . . a guy on three-foot drywall stilts wearing nothing but a red, white, and blue thong bathing suit with an American flag sticking out from between his ass cheeks.

Inside the car, Big Gato pulled his hoodie over his head. Lil Gato raised his bandana over his nose. The other homeboys did the same.

Jake looked into the rearview mirror and found Z's black eyes; his image in the glass vibrated with every throb of the music.

What the fuck, dude?

Holy shit!

They pulled up their hoodies, too.

The car rolled past a street sign: Selma Avenue. As a family the Sulcovs had visited Selma, Alabama. They'd also gone to Washington, DC; they'd stood together on the spot at the Lincoln Memorial where Martin Luther King made his famous "I Have a Dream" speech. Jake's maternal grandparents had a limited edition Andy Warhol silkscreen of MLK in their living room, one of only twenty copies. It was worth millions; every rich black person in America wanted one for *his* living room, too, or that's what his dad said, anyway.

Big Gato kept the car in the right hand lane, behind a long articulated bus. He lowered the windows on the passenger side of the Impala, front and back.

The fresh air felt good. Jake breathed deeply through his nose. *Do not barf!* he repeated to himself, a mantra. He pursed his lips, blew out a steady stream of air. He imagined his dad holding his hand, telling him everything would be fine. He didn't want to imagine what would happen if he threw up in Big Gato's car.

The subwoofers pounded, rumbling Jake's innards. The brass wailed. Siren effects, gunshots, car crash sounds, twisting metal— a powerful wall of sound flooded out of the car and into the street like suds flooding from a broken washing machine in some old sitcom on *Nick at Nite*, which Sulcov let him watch even though Tish disapproved.

Lil Gato reached down beneath the seat and retrieved a sawed-off shotgun. Jake stole another look in the rear view, caught a glimpse of Z. The vato to his right was holding a black metal handgun, some kind of automatic.

As they rolled past the wonderfully renovated mixed-use building that housed the offices of RAP Records, the *vatos* opened fire.

The noise was deafening, much louder than Jake ever imagined real gunfire would be; none of the simulated war games on Xbox came close to preparing him for the concussive volume of *actual* small arms.

Lil Gato pumped and squeezed the trigger again and again; Jake could feel the recoil passing through the shooter's body and into his own, pinning him between the two gangstas, taking away his breath.

The smell of sweat and farts and cordite was thick. Everybody in the car was yelling and laughing and cursing—Jake's ears rang with white noise, his hearing temporarily short-circuited.

And then Big Gato floored it.

The baby blue metalflake Impala fishtailed south on Vine Street, in the direction of home.

22

The Receptive Interval

Sulcov hunched over his cell phone, clumsily thumb-toggling a text message to his son.

HEY BUDDY WHAT UP?

He was sitting in his favorite chair, at his father's old desk in his pool house/office. The six-hundred-square-foot structure, semicylindrical in shape, was built of wood, steel, and glass; it was designed to appear to be floating over the edge of the canyon, "like a barrel over verdant falls," according to the architect Arnold Stevenson, the words handwritten in his leather-bound journal, which had conveyed with the purchase of the house. The front door was set at ground level, off the flagstone deck surrounding the pool, with a bath/changing area to the immediate left. A nautically inspired ladder-staircase led steeply down into the main room, which was dominated by windows, allowing for "intimate communion with Mother Nature."

From the first showing, Sulcov was drawn to this space—as a child growing up in the city he often daydreamed of tree houses. To the present it remained the only part of their importantly pedigreed residence in which he truly felt at home . . . and the only room for which he'd been allowed to choose his own furnishings. Some guys had plush corporate offices. Some guys had cubicles. Some guys hung out in their garage. Some guys went to the corner pub. This was his cave, his clubhouse, his studio, his sanctum sanctorum. It's where the magic happened, where he danced with the devil, where he pulled his pud. Nobody ever bothered him here: Daddy's office.

The haunted sounds of night birds and dizzy insects drifted through an open window. An owl hooted periodically from its usual perch in a high and fragrant eucalyptus tree directly across the canyon. The air smelled strongly of coastal sage and earth. In the morning he would drive downtown to the courthouse to swap vehicles with his buddy Bave, then out to Ventura to pick up the ground cover. Higinio needed to hurry up and plant; the winter rains were surely coming, as was the county inspector. The flat-screen TV behind him on the back wall was tuned to *The Daily Show with Jon Stewart*, popular for blurring the line between news and satire; pretty soon, nobody would know the difference anymore. Behind Stewart, on his studio monitor, viewers could see the hot topic *du jour*, rerunning in a continuous loop—the media had dubbed it the *Chillika Sex Tape*.

COACH SAID NO PRACTICE 2DAY SO WONDERING WHERE U B???

Texting was a slow and deliberate process with his outmoded Samsung flip phone. That he was a proud Luddite who stubbornly remained telephonically downscale was a pretty notion, but it would not last. In three months the Sulcov family's two-year phone plan would be at last eligible for termination; at that point they'd be able to take their digits and walk without a financial penalty. Tense negotiations over future carriers and plans had already begun; as the deadline neared, Tish and Jake's skirmishes had become more frequent—pitched battles over features, minutes, and phone styles offered, argued with encyclopedic command. To see the strong-willed Tish forced to do combat with her mirror image, to see her suffer herself the kind of frustration Sulcov always felt when trying to win a point from such a formidable spirit . . . Was it wrong of him to feel a little bit gratified even as he was playing referee?

Luddite or not, you needed text and e-mail on the go these days to keep pace with the rest of the world. Technophobes were no more interesting than people who claimed not to have a television. Every day Jake processed hundreds of text messages. After some amount of experimentation, Sulcov had realized that the boy was more likely to answer him when contacted by text—he was so unfailingly conditioned to respond to his self-programmed combo of bells and whistles, it didn't matter *who* texted. Additionally, his text answers tended to be more intelligible, good-natured, and complete than his spoken effort—an orderly row of somewhat recognizable (if misspelled) words and symbols vs. the mumbled hash that passed in teenville for verbal communication.

Usually life's best course is adaptation. If Sulcov was going to communicate meaningfully with his son through the difficult teenage years . . . clearly he was in need of a QWERTY keyboard.

CALL WHEN YOU GET A CHANCE, K? ILY, DADO

He pushed the send button and closed the silver clamshell, imagined his words winging toward the intended destination, a digital carrier pigeon with a little piece of his heart strapped to one leg.

Whether or not the kid would ultimately receive the message— or read it to conclusion—was another digression. Jake's cell phone could easily be dead or lost or dropped down a Jiffy John, as had been the case last summer at a tournament in Las Vegas.

Despite the casual syntax of his text, Sulcov was more than a little worried. He hadn't heard from the little pisher in over twenty-four hours. He wondered what he was doing. If he was hungry. What clothes he was wearing, if they were dirty, if they smelled like boy. He wondered, for the zillionth time, if Z's incredibly hot, single-mom-elder-sister—big black Keane eyes, pressed hair, they called her Flaca— was teaching his son things he wasn't ready to learn. There were guns, drugs, all kinds of bad stuff floating around in Venice . . . even in Z's house, he was sure.

Now there was this business with Chill and Sleeper and *Los Vatos*. Who knew what hornet's nest had been stirred? A drive-by shooting at Chill's corporate headquarters? In broad daylight? *Jesus*

H. Christ. The local news was on full alert, interrupting regular programming for updates. Police were saying the events had unfolded so quickly and unexpectedly that eyewitness accounts were wildly variable—meaning: they had no clue. It had to be payback from Venice, Sulcov figured. Why couldn't the cops figure it out?

Maybe I should drive down to Z's.

Great. Daddy shows up to yank him home. You gotta give him his manhood.

He's just a little boy.

Sulcov opened his Samsung again and started to poke the number 1, speed dial for Jake.

And quickly snapped it shut, placed it on the desk beside a small blue-glass canister. Unscrewing the lid, he extracted a half-smoked joint of Abusive Kush Private Reserve.

Yes, Sulcov was also on the list, too.

A partial share.

Co-owned with . . . *Zondo*, who'd left no Hollywood perk unsampled in his rise up the A-list. At least he'd been kind enough to share.

Under the arrangement, Sulcov was entitled to one-half of an ounce of the designer primo every two months. Upon e-mail notification, he had one week to claim his share—otherwise it was sold out from under. He had two days left. As you could imagine, there was no shortage of takers.

As was his custom, Sulcov made a note on a neon-orange Post-it: *Malibu Green's,* taking care to get the apostrophe correct. He affixed it to the bottom frame of his computer monitor, the screen open to Facebook and Outlook mail. Down the right edge of the monitor's frame were a number of sun-faded, tennis-ball-green Post-its—the plot points for his next *High Tolerance* script. He'd just started to work it when they called the strike. His eyes lingered over the sorrowful squares, the black ink faded to blue, the edges curled up at the bottoms. His heart felt heavy—like he was viewing the sonogram of a stillborn child.

The strike couldn't have come at a worse time, for Sulcov or for his show. *High Tolerance* had been number one on the Nielsen list since its second week—a phenomenon on the order of *Lost* or *Law and Order*. It had buzz; it had quality and longevity. It even plumbed original territory at times, mixing as it did the subjects of current events, journalism, and sleuthing, with sophisticated camera work and a healthy dose of special effects. As a writer, Sulcov was coming off an Emmy nomination. His scripts were evermore nuanced and stylized. He felt challenged but in control, an artist hitting his stride.

Though at the moment he wasn't writing anything at all.

Except Post-its.

It was hard to even remember anymore what it felt like to be writing. Without the discipline of sitting down to type every day, without the lighthouse of a project to direct him, he felt like a man adrift in a sea of nonbiodegradable plastic—he'd read about such a place in the *Times*, five hundred miles off the coast of Southern California, where a continent-size stew of unrecycled debris has collected in the nexus of the swirling tides.

A ticket to the writing game is a box seat in a stadium of self-doubt. Going through the turnstile he had a pretty good idea he wasn't going to end up being the next George Orwell or Truman Capote, but still he soldiered on, the work a reward in itself—the sitting and typing, the words appearing magically on the computer screen, the characters taking form, the action flowing . . . And all of it materializing eventually on a screen in people's living rooms—almost exactly as he'd imagined it. Actors saying *his* lines (more or less); people all over town (all over the world!) talking about *his* characters . . . as if they really existed . . . which they did now, thanks to his typing, his script. (Not to mention the young actors whose careers he'd created.)

On talk shows, Hollywood people are always saying how it's "all about the work." It sounds dippy, but it's true. The point is, people who create need to be constantly creating. Otherwise they start breaking down. Doing weird shit, fucking up, self-destructing. When Sulcov was working, when he was engaged in thinking about things other than himself, when he was projecting his fruitful imagination into a script . . . that's when he felt happiest.

Because he understood: to create a story is to become a god.

After that, everything else feels a little hollow.

Sulcov raised his eyes, took stock of his ghoulish, top-lit reflection in the large darkened window. Liquid sounds emanated from his midsection; his prominent lower lip bulged involuntarily, making his weakish chin appear nonexistent. When he was young and about to cry his father would tell him, "Pull in your lower lip, you're going through a tunnel." Now Marv Sulcov, the esteemed ob-gyn and ladies man, was apparently suffering from some kind of dementia or early-stage Alzheimer's.

He wrote another Post-it: *find neuro doc for Marv.*

Without further ado, he affixed the roach to a hemostat and helped himself to several therapeutic hits of Abusive.

Almost immediately he felt his spirit leaven, an actual lifting of his brow.

He stood up, walked over to the open window, took a deep breath. Like a sailboat changing tack, he could feel his state of mind making a course correction.

Lighten up, motherfucker. You have your health. You have a roof over your head and plenty of money. You have an amazing son who loves and respects you. And if you never work again, you won't starve. You have it all, my brother—including a hot wife waiting for you in the bedroom. What the fuck are you still doing in here?

On this rare night when their schedules had dovetailed, the Sulcovs had in fact dined together at a fond neighborhood bistro, a comfy spot where they regularly shared the *pullet*. The skin was crispy, infused with garlic—the inspiration behind his stomach's increasingly lively monologue. This was the upside of Jake's frequent absences from the household: they had the place to *themselves*.

Somewhat surprisingly, their impromptu date had been splendid, even magical, evocative of the couple's better days. They'd split a bottle of wine. For the first time in months, his jokes found her elusive funny bone; sweet laughter filled the space between them. It wasn't until coffee was served that the light bulb went off and he did some counting backward on his mental calendar.

The receptive interval!

Three to five precious days at the center of the menstrual cycle, the time of ovulation.

During this brief Edenic period, thanks to the rose-tinted lenses of her hormones, Sulcov could practically do no wrong. (The rest of the month was a crapshoot.)

And he had every intention of taking advantage.

Tonight.

He took a last long hit and stubbed out the roach. He stowed the ashtray and the other paraphernalia in the drawer, went about closing down the room for the night—pulling the shades, locking the windows, placing lengths of PVC irrigation pipe along the bottoms of several of the window frames for added security; during their first few years there were problems with a persistent thief.

He climbed the ladder/stairs, stopped in the changing room to take a pee. Standing over the toilet, his state of mind by now pleasantly stabilized, he could see through the small round window the soft glow of his glass house, reflected in the still waters of his pool, the family Banyan tree so stately in silhouette.

You are a lucky man, he told himself, zipping his fly.

Noting that the bowl was a bit grungy, Sulcov held down the handle for a bit longer than usual—about a month ago, he'd purchased this nifty new water-conserving brand of commode, designed with two distinct flushing cycles for greater economy. According to the plumber, it was considered "the Prius of toilets."

As the water swirled strongly and efficiently around the bowl, Sulcov set the alarm, locked the deadbolt ... And fairly jogged the thirty-two steps to the house.

23

E'erbody on My Dick

Hordes of press, gawkers and concerned fans continued to gather outside the headquarters of RAP Records. The overflow spilled into Vine Street, which was cordoned off, north and south, at the intersections of Hollywood and Sunset.

The scene had the trippy, night-turned-day atmosphere of a rave or theater of war. Rainbow strobe lights from various official vehicles played off the concrete and glass buildings that formed the surrounding urban canyon. News trucks vied for space in a commandeered parking lot; an assortment of microwave towers and satellite dishes dominated the immediate airspace. The din of voices, the drone of generators powering lights and police command elements, the rumble of traffic from the surrounding streets, helicopters buzzing overhead. On the eastern side of Vine, directly across from RAP—in the office of the randomly murdered lawyer—a set of giant speakers faced out the windows of a third-floor office, music pumping. (A banner advertised the DJ's website; another Tinseltown hopeful looking for his big break.)

Unbelievably, given the fusillade of small arms rounds produced by the occupants of Big Gato's Impala, only one person was dead as a result of the drive-by—a seventy-six-year-old man who'd suffered a heart attack. Several others were slightly injured by flying glass or buckshot; a homeless woman sustained a shoulder wound, a clean through-and-through. In real time, the actual shooting had lasted no more than two or three seconds. As it happened, the cacophony of the shattering glass—the storefronts of ground-floor establishments including Amore's Pizza and Do Rag—drew attention toward the building, away from the source of the gunfire. When questioned, tourists and locals alike told police they'd been walking with their heads down, focused on the stars underfoot. This stretch featured, among others, John Belushi, Grace Kelly, Bud Abbott, Jack Lemmon, and next to him for all eternity, his *Odd Couple* partner, Walter Matthau.

Over the last several hours, police commanders on the scene had become aware of the increasingly vitriolic back-and-forth between two camps of onlookers. Latinos and African Americans—the beaners and the *miatas*—had come out in force to let their allegiance be known.

Separated only by a line of sawhorses, one cop on each side, the two opposing groups were, in and of themselves, a remarkable consortium of different community types. Busboys beside homeboys, church ladies beside gangbangers—from all appearances, the usual competing interests and societal stratifications had been put aside tonight in favor of a larger sense of racial communality. Just as a city takes pride in its championship sports team, the people in TV land felt personally affected by the news events of the past two days. Universal chords had been struck, heartstrings had been played. The ranks continued to swell.

The portico of the RAP building was occupied by a platoon-sized contingent of riot police outfitted with helmets and electrified riot shields. Perhaps because the entryway was located at the northern-most section of the frontage, the huge, beveled-glass lobby doors sustained no damage in the drive-by. Off to one side was a makeshift shrine to *Los Vatos*—a snowdrift of flowers, candles, handwritten messages, pictures of saints, and stuffed animals.

Now, the lobby doors slid open and out stepped Detective Kenyatta Ducksworth, looking smart in an Armani suit, complete with pocket square, and Italian cap-toe boots. He was followed by a phalanx of a LAPD uniforms, a total of six men surrounding four prisoners: the bodyguards Clevon and Eddie; the aide-de-camp TBone; and bringing up the rear, Thomas Washington Curry, a.k.a. Chill.

The entourage proceeded toward a black paddy wagon idling by the curb. As a courtesy, the mogul and his men had been cuffed with their hands in front instead of behind their backs. Likewise, nylon restraints had been substituted for the usual chrome-plated steel. (In no way did Ducksworth want to see this guy made into a martyr; at the same time, he could have elected to take him into custody without cuffs.)

The crowd pressed forward against the barricades at various points. Hailing from trailer park and ocean front, eastside and westside, suburban mini-manse and two-bedroom garden apartment ... they'd all come to this place tonight for the same reason: to make sure the world that occupied so much of their attention—this fabulous land of celebrity and privilege and drama—was really here. And because they wanted to be a part of it.

For their initiative, for their expense (not inconsiderable to the foreign tourists in the bunch, of which there were many) they'd been rewarded a front-row seat at the event everybody in the nation—and a good many parts of the world—would soon be talking about, if they weren't already watching live.

Someday they'd tell their grandchildren: *I was there when Chilly T Neegrow was arrested for murder.*

Reaching the paddy wagon, the police formed a perimeter. With some difficulty, the beefy Clevon hefted himself up into the truck, as did Eddie. For TBone, the whole process was muscle memory—he'd been here many times before.

Chill made the move upward in one athletic step.

But instead of ducking inside the van, he turned around to face the crowd.

There were hundreds gathered, maybe a thousand, and scores of media. Mirrored in his Hater Blockers, it seemed like many, many more.

A female voice: "We love you Chillyyyy!"

Cheers. Hoots. Applause.

And also a few jeers.

A male voice: "We got your back, my brother!"

A smattering of claps.

"Only the Strong Survive!" somebody hollered. It was the title of an early Chill hit, a rap cover of an old Jerry Butler song, previously covered by Elvis.

"Tell It on the Mountain!" Another hit.

"Fear a Black Planet."

More hoots and cheers.

Then the DJ up in the window launched Chill's all-time dance hall favorite: "E'erbody on My Dick," from the album of the same name. The sound flooded the concrete and glass canyon.

The familiar bass line worked its magic, and the bodies in the crowd began to move. Heads bobbed. Feet tapped. Hands rose— white hands, black hands, brown hands, delicate yellow hands with little fingers—all of them keeping the beat in the air, transported and transfixed, like so many worshippers in a primitive church moved by the spirit.

And then, as if on cue, the culturally disparate but rhythmically unified mass, people of all ages and colors and shapes and sizes, hailing from Stockholm and Serbia, Modesto and Philadelphia, from Beverly Hills and East *El Lay* and Soweto South of Pico, all of them united only by their steadfast and hearty consumption of the popular culture that had been woven so tightly into the fabrics of all of their lives, however different, all of these people joined together as one to sing out the chorus of the snappy and naughty little song that had spent eighteen months at the top of the charts and made Chill into a household name.

> *E'erbody on my dick*
> *Looking to turn a trick*
> *The time has come*
> *To be the one*
> *E'erbody on my dick*

Feeling that rush of adrenalin, that feeling of invincibility—what could possibly equal the experience of hearing an audience sing *your* song to *you?*—Chill raised his nylon-shackled wrists above his head, his fists clenched defiantly in a double black power salute, and issued his best and most defiant hundred K smile.

Setting off a spontaneous cheer.

And a barrage of flash pops.

The cover of his next hit album.

24

An Arrow of Certain Knowledge

"Hey there, *beauuuutiful.*"

Sulcov leaned rakishly against the doorframe of the upstairs master suite, admiring his life partner. Man or woman, gay or straight, everyone acknowledged her intelligence and beauty, which showed every sign of improving with age. Truly he'd loved her from the first moment he'd seen her, striding athletically through the storied forty-second floor newsroom of *NewsSource,* wearing a black worsted Chanel suit over a teal silk Gucci blouse, the neck opened casually to the third button, exposing a thin gold chain, a teasing glimpse of lingerie.

As she'd passed down a long aisle between the desk pods, heads turned, eyes bugged, people whispered and winked and smirked; a number of colleagues of both sexes, including Sulcov, swiveled around in their chairs to track her progress, the pleasing sway of her hips, the sculptured muscularity of her legs, the running shoes that completed the ensemble. In a workplace where the customary greeting was "What's the gossip?" she clearly was it.

Now it was fifteen years later. His Mulatto Barbie was propped in her usual reading position, two pillows against the headboard. A warm circle of light illuminated her book, Maya Angelou's *I Know Why the Caged Bird Sings*, this month's selection for the book club she'd help start for teen mothers in Crenshaw, another project sponsored by The Sisters. Even in her favorite thread-bare night shirt, her expensively straightened and augmented hair pulled back beneath a sleeping scarf—he thought of it as her *do-rag* but had never dared utter the words—she was still the woman he most desired in the world.

She regarded him over the top of her reading glasses. "Did you hear from Jake?" It sounded more like an admonishment than a question.

"I sent him a text."

"What did he say?"

He shrugged, palms turned upward in resignation. *I love the way her breasts feel through that shirt. I think I'm gonna leave it on tonight when we do it.*

"What good is a *Black*berry if you don't ever *answer* it?" she asked rhetorically. "*You* don't even have a *Black*berry."

"But I *will* have a Blackberry soon, right? Or an iPhone? Have you and Jake decided which carrier we're picking yet?"

She looked back down to her book. "I don't really care to debate carriers this minute, if you don't mind."

His face twisted into an awkward half smile, as if the software governing his range of facial expressions had glitched between happiness and discomfort.

"I don't see why he has to be at Z's *again* tonight," she protested. On the night table, her Blackberry vibrated. She reached over and picked it up, read a message, made a dozen keystrokes with her thumbs.

Sulcov waited. He thought about the new bikini wax she'd professed to have gotten. She'd always been dismissive of such extreme personal grooming; suddenly it was all the rage. *I can't wait to see the little landing strip she's been talking about.*

"This is a *school* night," she said, placing her cell down on the bed next to her and rejoining the conversation. "He has tests coming up."

Obviously Sulcov had been wrong about the receptive interval thing. He'd been in his office for scarcely twenty minutes—surely that was within the acceptable range of Date Night behavior: dinner, followed by a little personal time, followed by reunification in the marital bed. That was the routine, no?

"His best buddy's big brother was just shot and killed," he said righteously, stepping into the room. If sex was off the table, he might as well shoot for justice. "Sleeper called Jake *hermanito*—little brother. He was so proud of that."

"I know what *hermanito* means," she said icily.

"We might want to think about some grief counseling for the kids. We could pay for Z's too, I guess. Maybe we can find a therapist who would do a—"

"Your son hasn't been home in *three days!*"

"Two, actually." In the interest of accuracy, Sulcov counted on his fingers. "Last night; tonight." He couldn't help but notice as he did the tufts of wiry hair that had begun to sprout on his knuckles. The edges of his ears had been similarly productive of late, necessitating all sorts of extra grooming.

"What about yesterday?"

"*I* saw him yesterday," he reminded her. "I took him to school. I picked him up from practice. I took them to Z's. Given the circumstances, I thought it only right that he stay with Z. And after I dropped them off . . . remember? I picked up a pizza from Martini's and a bottle of wine, thinking we could watch a DVD or something. And you . . . "

He tugged at his chin hair the way he sometimes did when he was formulating.

" . . . didn't get my call. You were at your *girlfriend's* till midnight in that slinky dress. I called you and you didn't answer."

She looked at him.

An arrow of certain knowledge pierced his forehead and lodged itself into the back wall of his brain.

For one long beat, his life stopped.

His knees became rubber. Misjudging the distance, he sat down awkwardly on the sharp corner of the antique trunk at the foot of their bed, "*Oooof.*"

She arched a single threaded eyebrow. "Sit much?"

His anus smarting, Sulcov readjusted himself on the trunk, which was filled with down comforters, ready for that moment when the big freeze hit Southern California. Reaching into his quiver of snappy comebacks . . . he found nothing.

Silence settled between them.

She stared him down.

"Tell me," he croaked.

Her familiar and arresting blue eyes blazed a mixed message: Helplessness. Remorse. Ruthless animal desire.

It was pretty clear the ruthless animal desire part was not directed toward him.

25

What Do You Think About Me?

Like a conquering warlord, Calvin Scott was pillow-propped on one of the large lounging beds that served as furniture at the Sky Bar at the Mondrian Hotel, the well-known celebrity retreat on Sunset Boulevard in West Hollywood.

The centerpiece of the club was the hotel's pool; steam rose enchantingly from the glowing topaz surface. The thumping repetitive music worked its hypnotic effect. Multi-culti model/waitresses with cute cropped tees and booty-hugging lava-lava wrap skirts circulated among the beautiful and ambitious crowd. The air was ripe with perfume and pheromones, bringing to mind rainy season on the African veldt—so many exotic species gathered around the watering hole, eyes wide and unblinking, attending to animal needs. It was Wednesday night. It was late. Nobody was going home alone.

In the area occupied by the bar, a raised platform with a faux thatched roof and a commanding view of the twinkling city lights, the customary wall-mounted televisions were tuned to various news broadcasts. All over the world, on digital monitors of every type and size—from the Jumbotron in Manhattan's Times Square, to computer screens in Tel Aviv and Tokyo, to cell phone screens in Mumbai and Johannesburg—people were watching the same thing: endlessly looped clips of the Chillika sex tape. In the twenty-four hours since it was uploaded, it had become the most viewed YouTube offering, ever.

And burned into the bottom right corner of every frame . . . the friendly and increasingly familiar logo of *StarNewsNetwork*.

Following Chill's arrest, Scott and the staff at *StarNews* had labored mightily to produce a package of in-depth coverage—magically turning an X-rated sex tape (an invasion of privacy at the very least?) into an Important News Event, requiring around-the-clock coverage, endless analysis and guest commentators, further deep probing. Bringing together the several relatable events of the last two days, the summary indeed looked grave. Five deaths, a dozen injuries. Millions of dollars of property damage and police time. Four arrests, including one of the most famous men on the planet. A car full of sociopaths still at large somewhere in this important and emblematic city.

And then there was the added complication of Chill's "misogynistic and racially charged statements," as the *New York Times* had reported. The product of Scott's interviews with the mogul, the sound-bites had been used out of context for promotions and cutaways:

"White people have an attitude of entitlement. They expect things to come their way, go their way, or get out of their way . . . "

"You know what they say about white women: you can't bring em home to momma, but you can turn em out for twice the price . . ."

"You *practice* on the white girls, but you *marry* your own kind . . ."

If the murder, mayhem, and celebrity sex gossip hadn't drawn people into the story, Chill's apparent abuse of his First Amendment freedoms certainly had, further fueling speculation that the *Los Vatos* shooting might have carried the undertones of a hate crime. Pundits and chat show hosts were chowing down on the news feast—as was anyone with axe to grind against Chill, the genre of hip-hop, liberal politics . . . or blacks or Latinos or celebrities in general. "Chill's statements are a heinous crime against societal harmony and good taste," said an op-ed piece in the *LA Times*.

Scott had been surrounded all evening at the Mondrian by his new compadres, members of the wacky, diverse, and hardworking staff of *StarNews'* LA bureau. The call for celebratory drinks after work had led to this impromptu gathering; text messages went out across the city, summoning friends, and friends of friends. What glory Scott had brought himself he'd brought to the rest of the team, from the lowly interns to the boardroom suits.

Tonight, this was the place to be—the exact epicenter of the universal buzz. No cheesy rental searchlights were needed to make the point:

StarNews was the network of the moment.

And Calvin Scott was the man.

As the party grew, as the corps of paparazzi massed outside—behind the requisite velvet rope, snaking west along the southern sidewalk on Sunset Boulevard—the story of Scott's fall and rise over the last forty-eight hours was told and retold among the gathered, a sacred tribal legend:

The months of negotiation to gain access to Chill's camp; the weeks gaining Chill's trust and actual proximity; the unfortunate timing of Scott's meeting with his agent; his fortunate re-entry into the building minutes before police arrived; his daring, you-are-there text dispatches from a bathroom stall . . .

And then: His early morning quest along an abandoned stretch of Malibu beach. His intuitive decision to investigate a distant, light-filled sliding glass door. His absolute surprise to find Chilly T. Neegrow—rapper, mogul, television reality star, and self-proclaimed "Mandingo Nigga U Luv 2 H8"—making a midnight booty call on America's favorite white girl.

Paramount among all things was Scott's amazing footage—*bang bang indeed!*—shot from a perfect vantage point inside a large wooden enclosure built for trashcans and beach paraphernalia. (Note to young journalists: the Leatherman Multi-Tool he was carrying included a small but healthy saw element that proved extremely useful.)

Combined with the extensive interviews and exclusive reporting and access, Scott's scoop was being hailed by some as good, hard journalistic enterprise, shoe-leather paying proceeds. For the first time in its short history, the tabloidish StarNews Media Group was being perceived worldwide as a serious news-gathering organization. Even the straight-laced *Washington Post* grabbed a frame of the video for its front page (with tasteful black censor bars employed).

Joining Scott on the mattress tonight was his LA editor and two youngish female journos, each arranged into her own still life of semisodden repose. The one to Scott's left wore oversized glasses and black Cleopatra bangs. Forty-five minutes ago, she'd plopped herself down a bit too close, offered Marlboro Reds all around, and started peppering Scott with questions. It had come as no surprise that she worked for the *LA Weekly*—they'd spent their first few moments establishing that their chat would be *off* the record.

Scott raised a distinctively shaped bottle of tequila—Patrón Añejo, the expensive stuff, homage to Chill's particular drink of choice and method of imbibing. "For all the jailed homies," he said fatuously. He took a swig and passed the bottle to his wingman, Peter Griffin. Respected as he was, nobody in the office dared mention that he'd been forced by fate to share his name with a buffoonish and wildly popular cartoon character.

"How long were you actually inside the trash chute?" the *LA Weekly* girl asked. Her bright and curious eyes were obscured behind the curtain of bangs and the additional rampart of her stolid ophthalmological gear. "The smell must have been awful."

"Everything went to the cleaners, but I fear the worst," Scott said solemnly.

The *LA Weekly* girl laughed and lit another cig. Besides the obvious draws of the Sky Bar, probably the most enduringly profitable feature was ... the sky. That the place lacked a roof, and was therefore technically outside, meant patrons could smoke cigarettes while imbibing—a rare and wonderful treat in Wellville.

"Is it weird that you're part of the story now? Those paparazzi outside are waiting for you, you know. "

The opportunities for triumph in life were few, Scott reflected, taking the bottle back from Griffin. A proper celebration called for good food, good drink, good friends, and good sex—a triumphant night-capping shag for the conquering hero.

"Enough about me," he said, thrusting the bottle beneath her chin, a newsman with a microphone. "What do *you* think about me?"

She snatched the Patron from his hand, gulped down a macho hit.

"She drank Vince Neil under the fuckin table at the last *Flaunt* party," Griffin said matter-of-factly.

LA Weekly passed the bottle back to Scott. "Doesn't it bother you just a *little* bit that this big story is really about two consenting adults doing what everybody does?" By her vehemence, her slight slur, you could tell she was getting pretty drunk. "At the end of the day, is this story really even *newsworthy*?"

Scott took another hit from the bottle and handed it off to Griffin's girl. "You know what the scariest thing is?" he told the assembled. "I don't really give a shit."

By the expression on his face, you could tell he was lying.

26

A Riderless Horse Headed Back to the Barn

Sulcov staggered across the flagstone deck, tracing by instinct his cherished thirty-two-step commute from the sliding door off the great room to his pool house/office, a riderless horse headed back to the barn.

She is contemplating an affair, he told himself, reviewing.

Who confesses to CONTEMPLATING an affair?

Someone who's not telling the truth?

The marine layer had lifted; the sky was inky blue-black and glittery with uncountable perfect pinpoints of light—briefly he was reminded of the ceiling in their neighbor's expensively decorated nursery, four thousand tiny halogen bulbs arranged in the shapes of the constellations. There had been an unveiling. The whole street was invited. A FatBurger truck in the driveway, a humongous bouncy castle for the kids in the backyard.

Maybe she IS telling the truth. Maybe she's REALLY just THINKING about having an affair. Maybe I cut her off at the pass.

Or maybe she's already made a bunch of trips to Cheater's Gulch, and she's lying her ass off.

We have history. We have love. We have a child together. Maybe she's having a rough patch. We all falter. She's just looking before she leaps. She needs someone to talk to. She's talking to me, her best friend—those were her words, right?

His throat was tight and sore from talk and emotion. The air was cool, his scalp was clammy, he couldn't breathe. He felt raw and pink and exposed, as if someone had just removed the top layer of his skin.

I CONTEMPLATE fucking other women every single day.

But you never do shit.

So, what . . . I'm a wuss?

Or nobody wants you.

Or maybe I'm just . . . faithful.

Each step seemed like a million. Everything familiar seemed strange. The menthol scent of the eucalyptus. The chlorine tang of the pool. The lively chatter of the night creatures in the canyon. The hooting owl in the distant tree. The fluky marimba tones of the bamboo swaying in the breeze. It was like he'd been born again, though not in a good way.

She says she hasn't done anything.

"Yet."

"Just good friends."

With D'Shawn Fireman, the six foot eight former starting small forward for the NBA champion Los Angeles Lakers.

He's into charity. Has his own foundation.

And three championship rings.

And two ex-wives.

Didn't he fuck Halle Berry?

Sulcov fumbled with the keys. Punched the security code . . .

The arms on that guy!

Chiseled onyx.

She probably talks about you: "He comes too fast . . ."

When you only have sex once a month, you're fast. It's lack of practice. It's performance anxiety. I Googled it.

Remember that Maxim magazine poll? Forty-seven percent of women rate "stamina" as Very Important.

Well, I happen to rate "fidelity" as Very Important.
She probably sucked his dick.

He vomited into a ceramic planter, home to a rare elephant foot tree—a flume of garlic chicken, red wine, espresso and bile, mixed with the masticated chunks of his ego, the shreds of a life he'd loved so well.

Leaning against the prickly stucco wall, gathering himself, he became aware of a curious sound.

A whooshing noise.

Like water flowing.

A fountain?

At their previous residence, on Henry Street in Brooklyn, the Sulcovs' front "lawn" had measured three feet by three—two holly bushes and four perennials, conspiring together to hide the unsightly gas meter. Instead of a back yard, there was a garage appended to the rear—he used to barbeque on the flat tar roof; they called it "Brooklyn Beach." It was a basic house, nothing fancy, a handyman's special. Everything was old and simple.

In their important Arnold Stevenson Treehouse, as in their new milieu, *nothing* was simple. The lord master of a small compound, Sulcov was attended by all manner of domestic machinery—a squad of marginally "smart" automated systems, controlled by a series of timers and computer interfaces, over which he had titular control. There were solar heaters, electric blinds and shades, security alarms, pool and Jacuzzi motors and filters, in-ground sprinklers . . . all of it required expensive professional intervention from time to time. On a daily basis, components here and there cycled on and off, going through their involuntary paces, creating a distinct set of *clicks* and *whirrs* and *hums* and *tha-rumps*. As the traffic noise, the flap of pigeon wings and the rumble of the subway had been his soundscape in Brooklyn, these aural signposts helped define his new environment. He knew every one of them intimately.

But *this* sound was something unusual.

He opened the door of his office, turned on the light.

The Prius of Toilets was overflowing!

Water poured copiously from the bowl, cascaded onto the floor of the bath/changing room and down the steps into the naturally harmonious sunken office.

His sanctum sanctorum had become a wading pool.

He fell to his knees, groping for the shutoff valve.

And wept.

PART THREE

27

The Face of Hate

Traveling in tight formation, three identical Cadillac Escalades sped southward along the 101 Freeway, one of a tangle of rutted thoroughfares and soaring overpasses that merge vertiginously at the graffiti-strewn epicenter of downtown Los Angeles.

The convoy exited at Broadway, turned left onto West Temple Street, sidled up to the curb at the front entrance of the Clara Shortridge Foltz Criminal Justice Center.

Known previously as the Criminal Courts building, the edifice had been renamed in a statewide effort to make government more gender-inclusive. A little research reveals Ms. Foltz an excellent choice of namesake; clearly she was a woman to be reckoned with. After she and her five children were deserted by her husband, Foltz began studying law with a local judge. Denied admission to law school because of her gender, she sued, argued her own case, and won admission. She passed the bar exam in 1878, but California law at the time allowed only white males to become members of the bar. Foltz authored a bill in the state legislature that replaced the words "white male" with "person" and pushed it through to passage.

In September 1878, she became the first woman admitted to the California bar.

The twenty-one-story building dwarfed its immediate neighbors; the peculiar architectural style put one in mind of a towering chunk of white honeycomb. It was a familiar visual image in the city's colorful criminal history, perhaps most remembered as the venue for the murder trial of the fallen USC football hero, O. J. Simpson. The judge in that case, the diminutive Lance Ito, still presided two days a week. He had an office down the hall from Sulcov's buddy, Judge Kenneth Lee Baverman.

At seven in the morning the traffic downtown was not yet heavy; there was a lingering sleepiness in the streets. Homeless people gathered belongings from doorways, steam grates, and hidden crevasses between buildings. Hot dog vendors set up wagons—opening umbrellas, plucking frozen tubes of meat-by-product from plastic packaging, boiling water, filling mustard dispensers. Street sweepers rumbled along curbsides; a golf cart equipped with a giant vacuum hose sucked up larger items of refuse. Articulated buses hissed to a stop, rubber accordion midsections aquiver, bringing to work the dark-skinned labor force, laden with backpacks and plastic shopping bags, their faces dulled with the rigors of minimum wage. Vast parking lots and multi-leveled structures began to fill, each vehicle a personal reflection. In Los Angeles, as much as you are white or black, a clerk or a lawyer, a Muslim or a Christian . . . you are a Bimmer or a Prius or a heavy-duty pickup truck with rugged all-terrain wheels that never touched actual dirt; you are a rice burner, a pimp mobile, a Jew canoe, a Nazi box, a spoiled little shit in a Maserati. They jammed the highways and clogged the exits, filed one by one though the automated gates, blithely burning fossil fuel.

Pulling in trio to the curb in front of the Foltz Center, the black Escalades made their own statement. All three passenger doors of the first Escalade opened simultaneously.

Out stepped three buff black men in dark, skinny suits and bow ties, Fruit of Islam bodyguards. The Fruit were to personal protection what Israel's Mossad was to espionage or Nepal's Gorkha Regiment was to ground combat. If you wanted the best, these were the dudes to call. (You certainly never wanted to find yourself working *against* them.)

Behind the Fruit emerged Chill's fez-haired assistant. He had a clipboard in one hand; a Bluetooth earpiece glowed against the side of his head. With the boss and TBone in custody, he was all that remained of Chill's inner executive branch.

The rap mogul and his entourage had spent the night in the Bradley Memorial County Jail, an hour east of downtown. Booking and transfer was an arduous journey through the bowels of the penal system; by the time they reached their cots, they only had an hour to sleep; the regularly scheduled inmate transport to the Foltz Center departed at four a.m. The arraignments were scheduled for nine a.m. in Division 30. At that time the charges would be read, and then bail would be set—presumably. The lawyer expected that Chill and the rest would be home by "2 p.m. at the very latest, barring unforeseen circumstances."

The security team moved toward the second Escalade—heads on swivels, eyes scanning the rooftops, weight evenly balanced on the balls of their outsized wing-tip shoes . . . think Alvin Ailey meets the Navy Seals. On a nod from the leader, they opened all three passenger doors simultaneously.

From the shotgun seat emerged Kisha, friend/makeup artist.

From the seat behind the driver emerged JamieLynn, faithful assistant.

And from the catbird seat . . . Angelika Collette.

Two days earlier, had you asked anyone in America to list their favorite celebrities, Angelika's name would have been at the top of the list, one of those first-name superstars who crossed all demographics.

There was Brad and Angie. Michael, JLo, Kobe, Jack. And there was Angelika—a Grammy- and Oscar-winning triple threat who could open a movie, fill a stadium, even throw down a flawless song-and-dance number as a last-minute replacement to kick off the Academy Awards.

People magazine's Hottest Woman. *Esquire*'s Sexiest Woman Alive. *Marie Claire's* "Superwoman of the Aughts." When she changed her hairstyle, salons across the country worked overtime, adding chunky streaks or asymmetrical bangs. The fact that she'd been through the wringer with that awful narcissistic Christopher Stone had only served to cement her bond with the public—clearly she was vulnerable and human just like them, like people they knew, friends and family. People felt *invested*.

That she'd emerged from her dark times as a role model for single working moms had imbued her with near-saintly status. Important parties had stepped forward, asking her to select a signature charity on which to focus. There was even talk of a UN appointment.

At work, she was a friend of *Friends* no more, commanding upward of $15 million a film. The previous year, her line of seven fragrances had grossed $100 million *wholesale*; there were seventeen product lines in development (from shoes to sunglasses to scrapbooking and collage kits—remember the cigar/stash box?). She was more than just a star. She was the president and CEO of a diverse business enterprise. She was a brand, a household name worldwide, with stores in twenty-two countries, including the Ukraine, Macau, and Dubai, where she'd recently done two private concerts for a cool twenty mil.

Now all of that was in jeopardy.

"RAPPER MADE MIDNIGHT SEX VISITS TO AMERICA'S GIRL NEXT DOOR," screamed the *National Enquirer*.

"ANGELIKA'S SHAME," admonished *The Globe*.

"Scandal Could Devalue Market for Rapper's, Starlet's Brands," explained a lengthy thumb-sucker in the Business Section of the *LA Times*.

"A wanton ho-bag," huffed Rush Limbaugh.

David Letterman: Top Ten Presents to Bring When Making a Booty Call on Angelika Collette.

For the second day running, the news channels were on twenty-four-hour alert. Websites were updated instantaneously. Pundits yammered. Hosts posited rhetorical questions. Elaborately scored highlight packages were played and replayed; commentators compared the spectacle to the death of Princess Di—except *this* coverage included dynamite music, amazing abs, and interracial sex. As you would expect, Angelika's "Ass of the Ages" photo was featured prominently . . . as were the images of herself and Chill doing what ordinary people do every day. (Though perhaps in a somewhat less aesthetically pleasing manner. Given the participants, and the rigorous expression of their mutual passion, the footage was being hailed by sexperts as an instant classic. Wrote **XXX** Industry historian Bill Margold: "The hottest and most compelling coupling ever caught on film.")

Meanwhile, a crafty hobbyist had digitized and enhanced the available footage, allowing for super-realistic close-ups. Lawyers for both Chill and Angelika were working vainly to have the URLs quashed or injuncted. But as the vintage TV host Larry King sagely opined: "once something is up on the web, taking it down is about as easy as putting Silly String back in the can."

After multiple entreaties from Chill's fez-haired assistant, messages from his lawyer and his manager, and finally a call to Angelika's personal cell from Chill's *momma* herself, Angelika had overruled her initial instincts and agreed to a face-to-face meeting with the mogul before his arraignment. (Chill's emissaries had further sweetened the pot with the offer of the limos and the bodyguards.)

Once that decision was made, Angelika's people opted to alert the sheriff's department of their plans to visit the Foltz Center. Wherever she went, the starlet caused a disturbance; everybody just seemed to go a little bit nuts at the sight of her. Over the years, her camp had cultivated good relations with law enforcement. It just made sense.

At the same time, Angelika's team had been advised by lawyers from both sides *not* to be forthcoming with authorities as to the exact reasons for her visit to the Foltz Center. Her seeing Chill at this juncture in his relationship with the criminal justice system was not at all regular . . . or even allowed. At the moment, he was still officially in the legal custody of the LA County Sheriff's department, a condition that granted him few civil rights. Without deviation, Angelika had been instructed, this visit was to be cast as a meeting with Chill's *lawyer*. Once inside the conference room—a safe haven of attorney/client privilege—you never knew what could go down.

Seeking anonymity, Angelika had dressed herself for this mission in a hooded, ankle-length sweater-coat. A kente cloth scarf obscured the lower half of her face. Completing the ensemble was an overly large pair of Dolce & Gabbana sunglasses.

A modest granite plaza marked the entrance to the Foltz Center. Off to one side and slightly raised was a meditative rose garden with a bust of Clara Foltz, a stolid woman with a determined face. Angelika lingered for a moment by the door of her blacked-out chariot, taking full measure of her surroundings—you would have thought she was viewing for the first time a Tuscan hillside or the Sphinx. Of course, she'd Googled the histories of Clara and the building—she was also interested to know that this had been the site of motorist Rodney King's historic press conference, when he called for calm after the acquittal of the four police officers accused of brutally beating him had touched off riots in South Central. "People, I just want to say, you know, can we all get along?"

Like a flock of pigeons startled into flight, a tingle of excitement ran through the immediate area. Swaddled in her laughably conspicuous, inconspicuous costume, you couldn't tell exactly who Angelika was. But you *could* tell she was *somebody*—no ordinary civilian needed three Escalades and a crew of bodyguards to go to the courthouse. Pedestrians slowed and stared in her direction, elbowing one another, reaching for cell phone cameras, not really sure why. The journalists and paparazzi enterprising enough to be on site early for Chill's arraignment were already on the move—Indians chasing the wagon train.

The fez-haired assistant and the bodyguards quickly escorted their three female charges toward the entryway, where they were joined by the occupants of the third Escalade—Angelika's lawyer, her agent, her manager, and Troy the PR guy. A U.S. marshal escorted the group into the portico and down several steps, through the glass front doors of the building.

To accommodate the added security problems associated with the starlet's visit, the ranking U.S. marshal had opted to shut down two of the three metal detector lines that usually funneled the public through the vast lobby and toward the elevators. In terms of crowd control, went the thinking, fewer lines meant easier supervision.

It also created a bottleneck—another traffic jam to be endured by already-frayed morning commuters, a diverse population of sleepy, annoyed, and self-entitled people of every race and class—many of them not yet caffeinated (there was a Starbucks on the mezzanine). Attorneys and judges and potential jurors stood butts to nuts with cops and felons and complicated family units headed to juvenile hearings.

As the celebrity convoy moved on foot toward its destination, Angelika did as she'd been trained: she kept her head down, focused her energy inward, and followed the broad back of the bodyguard in front of her. As she'd told the *New York Times*: "I just have to find a way to tune things out. Sometimes there are so many flashes going off at once I start, like, twitching. It gets really, I don't know, *overwhelming*. I feel like I'm having an epileptic fit or something—it's like you've been struck by lightning. Your fingers tingle. It takes hours to wear off."

Often, when traversing a particularly frenzied crowd, she imagined herself to be a fancy midcentury railcar, one link in a longer luxury train, a private parlor with fringed velvet curtains and Tiffany lamps and an overstuffed fainting couch. Safely hitched, physically inert, moved involuntarily toward the metal detector, behooded and begoggled, singing to herself, click-clacking along the safe tracks provided by her security team . . .

A gruff voice: "Excuse me, miss."

Existing in her *happy place* . . .

Louder: "*Miss?*"

Totally oblivious . . .

"HALT RIGHT THERE!"

A hush fell over the lobby.

A jowly man with white eyebrows and an angry pink face. He was wearing a blue uniform with lots of stripes on the sleeve.

Angelika issued her best, red-carpet smile. "Is there a problem, officer?"

"I need you to remove your—" he waved a sausagey index finger in the starlet's general direction, searching for the right word to describe her get-up. The look on his face reminded her of baby Eleanor experiencing a disagreeable taste, that moment just prior to the one where the offending mouthful was spit out.

And that's when it happened.

Right then. Right there. Angelika got it.

What JamieLynn and Kisha had been gently trying to tell her on the way from Malibu.

About the *public*. About the *reaction*.

About people's not-exactly supportive take on her decision to cross the color line with Chill.

In the limo, she'd laughed it off. "What is this, *West Side Story?* Who cares who I date—red, black, yellow, or frickin purple? I'm over twenty-one. This is the twenty-first century. Who the *frick* cares? This is *crazy!*"

But now she understood.

Everyone cared.

And if the message wasn't clear enough, all she had to do was look at this grandfatherly U.S. marshal standing right in front of her—his jug ears flushing pink with rage, his thoughts perfectly transparent:

You fucked that militant nigger. You disgust me.

The breath went out of her. All systems shut down momentarily as her brain updated itself, as these new bits of critical understanding traveled through the hallways and corridors of her personal archives, making the appropriate corrections, sweeping away any last shards of her cosseted poetic innocence.

She turned around robotically and submitted herself to Kisha, who plucked the dark glasses from her friend/employer's face and placed them in one of the small baskets, as directed, then set about unwrapping the kente cloth scarf.

28

The Powerful Pull of This Other Person

The CEO of RAP Records sat behind a metal conference table, wearing an orange jumpsuit. The laces of his Jordans had been confiscated along with his fancy watch and the uppers and lowers of his hundred K smile.

Chill looked haggard. He hadn't slept for two nights. His eyes were puffy and bloodshot. The mascara-sharp lines of his carefully sculpted facial hair were smudged with new growth. His hands were shackled at the wrists, as were his feet at the ankles; a third chain connected one pair of limbs to the other.

He'd been here before. Not *here* here, in this particular conference room in the Foltz center, but in this position, shackled and shit out of luck. As Thomas Washington Curry, prep athlete/disappointment, he'd done some big-boy time, a six-to-twelve-year sentence for armed robbery, with an additional six-to-twelve for aggravated assault, served concurrently. (The drug charges he was known for were actually thrown out.) Lucky for Chill, his raps and gift for word play were prodigious enough to impress even the hardest OGs in the joint—when there's nothing but empty time on your hands, you can't put too high a premium on a guy who can spontaneously entertain. The lifers took him under wing, protected him from the Aryans and the beaners. And made sure the experiences of his thirty-six-month stint (time off for good behavior) in the big house at Chino played forever in his memory like a season of *Scared Straight*. Never had Chill imagined that he'd be back behind bars.

The conference room was decorated in a manner that suggested the purgatory of Chill's legal status, somewhere between prison institutional and the implied blind grandness of the courts. The tabletop was carved with gang signs and graffiti, the impotent angry doodles of previous occupants. A sheriff's deputy stood off to one side.

Standing to the other side of Chill was his lawyer. He wore an expensive suit but no tie. His consoling moist palm rested upon his client's shoulder; with his free hand he worried the change in his pants pocket, the only sound in the room besides the blowing ventilation and Chill's rumbling gut. It had been some time since he'd eaten anything, lunch the day before. He felt nauseous and lightheaded. No doubt his blood sugar was low. A bottle of electrolyte water was sitting on the table in front of him for the purpose of rehydration.

And then the door opened.

In swept Angelika Collette, preceded by a guard and her lawyer.

Her long sweater-coat was unbuttoned to reveal a Juicy sweatsuit of black velour. She took down the hood and shook out her hair. Even in this dingy room, she was a dazzling presence, something otherworldly.

At the sight of her Chill felt a powerful tug. The last time they'd been together, he hadn't even known his feelings—or maybe he had, but he hadn't yet called them by name. Seeing her now, he was absolutely certain. He wanted to blurt it out: *I LOVE YOU.*

"Thanks for coming," he managed.

She felt it too. The powerful pull of this other person. He was like no other man she'd ever been with, a guy who'd dreamed himself an empire. Since the debacle of Christopher, her notion of the ideal man included someone who could stand up to her as an equal partner. If you weren't equals in life, how could you ever be equals in love?

Which always led to the next problem: how many people could be equal to a superstar?

"I didn't want to come," she said coolly. *He isn't good for me,* she reminded herself. *This is not a good time. We are not a good match. I'm feeling things for all the wrong reasons.*

"I'm glad you did."

Softening: "Your mother *insisted.*"

His pearly smile. "She have a way of getting what she want. She was my manager for the first five years, you know."

"Like Missy? I never knew that."

"Me and you kinda skipped all the historical chitchat, I guess."

Her smile faded and she crossed her arms. "I still don't know why I'm here."

"Did my lawyer e-mail you the interview transcripts?"

"With the applicable sections highlighted—very thorough, Mr. Curry."

"We can get you the audio if you want to verify anything. Them scripts is 100 percent legit. We hired a transcriber from the *LA Times.*"

She brought her hand to her mouth, suppressing a smirk of collegial admiration. "You record all your interviews?"

"Spy in the sky. We got video, too. The entire office is wired. We always got the *smoking gun.*" He nodded his head in the direction of his lawyer. "We got a motion in the courts right now seeking damages for taking my quotes out of context."

"Damages?"

"You gotta fight back or these people will air *anything.*"

"For insulting white women?"

"You *know* that shit outta context. I wasn't talking about *you.* I wasn't even talking about what I myself *believe.* It's there in the transcripts—another clear case of the white establishment using trickery to fan the flames of racism. It's like the way they took the—"

He started to say something about the sex video but thought better. He hadn't seen it yet, but he'd gotten some righteous *huzzas* from the brothers in the bullpen.

"Please believe me," he said humbly.

She didn't know what to say.

Looking to defuse emotions, the lawyer came around the table and pulled out a chair for the lady. He made a charming little flourish with his hand, playing maître d'.

Angelika considered her options for a beat, sat down.

"Can we get some privacy?" Chill entreated.

"I just want you to know, straight up," Chill said. "Those sound bites they're using—they *totally* out of context."

"Okay, I get it. Out of context," Angelika granted.

"I was just talkin some old school smack about my *uncles* and shit. Stuff *they* used to say to *me* when I was little. And the reporter took it *totally* wrong. None of that shit is about *you*."

Frustrated: "I know it's not about *me*. I read the transcripts, Thomas. But you said it, didn't you? It's misogynistic. It's anti-white. It's racist and sexist. Sometimes I think *black* people are more racist than *anybody*."

"We got four hundred years of resentments built up. Payback a bitch, you know what I'm sayin?"

"You become what you project. All successful people know that."

"Listen, baby. I was in the studio laying down some tracks with AI and the *StarNews* motherfucker was asking me these off-the-wall questions. It was stupid of me, I admit. I was preoccupied. The shooting had just happened, all this shit was going down—it was right before they arrested me. I was only half paying attention—the reporter guy's been attached to me like a sucker fish."

"I don't know why you let your people talk you into these interviews that you don't need to do," she admonished. "They've tried it with me over and over, but I've always said, 'No way.' It's something Jen and Brad taught me when I was first doing *Friends*. PR people are the devil. They book stuff and they don't ask you; they don't even *tell* you about it until the last minute, and then they try to act like they told you but you forgot. What do I look like, somebody's intern? You're telling me you told me something and I forgot? You think I can't remember what you tell me and what you don't?"

The pearly smile: "Listen to *you*."

She looked at him blankly.

"I just want you to be clear," he said. "Cause listen . . . I gotta be honest. Since I started going out with you . . ." He looked into his lap, his shackled hands.

"What?"

"It's just . . . You know. You *different*."

"Don't try to tell me you've never *dealt* with no white girl before."

Her use of the Ebonics made him chuckle. "It ain't important."

Annoyed/defensive: "We don't have a lot of time, Thomas."

He shrugged.

"Could it be that Chilly Tom Neegrow is *actually* at a *loss* for words*?*"

"I think I'm falling in love with you," he blurted.

She checked her watch. Their time was running out.

"I have to ask my people if we can stay downtown for your arraignment thing," she said, taking a businessy tone. "The lawyer says you'll be home by this afternoon. Let's have dinner like two civil adults, shall we? Talk about it then?"

"It might not be that simple."

Softening: "What do you mean?"

"I mean, I might not be getting out today. I might have to stay here a while."

"But you said you didn't do anything."

"That is correct. The truth. I did not do *anything*."

"So what's the problem?"

Silence hung between them like the mesh-reinforced glass through which ordinary prisoners had to see their loved ones.

Chill sighed. "They want me to say some things I don't want to have to say."

"What is *that* supposed to mean?"

He leaned forward and whispered: "Somebody mighta did something stupid. Somebody close to me. And there's a murder charge behind it."

"Do you mean to say," she asked him evenly, speaking the King's English at a polite conversational level, "that you could be *out* of here if you just told the authorities the truth about what really happened? Is this some kind of gangsta brotherhood thingy? Because if it is—"

"Baby. Whoa. Please. *Please.* It's complicated, *you know what I'm sayin?*"

He raised his hands to comfort her but was jerked to ground by his shackles, a leashed dog at the end of his run.

29

KISS THIS

Sulcov stood dumbly in the opulent foyer outside the judges' chambers on the tenth floor of the Foltz Center, awaiting the down elevator.

He'd just traded the key fob to his Bimmer for the fob to Judge Baverman's fancy pickup truck, a high-end, tricked-out vehicle that seemed more appropriate to a radical eco-mercenary or extreme off-road racer than to a respected judge who presided over major criminal cases in an antiquated black robe. Tied up in trial and unable to see him personally, Bave had let his clerk handle the transaction.

Watching the Art Deco–style numbers illuminate and fade along the elevator's brass and glass display, Sulcov felt removed from himself, here but not here. Like a computer monitor operating on safe mode, everything around him seemed monochrome and slow.

Last night, sitting at dinner at his favorite little bistro in the neighborhood, Sulcov was a man who knew himself, who knew his place in the world. He was a husband and a father, a resident of Pacific Palisades, a proud and deeply involved family man who had every intention of growing old with his wife, for better or worse. He knew his role and he loved it, he understood it, he'd hunkered down these many years and carried it out conscientiously.

And two very special people loved him for it.

Or so he'd thought.

Last night, a seemingly ordinary Wednesday in January, Sulcov's already-crumbling world had completed its disintegration. The writer's strike had taken his work, his sense of self, and any pretense that he wasn't living on his wife's family money. His father, he'd just learned, had some sort of early dementia. His thirteen-year-old son had not been heard from in two days; Lord knows what he was doing with those gangbangers. And now his home office—his haven, the only place in the world where he felt truly comfortable—was off limits until further notice.

After discovering the flood, he'd found a wet vac in the garage. Tish had been kind enough to bring some old towels; when entreated, she agreed to call the insurance company. He'd sucked up and toted water until dawn, Mickey in the *Sorcerer's Apprentice*. At seven, a crew of dentally impaired ruffians in white hazmat suits and face masks descended upon the devastation and commenced removing ruined furniture and electronics and ripping out soggy floorboards and dry wall, setting up fans and dehumidifiers, treating for mold.

The deco numbers descended: Fifteen... Fourteen... Thirteen...

Maybe it'll all blow over.

Maybe you'll wake up with a full head of hair.

"I am considering having an affair."

Thanks for letting me know, bitch.

Ding.

The lobby of the Foltz Center was charged with excitement. Through the glass of the entryway, Sulcov could see a firestorm of strobe flashes. The visual effect was something akin to a sustained drum roll—a rapid progression of individual strikes, ebbing and flowing, blurring together into a single blinding silver light.

Seized by impulse, Sulcov crossed the lobby and pushed out the revolving door, into the roiling crowd.

With the renaming of the Foltz Center building, the portico entryway had received a facelift, including the creation of the Clara Foltz

Memorial Garden, complete with bust. Slightly elevated and crowned with a modest trellis, the garden served as a natural proscenium stage; over the years, even before the sprucing-up, it had become the designated site for impromptu press conferences. All the major players from the O. J. Simpson murder trial had taken their turns at microphones here, as had the Hillside Strangler, the Grim Sleeper, as well as a succession of troubled entertainers, including Michael Jackson, Charlie Sheen, Tom Sizemore, and Rick James.

Emerging from the scrum, Sulcov discovered immediately what all the commotion was about:

Angelika Collette was giving an impromptu press conference!

The beautiful fallen starlet was standing less than ten feet away, beneath the trellis. She was still wearing her long, clingy sweater-coat, which revealed nothing of her body while tracing perfectly her perfect shape. The sun had come out. The sky was robin's egg blue. Her eyes were hidden behind her D&G goggles.

News cameras were rolling live. The paparazzi oozed around the slightly raised "stage."

"Angelika! Look over here!"

"When did you start seeing Chill?"

"How did you two first hook up?"

"Is it true you're pregnant with Chill's baby?"

Angelika smiled and posed and twitched, a beautiful deaf robot, one hand on her hip.

Troy the PR guy, stepped forward. "Can I have your attention, please?" The sharp toe of his lizard skin cowboy boot was pointed forward, one hand on his hip, the same pose as his charge.

"People, *pl-eassssse*," Troy admonished sibilantly.

At last the crowd settled and Angelika stepped forward. She spoke into the bouquet of microphones.

"Thank you very much," she said, and then she faltered, a bit unsure how to continue. It was easier when you had a script.

A man in the crowd: "Don't be afraid, Angie."

"We *love* you girlfriend!" called a woman.

"We're all here for you!"

Warmed by the positive welcome, Angelika removed her sunglasses, touching off another squall of flash pops. She handed the specs absently to the person on her immediate right, who happened to be her lawyer. (Always position yourself to make the two-shot, he'd learned; you can't *buy* that kind of publicity.)

The flashes slowed to a trickle and then stopped, the last intermittent popping kernels in a bag of microwave popcorn. Everyone leaned forward, listening keenly. Even the photographers, a nonverbal lot used to hiding behind their cameras, seemed to want to hear what she had to say.

"I have just come from the courtroom where Thomas 'Chill' Curry, has been *remanded* to custody," Angelika said. "What that means, according to my lawyer," gesturing to her right, "is that this talented musician and entrepreneur, this role model for his community, this local kid who grew up only a few miles from here in Long Beach and attended a private school on scholarship—is being held like a common criminal without bond for crimes he did not commit. I do not know how such a miscarriage of justice could possibly occur in our so-called land of freedom."

Scattered polite applause, mostly from black people in the audience.

She pushed on. "I see there is a lot of press today," sweeping her hand in acknowledgement of the large group before her. "As you know, I'm usually running away from you guys."

Scattered laughter, nervous applause. A storm of flash pops.

"But today I'm here to help make your jobs a little easier, if you can believe that."

She paused a moment, the only sound the traffic echoing off the surrounding buildings. "I have a little clue for you: there is *evidence* out there that can shed light on the truth about these crimes and prove Chill's innocence in the unfortunate death of that poor attorney and the others. My prayers go out to the families. I can't say more at this time. But believe me. *Trust* me. There is *documentary evidence* of the crime being committed. So that's the takeaway, okay? That's the *biggest* story here. It's the *only* story."

"Can you tell us what you mean more specifically?"

She looked directly at the questioner. "Do I have to make the news and report it too?"

Big laugh from the crowd. Applause.

A fresh round of flash pops.

Emboldened, she continued. "Now I want to say a few things about something else. Can we talk for a moment about this *video?*"

A loud wolf whistle from somewhere within the safety of the mob.

"The Ass of the Ages!" somebody yelled.

A ripple of nervous laughter went through the crowd. A few claps.

"When I first saw the images of myself on TV I couldn't believe it," she said. "I felt so . . . humiliated. So *violated. OhmyGod!* Can you imagine if this was you? In what country, in what *world*, do consensual relations between two adults constitute news?"

She put her palms together, unconsciously forming a Buddhist wye, a gesture of worshipful respect. "Look, guys, I understand the game: The gossip. The media. The inability to go anywhere because the public has this supposed right to know what kind of tampons you use. I get it. I do. I *really* do. It's all about business.

"When I met Liza Minnelli, she told me, 'You have to learn to do the dance, babe.' And she was absolutely right. You *really* do. And you guys *know* me. I dance. I *tap* dance all over the place. I give a *lot* of interviews. Have you ever sat in a hotel room for forty-eight hours straight doing interviews with the foreign press for a movie? I don't complain. More publicity equals more sales. I'm not going to lie: I get a percentage of the back end. It's in my interest to cooperate with you guys.

"But this stuff with the video, all the salacious innuendo, the out-of-context racial slurs . . . Come on now, people, what the hell is that? There have to be standards. I'm frickin *sick to death* of all this *bullshit* that passes for news."

Stunned silence.

Did Angelika just say "bullshit" on live TV?

Hoots and hollers. Big applause. Scattered wolf whistles.

The sun was high overhead. A few beads of sweat could be seen forming in the cleft of Angelika's upper lip. Without fanfare she shrugged off her clingy knit sweater coat and handed it to the lawyer.

"I just have one more thing to say. And I'd like to dedicate it to all the paparazzi and the press. And to all the *haters* out there."

She took a step to her left—well clear of the mic stand—and executed a fluid 180-degree turn.

And struck a pose—one hand on hip, back arched, chin high.

Exposing perfectly the message riding her celebrated posterior, the oft-referenced Ass of the Ages, in three-inch high, neon-pink letters:

KISS THIS.

30

Dude, Are There Any Tortillas Left?

"Dude, are there any tortillas left?"

Jake handed Z the plate and his big friend commandeered the last half of a homemade tortilla. They'd been held captive since the previous afternoon in this detached garage behind Big Gato's *abuela's* house in Venice. It was here that Big Gato's baby blue metalflake Impala convertible had been mothballed while he served his sentence. At the moment the car was gone; they'd seen nothing of Biggie or his vehicle since yesterday's mayhem.

In between the cinderblock garage and the stoop-shouldered clapboard domicile was a large concrete area with a picnic table, a cinderblock barbeque pit, and a basketball hoop (the base weighted with cinderblocks), the height dialed down to eight feet. The previous afternoon, when they'd arrived, Jake recognized the setup immediately—the court on which he and his dad had first encountered Big Gato.

Notwithstanding the considerable shock and mental trauma of their participation in the drive-by—and their certain, dire, adolescent understanding that they were now wanted criminals with their futures in jeopardy (as they'd learned in Crim Jus: being in the car during the commission of a felony often carries the same weight as actually committing the crime yourself)—Jake and Z were in decent spirits.

They'd been treated kindly enough by their series of minders, who had come and gone in shifts. Most of them were well known to the boys—if you could pair the words fond and imprisonment, such was the tenor of things. Adding to the effect was the jailhouse cuisine: Flour tortillas heated on the stovetop and slathered with butter! Homemade bean and cheese burritos! Fresh churros from the bakery down the street! Jake loved eating in Z's neighborhood—though he did wonder why Z's relatives and neighbors never ate anything *besides* Mexican food. *It's not like we have fried chicken and greens or matzo ball soup all the time.* "Living here is like being in the best Mexican restaurant in the world," Jake would tell the *abuelas* who were always pushing food.

The boys' cell phones had long been dead; for good measure Big Gato had confiscated *all* of their instruments of technology—phones, watches, and iPods; he seemed worried about being outsmarted by these two little pussies from the fancy private school. To the boys, Big Gato's motivations were unfathomable. His actions brought to mind a ten-year-old at a piñata party—blindfolded, spun around until dizzy, handed a bat. There was no discernible logic in anything he'd done. Raw emotions, direct actions—the hallmarks of Thug Life.

The garage was dark and timeless, lit by a single bulb. It smelled strongly of cut grass and gasoline. Jake's allergies were acting up; he was wheezing a little bit. And there was no fresh air, which always made him uncomfortable.

The boys were sitting side by side on a futon. Last night, they'd slept fitfully together on the filthy thing. Like his dad, Jake had an active imagination; sometime during the wee hours, the idea of bedbugs crossed his mind, causing an outbreak of the itchies. When alerted, the symptoms spread to Z, and even to their minder. Nobody slept a wink after that.

This morning they'd beaten the futon half to death with an assortment of tools, a shovel and a broom proving the most efficacious.

Then they propped the mattress against a wall, creating for themselves a kind of sofa on which to sit, a series of tasks that had kept them occupied for nearly an hour—they were laughing and goofing around to such an extent they'd forgotten their dire situation for a while. Across the room was a weathered Barcalounger, usually occupied by their guard. At the moment, between shifts, the boys had been left alone. They'd already tried all the doors and windows—everything was locked or painted shut. They thought about breaking the window, but worried they'd get in trouble.

"So what do you think we should do?" Jake asked.

"I don't know." Z shoved the last bit of cold tortilla into his mouth.

Though Z was bigger, Jake was older; it was he who usually called the shots. Annoyed: "It's *your* hood, dude."

"Things are fucked without Sleeper," Z said.

"I keep thinking I'm gonna look up and see him come walking into the room, like this was just a big joke, you know?"

"Big Gato woulda never disrespected us like this if he was alive."

"That's what I'm *talkin* about."

"Cause Sleeper would kick his ass."

"Or pop a cap in it!"

"Shit yeah."

"He'd fuck him up."

"Hella waste him, dude."

They reached out and patted palms, bumped fists, their customary series of comforting touches. Z's hand was the size of a paper plate. The varsity track coach was already after him to throw discus and shot. Jake's longish slender fingers were swallowed in the dance of their hands, as if by a larger fish. There was a lingering quality to their movements this time; less casual than usual, more weighted. They'd been through a lot together on the court, in the classroom, even along the Venice boardwalk—*The birthplace of crazy*, Sleeper called it, always an adventure, every single day.

But never had they been in a fix like this.

"I'm still hungry," Z groaned.

Jake cracked up. "Dude, what else is *new?*"

"Lunch should have been a while ago."

"How do you know what time it is?"

"My stomach knows." On cue, Z's stomach rumbled mightily.

Jake giggled—a vulnerable, regressive sound in a higher register. "Now I'm *really* scared. If you fart I'm gonna have to kill you."

"Ha *haaa,*" Z offered sarcastically.

"Remember that huge burrito you made that night? "

"The Ultimate Dessert Burrito? Your dad keeps the best junk in the pool house."

"His 'trove of contraband'? We shoulda got a picture of it."

"Another award-winning creation by Chef Z."

"A large tortilla with a layer of peanut butter—"

"Pretzel M&M's, Reese's Pieces, a few Gummy Bears, crumbled up chocolate chip cookies—"

"And a pack of cheese crackers, crushed."

"And some hot fudge sauce—but not too much."

"Heated *gently* in the microwave."

"Oh my God!" Z exclaimed. "That was my greatest *ever.*"

"You ate all my dad's sesame almonds, *dude.*"

"I left *some.*"

"Like, *four.*"

"Shut up!" Z laughed. He reached out playfully with one of his huge paws and shoved his smaller friend . . . rolling him off the futon.

Recovering, Jake sprang at the larger boy and a play fight ensued . . .

Whereupon the garage door began to lift—a rusty metallic squeal, the interior flooding with bright afternoon light.

Blinded, the boys froze. Z had Jake over his shoulder.

"Wat up, *homies?*"

His name was Diego. He looked like a guy who was probably most at home crawling through somebody's bedroom window in the middle of the night with a knife between his teeth. Before Z was born, when the Venice Gang had been known for selling black tar heroin, many homeboys, Big Gato among them, had made a lot of *fedia.* Diego had been more of a customer, addicted to *chiva* for as long as Z could remember. He was probably about forty-five; he looked seventy.

With some difficulty, Diego muscled the garage door closed behind him.

Z replaced Jake onto terra firma.

"I'm sorry about your brother, homes," Diego told Z. He tapped his chest with his fist.

"You know my boy Jake, right?"

"The man who feeds the ball to Big Z! What up lil homie?"

A cell phone rang. Diego pulled a prepaid out of his pocket, squinted at the digits, declined to take the call. Lowering himself into the Barcalounger gingerly, like an old man getting into a hot bath, he placed his phone on the convenient lamp table to his left.

To Jake: "Get me one of them beers out the fridge, *ese.*"

31

A Stoned-Out-Looking Green Smiley Face

Sulcov pulled into a liquor store parking lot a half-mile north of Malibu Green's Farmacy, across the Pacific Coast Highway from the ocean.

Dismounting from the captain's chair of Judge Baverman's eco-sporty Nissan Xterra truck, he walked around the back to check the flats of ground cover, secured in the bed under a tarp. Over the years, Bave had owned a number of odd and remarkable vehicles, among them a DeLorean, an Excalibur, an MGB, and a red fire truck. Who knows what moves a man to spend his money on such things? Like sexual proclivities or relations with your wife, some subjects are better left undiscussed between the best of male friends, perhaps one reason they remain so. (Sulcov always wondered what Bave wore under the robe. That subject never came up, either.)

He set off on foot in a southerly direction, along the sidewalk bordering the busy thoroughfare, the facing traffic heading northward toward Ojai, Santa Barbara, and beyond.

Maybe you should come back later in Tish's Prius.

But I'm already here. I'm already walking.

What if you get pulled over with pot in the judge's truck? It'll only take ten minutes to drive home.

Fifteen. And fifteen back. Who knows if her car is even there? Or if she's coming home.

She's probably huddled up with basketball boy, telling him all about last night.

Behind his rose-colored Maui Jim sunglasses, tears began to flow. He wiped his face with the arm of his sweatshirt. He wondered if the people speeding by could tell he was crying. He thought about the scene in the bedroom the night before; about the way she stopped talking to him to pick up her phone and answer a text. *You know that was him!* He wondered if he should get a lawyer. He wondered how the demolition was going in his poolhouse/office. He wondered where in his own home he would now spend his time. The den? The living room? Where would he type? *Maybe I'll have to get an apartment.*

Approaching a familiar construction zone, Sulcov was momentarily distracted by the progress of work on a steep, eroded hill. There'd been a mudslide, all kinds of publicity. People had lost multimillion-dollar houses. He hadn't been up this way in two months, the last time his order was in—the truth was he didn't like parking his own car in front of the Farmacy, either.

By now the low fencing, wood stakes, sandbags, and other trappings of the disaster were largely gone. An artfully designed concrete barrier was rising along the shoulder of the road. According to the artist's depiction on a small billboard, the end product would resemble faithfully a rugged cliff face—another clever weapon against nature's cycle of degradation and rebirth that humans in general, and Californians in particular, were eternally attempting to derail. He thought about a different man-made barrier, the fence the U.S. government was building across the border with Mexico. He'd seen it recently on a restaurant excursion to Tijuana. It came to an end in the shallow waters of the Pacific, some thirty miles south of San Diego. He was amazed to see how easy it would have been to just *swim* around the fence from Mexico to America; it wouldn't take a minute to breaststroke from the Third World to the Land of Opportunity. He always wondered: *why do some Mexicans have to be smuggled across the desert by coyotes when others can just drive across the border and go shopping in La Jolla?*

He walked past a vacant lot filled with weed trees . . . a series of smallish detached apartment buildings . . . another vacant lot. At last he arrived at his destination, a rustic-looking strip mall anchored at either end by a Thai health food restaurant and a personal training facility. Hanging discreetly from a second-story railing could be seen the logo of Malibu Green's Farmacy—two smoking joints crossed like bones beneath a stoned-out-looking green smiley face. The Farmacy was located on the backside of the building, facing east. There was a stairway at either end of the mall. The elevator was centered in the front entryway, which had been recently upgraded with a canopy.

The ocean was just across the street—presumably. The view was mostly obscured by the walls and houses belonging to the people who were wealthy enough to live on that side. At one spot—between an old ruin of a cottage and brand new architectural gem—a public access point was provided. (The beach was open to the public, even if the view generally was not.) Often, you would see workmen pulled over eating sandwiches, a pair of lovers in deep discussion, two dudes smoking a joint. At the moment, Sulcov noticed, the access was occupied by a beautifully restored, sixties vintage Chevy Impala, painted baby blue metalflake.

Jake would love that Chevy.

It looks so familiar.

Didn't you buy him a toy like that once?

If I had my new smart phone I could send him a photo.

You need to call the school when you get done here.

Parked illegally in front of the strip mall entryway was a fancy blacked-out Escalade. Two large black men in skinny suits and bow ties were standing beside the driver's door.

Maintaining the appropriate discreet distance from this obvious celebrity chariot, Sulcov headed toward the stairs at the southern end.

32

Drama Playing Out in Tiny Bird Brains

Parked at the public access with his trio of homies, Big Gato looked out thoughtfully through the windshield of his Chevy Impala toward the expanse of the blue Pacific, the darker ocean meeting the pale sky at the horizon, a band of rose at the lip, like a Tupperware bowl sealed with an airtight top molded of gossamer particulate haze. A tidy formation of seabirds winged along the shoreline; the order and precision of their ranks, the implied sense of common goal, made Biggie's heart swell. Wherever they were going, whatever they were doing, whatever drama was playing out in those tiny little bird brains of theirs, they were in it together, for the good of the flock. They knew nothing else.

To be a member of the V-13, to hail from the Venice neighborhood, to be one of its strong soldiers, was to know your place in the world, too. Outside Venice, Higinio Jesus Fernandez was a fatherless middle school dropout and convicted felon, unemployed and unskilled, a deadbeat dad with a crucifixion tattooed on the side of his face. But within the neighborhood he was a *veterano*, an OG, a man valued for his loyalty and leadership, an elder upon whom his brothers depended as a beacon of strength in these difficult times. With Sleeper gone, it was up to him. A tear formed in the corner of his yellowish, bloodshot eye, dripped along the path already occupied by the three etched in permanent blue-black ink.

Discreetly Big Gato knuckled away the moisture. He made himself think of Sleeper and Yogi and Roc, and of Sleeper's brother Big Juan, and of his own *hermano de sangre*, Pistolo, jumped by a pack of Shoreline Crips one night at the beach and beaten to death with his own namesake .38. He made himself think of Chilly Tom Neegrow, and of all the thievin *miatas* who'd fucked with him in elementary school and in juvvie and in prison, and how they'd stolen the drug business from under the homies. His eyes narrowed. *Payback a motherfucker*. He reached between his thighs and grabbed the stubby neck of the forty-ounce bottle of malt liquor that was nestled there. In one gulp, he killed off the last 20 percent.

"*Hija de puta*," he groaned, "now I *really* gotta *piss*."

"We can go back to McDonalds, it's a half-mile north," Lil Gato offered helpfully. His real name was Romero Delante Esquival. In order to become "Lil" Gato, he'd had to go to Big Gato and ask his permission. Biggie was fine with it. Only one problem—there was *already* a Lil Gato. If Romero wanted the name, he'd have to beat up the other homeboy and take it away, thus proving his worth.

"We got this Styrofoam cup back here if you need it, Biggie," said Joker, the homie sitting behind Lil Gato.

"Maybe you wanna hold it for me, *ese*?" Big Gato cackled.

The laughter swelled and broke, relieving the tension, giving way again to the cacophonous white noise of the pounding waves.

The way they were parked, facing south toward Santa Monica and home, Big Gato could see lots of pretty white people in expensive outfits jogging and walking in pairs along the beach. Surfers plied the waves. A couple of guys on longboards stood and paddled. "If we didn't have them Crips blockin the way," he said wistfully, "we'd have this kinda ocean view 24/7, homes."

"Back in the day, didn't you used to go to the beach alla time?"

"We'd roll down to that lot off Rose Street and park the cars."

"Peel down to your wifebeaters, right? Fold your Pendletons over the bench seat."

"Never mess the pleats, *ese*."

"*Never* mess the pleats," the youngsters chorused, imitating Biggie's thick old school singsong.

"They had a truce over the boardwalk. You got *everybody* down there. We'd have *heinas* coming past from all over—East LA, inland, you name it. Fun in the sun, homes, you know what I'm sayin?"

"Don't seem fair the Shorelines get it now," Lil Gato said, taking a swig from his own bottle of malt.

"The rich folks got the view, homes. The Shorelines just control the right-of-way."

"You mean like how we gotta go down to the marina, or up to the Santa Monica Pier, to get to the beach?"

"It ain't no different from this lil spot right here," Big Gato said. "See that sign there?"

Lil Gato, downed the last third of his beer, wiped his mouth with the back of his hand: "*Public Access. No Parking.*"

"*Bueno.* You know why they got this spot?"

"Cause the beach is public but all the houses block it off?"

"That's right. The beach is public. But the rich folks make it difficult to actually get to it."

"And there's no parking anywhere, neither," said Joker.

"Turf," Big Gato said. "It all about turf."

"Everybody tryin to protect they own," Lil Gato said.

"I heard dat," said Joker.

"*Claro que si,*" concluded Big Gato.

The waves broke; the car was parked close enough that the *vatos* could hear the Rice Krispies fizzle of the bubbles that washed up on the sand between the detonations of the four-foot swells.

"Now I gotta piss, too," Lil Gato declared, eliciting titters from the back seat.

33

You're Not the Only Celebrity Who Comes In Here

To gain entry into Malibu Green's Farmacy, you had to first enter a phone booth–size reception area—without a proper license, nobody could venture inside. A surveillance camera spied down from overhead, one of a dozen placed throughout the facility; the fixed, one-eyed dumbness of the devices, jutting out from the crotch between wall and ceiling, always reminded Sulcov of the business end of a penis.

His image was fed to a bank of monitors located in the back office, the realm of the manager/licensed security guard, who could usually be found playing World of Warcraft on a tricked-out laptop—in an alternate and digitized reality system, he was a Level 80 Elite Tauren Chieftain, feared and worshipped by millions.

The inner door buzzed. Stepping across the threshold, Sulcov could feel immediately that something was different inside the modest square-footage that comprised the entirety of the store. A certain vibrant energy filled the space, an unmistakable presence. All three of the regular Farmacy staffers, including the Warcraft guy, were crowded behind the glass case where the various medicinal offerings were displayed in fancy airtight canisters. A colorful chalkboard on the wall listed daily specials—Blue Dream, Purple Moonshine, Headband, Chemdawg, Afgooey, Raging Slut.

Standing on the customer's side of the case, with her back to Sulcov, was a woman wearing a long, knitted hoodie that hugged her body like a second skin.

Sulcov stood there a moment, unnoticed. "How's it going, people?"

"Hey, Mr. Sulcov. Wat up?"

The respectful tone in Warcraft guy's voice caused the other two employees to follow suit.

"Wat up, dude?"

"Howzit, bra?"

Made curious by the warm reception—*You're not the only celebrity who comes in here, you know*—Angelika Collette twirled around in place to see what all the boy-fuss was about.

Sulcov's heart fluttered as his already-taxed system took another hit of adrenalin.

"Hey, Angelika. Remember me?"

Remember me?

Are you serious?

She was holding in one hand a pair of chopsticks used to pluck choice buds from the storage canister without disturbing the sticky crystals of THC. The lesbian couple who owned the Farmacy were raw vegan Buddhists. They believed mightily in ritual and ceremony; it's what their "patients" had come to expect. Sulcov had learned (embarrassingly) that the Farmacy didn't sell weed, pot or herb; medical marijuana was always referred to as "medicine," which came in different "strains." And it didn't get you *high*. It had "varying medicinal effects." You didn't say, for instance, that you wanted to purchase strong, speedy pot that made you so high you forgot proper nouns; instead you said you favored sativas that offered an intense cerebral effect. Old-fashioned pharmacy scales were used to weigh the "prescription," adding to the new-age medical ambiance. The counterweights in their precious velvet case were said to be pure gold, as was this location.

Angelika continued to smile woodenly at Sulcov, her discomfort painfully evident—clearly, she didn't know who the hell he was.

Warcraft guy: "Didn't you two work together on an episode of *High Tolerance?*"

Her brow furrowed as she narrowed the search parameters for her internal files. She met so many people in the course of a week, a month, a year. . . . Everybody knew *her* name. She couldn't possibly begin to know all of *theirs*.

"Nate Sulcov?" he offered. The SoCal uptick, an immigrant's adaptation, made it sound like he wasn't quite sure of his own name.

She pointed with the chopsticks. "The *writer*, right?"—she beamed at him as if she'd just unearthed a rare and unusual fact. Whether she was impressed to see him, or impressed with her own power of recall, was uncertain. Either way, she seemed properly enthused.

"And cocreator," he added brightly.

Her memory focusing: "You helped me with the new scenes."

"Wrote them," he added, dropping the personal pronoun for humility's sake.

"That teleplay was *amazing!*" she gushed.

Sulcov was charmed at her use of the antiquated word for a TV script. In the confines of his pool house/office, he used that word also.

Warcraft guy: "Wasn't there, like, talk of a Golden Globe nomination for that episode?"

"Emmy," Sulcov corrected. Sad smile. "But they say there might not *be* any Emmys this year."

In that instant, Angelika sensed Sulcov's deep well of grief. Things were not well in La La Land. Many were suffering. The more she got out into public these days, the more she could really feel it. Sulcov seemed so much older than when they'd last met. So burdened. When she took the opportunity to open herself, she'd come to learn, she was extremely sensitive to others; her mentor called it *exercising empathy*, it was an important part of *giving back to the universe*. It didn't take a lot of focusing for her to *grok* that Sulcov's woes extended much further than just the writer's strike.

"Awards or not," she assured him buoyantly, "it was a *brilliant* piece of writing."

"Brilliance lasts," Warcraft guy said.

"Making *High Tolerance* was so much fun," she said wistfully. "I think I actually *miss* TV."

"Not many people realize you did nearly three seasons of *Friends*," Warcraft guy said.

"Television is so . . . I don't know—" she searched for the right words. "So straightforward. So honest. It feels like having a regular job. You know what I mean? You get up, go to work, come home. There is a work life and a home life. There's a normal rhythm."

"Plus an episode only takes a week to shoot," Sulcov added. It took quite a lot longer to write . . . unless you were on deadline. Then it took exactly as long as you had.

"You feel like you've accomplished something," she said. "A movie drags on and on for months and years. By the time you're doing publicity, you hardly remember doing it."

"TV is the closest thing to instant gratification you're gonna get in this business—except for music or theater, I suppose," Sulcov said thoughtfully. "Being up there on stage, giving your best, getting immediate feedback from the crowd, putting it back into your work . . . that's gotta be the height of creativity right there."

"I don't know," she said bashfully. "I just get up there and do it. Writing is way harder than singing! Are you kidding?"

"You've never heard me sing," Sulcov said.

Angelika leaned her forearm on the glass case, exposing a bit of cleavage. "I remember he came to my trailer to work with me on my new lines," she told the gathered employees, initiating a kind of spontaneous, best-friend-ever intimacy with strangers that only a famous person can. "There was all this crap with my people and the network people. He rewrote the whole script in *one night*."

"Just the second, third, fourth, and fifth acts," Sulcov said, a tad sarcastic.

"Whatever you did, the script was killer," Warcraft guy said. "We're huge *High Tolerance* fans around here, aren't we, guys?"

"And huuuuge *Angelika* fans," added the minion to his right, overloud . . . and kind of *icky-creepy*.

All life appeared to drain from the superstarlet's person. She issued a large, vacuous smile. "Thank you *so* much," she said graciously.

Insufferable silence prevailed.

The four men exchanged glances. *What the hell did we do?*

Sulcov to Warcraft guy: "Can I ask you the obvious question?"

Picking up immediately: "You *know* I can't answer that."

"May I infer then, from the cherished special canister I see on the counter—"

"Are you trying to ask if I'm on the Abusive list?" Angelika trilled, suddenly reanimated.

She batted her lashes at Warcraft guy. "I've asked *this one* a million times but he won't tell me anyone who's on it! I only know of *one* other person."

"I'm not at liberty to divulge that information," Warcraft guy said, a well-rehearsed monotone. You could tell he enjoyed being the one who knew.

"I believe," offered the minion to his left, unsolicited, "that there is no express prohibition against *one* list member inquiring to *another* list member about his or her status on the list. I think we would be well within our protocols if we indicated that they would be safe talking to one another. In fact . . ."

As the assistant rambled on in nerdspeak, Nathan Sulcov and Angelika Collette exchanged looks, a sort of furtive secret handshake. In the world of celebrity, there was a time for friendly chitchat with fans and service people, a time for instant-Oprah-intimacy. These were, after all, members of the public, adoring fans and consumers, worshippers in the church of her celebrity. You had to treat them right—or suffer the consequences. A fan scorned is an indignant enemy for life. . . . Or possibly even a stalker, trespasser, or psycho assassin. The literature is full of examples.

But truthfully, how much mindless slobbering devotion can one person take—before it makes you start feeling like a worthless phony? How much bending of the rules and special treatment can you experience—before you begin to wonder, you know? You ask yourself: *What's wrong with this person that they need to spend so much energy fawning over me and doing me favors? They don't even know me.*

Though Angelika and Sulcov were by no means equals in the celebrity firmament, they had common ground, a status relationship that began perhaps with the very existence of their respective IMDB pages on the World Wide Web. In Hollywood, either you have credits or you don't. Either you're in the business or you're not. Either you're a gawker on a double-decker tour bus (leaving from the intersection of Hollywood and Vine on the hour) or you're chillin poolside as the tour bus is juddering past your house, hopefully well away from earshot, beyond an extra-high wall hidden by thick and tasteful foliage. In a room full of celebrities, Angelika and Sulcov would never be equals. But right here, right now, marooned together on this island of everymen at Malibu Green's Farmacy, they were the only two of their kind.

"My name is Nate Sulcov, and I'm on the Abusive list," he said solemnly.

She pointed a manicured nail playfully/not playfully at the four men in the room, each in turn. "Remember, I'm a *mother*. If this gets *out*, I know *exactly* who to have *killed,* you understand?" She sounded the way she did in her action movies when her futuristically clad alter ego had the villain on the ground, one metallic stiletto heel on his chest.

Warcraft guy made a cross over his heart. "Confidential doctor/patient relationship."

The assistants on either side of him made zipper motions across their lips.

Sulcov: "I'm *totally* with you. I have a thirteen-year-old."

Angelika beamed. "Boy or girl?"

"He's a Jake."

"I have a girl."

"What is she, about five now?" Sulcov asked.

"Eleanor," chimed Warcraft guy.

Angelika said nothing. Yes, yes. They knew her child's name and age, and probably the fact that two weekends ago, she'd had a

Western-themed birthday party, exclusively covered by E!, with a photo spread in *US*—a way of limiting the usual paparazzi overload. *How stupid of me to try and act like a normal human.*

Sulcov, sensing her discomfort: "When Jake was young, my wife and I referred to pot as 'Daddy's Medicine.' Then one day his kindergarten teacher asked the kids if any of their parents smoked cigarettes. And my son was like, 'My Daddy smokes *medicine*!' "

The starlet guffawed: "Shut *up*!"

"Thank God the teacher was an old hippy. And a pothead herself. She's been teaching kindergarten for like thirty-five years."

"You mean '*patient,*' right?"

"I don't see any other way you could *teach* kindergarten but 'medicated,' " Warcraft guy offered.

"*Daddy's medicine*!" Angelika repeated, genuinely amused. "Oh my God! That's *sooo* precious."

"Next time we get a new strain we should name it that," Warcraft guy said.

"I'm signing over my copyright here and now," Sulcov said, rapping his knuckle twice on the glass countertop, looking to Angelika for approval. Absently, he picked up one of the expensive, blown-glass Sherlock Holmes-style bubbler pipes on display and inspected it. "You won't believe this," he told the starlet, pointing the stem of the pipe towards her lampoonishly, "but this is actually the *second* time I've seen you today."

"I don't live far from here," she said cryptically. "Do you live in Malibu?"

"No, no. I mean *downtown*. I saw you downtown at the courthouse. Doing your press conference. My friend from college is a judge."

Alarmed: "Not Judge Alfred!"

"Is he the one who denied bail to Chill?"

Annoyed: "What a *douche bag*."

The men exchanged glances. *Did she just say douche bag?*

"My friend is named Baverman. I needed to borrow his truck—" He pointed northward, in the direction of the liquor store parking lot where the Xterra was stashed. "The city has demanded that I plant . . ."

Angelika turned to Warcraft guy and handed back her chopsticks. Her voice took a sweet, insistent tone that Kisha called her Jedi Mind Fuck. It worked on men and women alike, a form of celebrity hypnosis.

"Can you get me my oh-zee out of the back, *pleeeease*? With some of the big fat buds that I like? In one of your wonderful blue glass containers? Oh *shit. Shit! Shit!* That reminds me! I keep forgetting to bring the *other* containers back to recycle. I'm *sooo* sorry. I know you encourage that. Do you hate me? I'll send them over with my assistant this afternoon, *k*?"

Sulcov looked at his watch. "You might as well hook me up, too," he added brightly. He didn't bother mentioning the paltry amount of his own order, or his every-other month, half-ounce status—it was all recorded discreetly in the back room.

The assistant on the left was dispatched to fill the orders. Angelika busied herself looking at the various offerings on display atop and inside the counter. A roach clip that resembled a key. A joint case that resembled a pen. A pipe that resembled a cigarette.

Ignoring the obvious social cues—no one was completely immune from celebrity-*itis*—Sulcov addressed Angelika's back. "I loved what you said downtown today. I think it was so *important.*"

At the sound of that last adjective, the starlet reconnected. "Thank you," she said graciously. "It was from my heart."

"It was brave of you to speak the truth. Everybody in this town thinks that stuff, but nobody ever stands up and actually says it. You came across totally *genuine.*"

Angelika regarded Sulcov appraisingly. He wasn't so bad, tall with those beautiful Maybelline lashes, his chin nicely fortified by the beard. Possibly she was remembering more details about their intimate little rehearsal in her StarCarriage. "I forgot what a total *trip* you are, Nathan."

34

One Last Extra Mile

"So you're saying you can't help a brother out?"

Calvin Scott was getting nowhere chatting up the Fruit of Islam bodyguards waiting with the Escalade in the entryway of Malibu Green's strip mall.

That he was wearing his Kangol cap backward and spicing his dialect with some of the hip-hop patois he'd learned hanging with Chill showed his inexperience with the Fruit—from Elijah Mohammed down through Louis Farrakhan, the sect had a proud history of sterling diction. Not to mention an absolute policy against speaking to the press. *Showin love* to the *StarNews* was never in the cards. Calvin Scott might well have been invisible . . . or back in his hotel room sleeping off his vicious hangover.

Our intrepid reporter was not to be discouraged, however. For the first time in his career, he'd discovered the rewards of employing a work ethic to his chosen field. The idea that you reap what you sow? *Wow*. It was beginning to make sense to him.

He had gone the extra mile—literally, down the cold and misty beach. For his efforts and inconvenience he'd been rewarded many times over. There was no denying it: this story—*this footage!*—had made his middle career. He knew now that his contract would be renewed for at least another year—as much security as you could have in his line of work. He'd always told himself that getting the good breaks in life was all about having good luck; he'd just never had any. He'd always told himself he was born unlucky and ordered another vodka.

Now he saw it:

Effort brings reward.

You make your *own* breaks.

Sure, you need luck. Everyone does. And you need some talent for what you're trying to do—brain surgery, plumbing, even journalism.

But maybe luck comes a little easier when you're *doing* instead of *waiting*.

At the very least, it makes the time go faster.

It was in this new spirit that Scott had responded with haste to the phone tip from a source in the U.S. marshal's office that Angelika would be attending Chill's arraignment at the Foltz Center. He'd caught the tail end of her impromptu press conference, then followed the three Escalades carrying her party. When the formation broke and each vehicle took a different soaring highway ramp, he was left playing a shell game at eighty miles per hour.

The Escalade he'd chosen to follow, the middle one, took the 101 Freeway toward Calabasas and made two quick stops—an apartment complex, a Bank of America drive-through kiosk. Then it headed south along a vertiginous dual lane that snaked though picturesque canyons on the way to Malibu. By the time he reached the ocean, trailing at a proper distance, Scott was horribly carsick. Indeed, he was so intent on keeping his food down, and keeping his eyes on the Escalade, that he'd failed to notice the car following his—Big Gato's baby blue Chevy Impala.

When the Escalade pulled into the strip mall, Scott had parallel parked at the curb between the mall's two driveways, entry and exit, that were required by municipal law. Big Gato had rolled past, made a U turn, parked in the public access across the street. Scott observed as a Fruit bodyguard exited the door behind the driver. The passenger or passengers entered the mall from the other side. Same as the *vatos* in the Chevy, Scott was still unsure about who he'd been following.

Sitting there with the engine off, mulling his next move, the traffic whizzing past on the PCH, Scott noted for the first time that the car he'd rented at the airport nearly five weeks ago—the floor in the back was ankle-deep in Starbucks cups—happened to be a Chevy Malibu.

I'm in Malibu in a Malibu, he told himself.

Yes, here he was, in the center of the center of the Southern California Lifestyle—a decades-old marketing juggernaut, the showcase of the American Dream, dating back to the Gold Rush and Steinbeck's Joads, Annette Funicello, and the Beach Boys . . . the absolute epitome of human habitat. All over the world, people know Malibu, our fabled Hollywoodland by the sea, a location that had itself become a star, a place where everything is the very best; and if it's not the best, it *thinks* it is and acts the part, a Pilates butt in yoga pants by Lululemon. The air was cool and smelled wonderfully salty and rejuvenative. The sun through the windshield was as warm as a heating pad on his lap. A pair of barefoot surfer girls strolled past on the sidewalk, confident and carefree, their golden hair floating like kite tails, hips swaying in breezy unison. It was *January*, for chrissakes. Right now in Manhattan, where he lived in a dismal, rent-controlled efficiency near Clinton and Delancey streets, the temperature was just above freezing.

At the moment the two Fruits were standing on either side of the driver's door, toy soldiers with hands clasped restfully over their respective junk. Forming a trio in this snapshot was the driver of the Escalade—Asian with a Mohawk, the tips dyed magenta, his Bluetooth wireless headset glowing on one ear.

Thinking that direct contact would be the most efficient, Scott had approached the Fruits and introduced himself with a hearty "What up, my brothas?" Thus far, his efforts had gone for naught; it was like trying to talk to the guards at Buckingham Palace, only these guys were hatless, deep ebony, and wearing bow ties.

Inherent in their noncommunication was a certain rudeness Scott often felt from strangers in the course of performing his professional role. The general public assumed a liberty to treat him with disrespect, as if he was responsible for the bad behavior of all the journos who came before, as if *he* had been one of the guys chasing Princess Di to her death in that fateful tunnel. No matter what he did, he'd always be considered one of the faceless mass. Who he was, *personally*, didn't matter. To them he was The Press.

Scott reached for his back pocket. "What if I say there's a twenty in it for you?"

Continued silence.

"Forty?"

A beat.

"I can go to a hundred," he said, "but I'm gonna need you to name names, my *man*."

The Fruit on the left finally spoke. His voice was impossibly deep, think of the actor James Earl Jones. "First of all," he said calmly, "I am *not* your *brother*. Neither am I your *man*, your *dude*, your *bro*, or your *big guy*."

"There's no love here," the driver said, translating derisively. "Can you feel me, *dawg?*"

"Look," Scott said, "I'm a working man, just like you. I'm just trying to do my job. Give me a little tidbit or something to bring to my editors and I will scuttle away. I promise. It's nothing personal. How about it, fellas? Can you tell me who you're driving today? What you're doing here? I hear that's a great restaurant," indicating the Thai health food place over his shoulder.

Cars sped past. Waves crashed. Behind their dark sunglasses, it was hard to gauge if the Fruits were even listening.

Scott turned away, bitter and determined.

As a public citizen he had a right to visit all the businesses in the strip mall. And so he would.

35

Yukking it Up Like Old Pals

In the entryway of the strip mall, the elevator door opened.

Out stepped Angelika Collette and Nate Sulcov, yukking it up like old pals.

36

If She Knew Me Personally, She'd Like Me

Lil Gato was the first to spot the superstarlet exiting the elevator.

"Biggie! Check it out!"

Big Gato keyed the engine and floored it. Tires smoking, the Chevy fishtailed out of the public access area and crossed all four lanes of the PCH.

Cars honked, brakes squealed. A minivan hit a Toyota, sending it into a spin.

Gaining speed, the heavy old Chevy Impala bounced into the southernmost driveway of the strip mall parking lot, bottoming out, throwing sparks.

The *vatos* opened fire.

As was their tradition, the Fruits were unarmed. They hit the deck and rolled under the Escalade. Using the door as cover, the driver with the Mohawk whipped out his registered .38 and returned fire.

Briefly this parking lot in paradise became a battlefield. Bright muzzle flashes, the *pop pop pop* of handguns, the *BOOM-BOOM* of the sawed-off shotgun, the sizzling sound of lead ripping the air. Shouts and curses, a woman's scream, the acrid smell of gunpowder.

And then the crash, the crunch of metal, the shattering glass. The Chevy's horn stuck, a custom installation, a piercing Road Runner *Meeeeeeeeeeeeeep!* The ringing alarm from the Pilates studio, its expensively rendered storefront breached.

Calvin Scott was struck once in the back. The 9 mm bullet pierced his lung and his aorta and came to rest against his sternum.

His last earthly vision: Angelika emerging from the elevator.

His last earthly thought: *If she knew me personally, I know she'd like me. I'm different from all the rest.*

37

The Imperiled Heroine in the Bucket Seat Beside You

Rigorously cross-trained and organically fed, riding a maximum adrenalin surge, Sulcov and Angelika galloped the half mile back to the liquor store parking lot—he in his Adidas, she in her bare feet, having run out of her high heels about three strides into their getaway.

He led them stealthily northward along an old game trail, behind the apartment buildings, through the stand of weed trees previously described . . . past one startled backyard sun worshipper. They emerged at the southern edge of the hillside erosion project, then walk/jogged the rest of the way to Bave's truck, trying not to look too conspicuous.

Sulcov turned the vehicle northward on the PCH, away from Malibu Green's. Having stashed their pot in the glove box, alongside Bave's judicial parking pass, they drove in silence, the only sound between them the road noise and their own ragged breathing.

Angelika pulled her bare feet up into the bucket seat with her, knees to chest. From between two toes she plucked a piece of gravel.

"Are you . . . okay?" Sulcov panted. He was still wearing his rose-colored Maui Jims.

"Except for . . . my sprained ankle."

Alarmed: "Do we need . . . a hospital? A friend of mine . . . an orthopedist—"

She held up the small, glittery white rock she'd harvested from between her toes and turned it over this way and that, inspecting it like a precious gem. "Do you think . . . we should call the cops?"

Reminding himself to keep his eyes on the road: "Was that . . . your limo?"

She dropped the rock into the console between the seats, picked up a pair of Bave's antique RayBan aviator sunglasses. "I didn't hire it . . . but yes, I was *riding* in it."

"Did you leave anything behind? Personal items?"

"My *purse* . . . *Shit.* And my *phone!*"

"Do you need to call anyone—let anyone know where you are?"

"Probably the *cops,*" she said again, growing annoyed. On Planet Angelika, a suggestion was just a nice way of issuing a command.

Looking over the top of his sunglasses. "Do you want the world to know you were buying pot at Malibu Green's?"

"Won't the cops know I was there when they find my stuff in the limo?"

"You can explain that: you could have left your purse behind by mistake. Did you make any stops between the courthouse and Malibu Green's?"

"We dropped my stylist and my assistant at her apartment in Calabasas—they were going to lunch together. And then I went to the bank to get cash for the Abusive."

He braked for a light, three cars back from the crosswalk. A man in an SUV to their right spotted Angelika and began waving enthusiastically.

Reflexively she pulled up her hoodie.

Sulcov leaned forward and shot the lookie-loo a mad-dog stare—a gang-thing he'd learned one lazy afternoon from Z. They'd had the best time, the boys and he, practicing their mad-dog faces in Jake's closet-door mirror. Z said that mad-dogging was intermediate between cussing someone out and actually fighting them. Or sometimes it meant you wanted to kill them. You had to be careful not to use it incorrectly.

Intimidated, the lookie-loo looked away. Sulcov felt a surge of protective pride. "It must get really old."

"Just to go *shopping*," she said wistfully. "I used to love to *schmy* along Melrose. Or riding a bike on the Venice boardwalk! *Oh my God!* I'd stop for a slice and a coke and watch the people."

"And nobody watching *you*."

"My mom and I used to be hiking *fanatics*. This was before *Friends*. We'd have a day with no auditions and nothing going on. We couldn't afford a gym, so we'd go on hikes. Missy—that's my mom—she used to call it our 'Stairmaster With a View.' We'd go all over. Runyan Canyon. Rustic Canyon. Temescal Loop. The Venice Canals."

"I love hiking. I like to go to—"

"And Malibu Creek. Oh my God! Have you ever been to Malibu Creek? It's a wonderful, wonderful place. Reflecting pools, volcanic walls—it's *captivating*. Just so amazing. When you're there, you feel like you've been teleported back in time. Very ancient and very centered, very close to the earth." She hugged her knees, embracing the memory.

Sulcov: "Have you ever been to *Solstice* Canyon?"

Bave's RayBans were dark green and hid her eyes completely. She made no response.

"There's this amazing waterfall," he said. "*Seriously* a-*mazing*. It's like five minutes from here. We could go there right now and try the new Abusive. I have some papers. What do you say?"

"I don't have any shoes."

Sulcov reached behind the seat and fished out a pair of pink flip-flops belonging to one of Bave's three daughters. "We won't have to hike," he said cryptically.

Angelika didn't particularly appreciate the way things were developing but she wasn't sure what to do. "What happened to calling the cops?"

For some reason, it occurred to Sulcov at that moment that if Tish left, if they got separated or divorced or whatever, he would have to get his own cell phone account.

I guess I'll have to figure out myself which plan to choose.

He thought of all the divorced couples they had known over the years and how awkward it always was for them and their kids and everyone else. He thought of attorneys and visitation. Moving his clothes out of the house. Losing his beloved pool house/office. His throat tightened, his emotions welled . . .

Pull yourself together, man. The imperiled heroine is sitting in the bucket seat next to you.

Taking control of himself, he dug into the pocket of his jeans and extracted his outmoded flip phone and handed it to her.

She turned it over this way and that, something quaint she might consider buying in an antique shop.

"At the time of the shooting, you were upstairs, in the back of the strip mall, window shopping at the bikini boutique," Sulcov offered. "You didn't see a thing. You heard the shots. You ran the back way because you were scared. You bumped into me at the liquor store parking lot. You're safe with friends and available at this number. "

The light turned green.

He shifted into first gear and pulled away.

38

A Set of Hard, Incontrovertible Facts

Kenyatta Ducksworth strode into the audio/visual room at the Hollywood Station precinct house, a manila envelope in one hand. Those familiar with the usually understated detective—dressed for work today in his best A.P.C. denims, a dark tweed vest, and a caramel-colored corduroy blazer—might have noted an uncharacteristic swagger as he made his way through the station house. After all these years of chasing down puzzle pieces and sifting through people's selfish takes on truth, nothing made him happier than a set of hard, incontrovertible facts.

"Dude!" exclaimed Colin Wee, the young forensic scientist. He was sitting at a large, studio-quality editing console. His single pigtail had been let down; one side of his face was partially hidden by a veil of black hair.

Ducksworth opened the envelope. Inside were five DVDs just burned for him at Roots American Productions. He fanned out the disks like playing cards. "Which do you want to see first?"

"The TEC-9 footage."

"You'd rather see that than the shooting?"

"Come on, give it up—the penlight idea was *genius*."

"Be glad it wasn't *you* downtown having to *sell* it. They'd have taken my badge if you were wrong, *dude*."

As it happened a day earlier, Duckworth's very first steps into the reception area of the mayor's suite of offices were met with the breaking news of Big Gato's retaliatory drive-by shooting—at Hollywood and Vine, in broad daylight, a little over a mile from the station house (from whence he and his two superior officers had just driven in three separate LAPD vehicles, two of them with drivers).

And not a single witness.

The deputy mayor was a Stanford law graduate, Alfonso Gutierrez-Garcia. His father was a migrant farm worker; Alfonso himself had picked fruit and vegetables as a boy. Now he was an unbending loyalist assigned to protect the mayor's throwing arm. As the meeting opened, he lit into Ducksworth for . . . well, basically for doing his job the way it was supposed to be done: Considering the evidence. Making inquiries. Working his way through multiple scenarios. Taking his time to figure out what had actually happened before looking to arrest folks, whether he liked them personally or not.

"Do you have any idea how hard the mayor and his team have worked to revitalize central Hollywood, to attract businesses and professionals back to that historic and signature area of the city? Now look what we've got. A partner at a big firm gunned down by a random bullet while sitting at his desk in his corner office. A drive-by shooting in broad daylight. And now the press is playing the hate crimes card?" Gutierrez-Garcia seethed. "The feds are licking their chops." Underneath the fancy Stanford diction was an unmistakable sing-song cadence. Ducksworth's immediate bosses sat dumbly nodding their heads.

Ducksworth steeled himself. Like running suicide drills or doing push-ups, he knew the requisite number would eventually be reached, that the pain would be exacted, that this tirade would eventually come to an end and he would still be alive. The state of his career would be another matter.

He was no dummy. He could see the bigger picture. Nobody wanted another 1992, when South Central Los Angeles had erupted

in spontaneous rioting after the acquittals of four white LAPD officers charged with assault and use of excessive force in the beating of
black motorist Rodney King.

This time it wasn't just the *miatas* vs. the crackers. This time,
it was everybody—the beaners, the yuppies, the rich and the poor,
celebs and wannabes . . . even the olive and yellow folks who owned
stores in potential riot corridors—any unrest would likely stretch all
across the Southland's crazy quilt of racial and ethnic communities.
Nobody would be untouched. Nearly everyone had a horse in this
race. It came down to simple DNA.

As far as the deputy mayor was concerned—it was given he
was speaking for the mayor—it was best for all if Chill's initial story
proved true and this case was closed quickly. In other words, it was
most politically expedient to blame the dead brown men for the white
lawyer's death. Yes, it would cost the mayor some political capital with
his own people, the Latino community. But let's face it. He was their
guy, El Queso Grande—the most powerful and highly placed among
them, the next choice to lead the National Conference of Mayors.
After that? Who could tell. Certainly there was higher office in his
future. What were they going to do, turn their backs on their *vato*?
There were way too many years and quinceaneras and done deals invested on all sides for that now.

When the deputy mayor concluded his speech, Ducksworth
pulled out the disk Wee had made for him, a video of the forensic
penlight experiment. Ducksworth's father had spent his entire working life as chemical compounder in a tire factory. He never missed a
day of work in forty-five years—he only retired because his wife, who
suffered from Alzheimer's, needed full-time care. Like his old man,
Ducksworth found comfort in honest effort. He never sought short-
cuts; he always played by the rules. He'd even cashed in the promise
of his expensive minority scholarship education for a job enforcing
them. He could have been a doctor, a lawyer, a partner in some kind of
big firm . . . Instead he'd chosen to become a cop. Police academy, foot
patrol, shit hours, advancement exams, the whole nine. He thought
he could help make a difference.

Closing a case at the whim of an elected official was not what he'd had in mind.

It took a lot of explaining, but after he cued up the disk, and the deputy mayor and his two superiors listened to Wee's voice-over explanation—and to Ducksworth's extensive re-explanation—it was decided that Chill and his party should be arrested. Surely one of them would crack.

Or it was Ducksworth's ass.

And then Angelika had spilled the beans at her press conference. A new search warrant for the RAP offices was hastily sought and granted; forensic techs discovered a complete network of high-quality cameras and microphones—installed by the producers of *Chillin with Chill* to enhance filming of the reality series.

These new disks were numbered with a black Sharpie. Ducksworth pulled out No. 4 and handed it to Wee, whose fingernails were lacquered black and bitten.

"High def and THX digital," Ducksworth said as the image appeared on the screen. "There's a monitoring station in a three-bedroom condo unit one floor below the penthouse offices. It's like a fuckin missile silo in there—key-card security, a three-person team on rotating twelve-hour shifts. A dorm and a living area. The kitchen has granite counters. You'll wanna skip forward to about 1902. Everything's coded rather than dated. We'll have to sort that out."

"By *we*, I assume you mean *I*?"

The POV was bird's-eye, a wide-angle shot, slightly distorted at the edges. As the scene opened, Chill's office was in its usual orderly state—except for the three bodies, belonging to Sleeper, Yogi, and Roc—lying between the undisturbed sofa and the bulletproof executive desk.

A large black man in a vintage Chilly T concert T-shirt entered the room carrying a TEC-9.

"They call him TBone," Ducksworth narrated. "He works for Chill, chief flunky or whathaveyou. He's married to Chill's younger sister."

TBone walked about ten steps into the room, just north of the doorway, the exact spot Wee had earlier hypothesized. Gripping the weapon with both hands, using his stomach paunch as a steadying platform, he proceeded to unleash a methodical, counter clockwise sweep, a house painter deploying a power sprayer.

Instant war zone.

As Wee had suggested, the last few bullets shattered the windows.

"I keep thinking about that lawyer," Ducksworth said. "Three fuckin kids. In elementary school."

"And if you think about it, the bullet went through two different plate glass windows. Each time the trajectory was slightly altered. A perfect kill shot. I wonder what were the odds?"

"You'll figure it out *after* you get this logged, I'm sure." Ducksworth handed over the remaining disks. "The meeting with *Los Vatos* starts near the end of No. 1. The shit sparks off on No. 2. Everything's all cozy until Sleeper flaunts his weapon. He never even pulls it. He doesn't even *go* for it. He just shows it off in his waistband. Fuckin opens his shirt and throws a pose. What the *fuck* was *he* thinking?"

Wee let his hair fall, curtaining one side of his face. "That he was filming a music video?"

"All they had to do was finish the meeting and sign the paperwork and walk back to accounting." From the inside breast pocket of his sport coat, Ducksworth fished out a check and unfolded it.

It was made out to *Los Vatos* for $1 million. He handed it to Wee.

"What was this dude thinking?"

"That's the answer we never get," Ducksworth said, shaking his head sadly. "If you fast forward to about 1408 on No. 5, Chill is dressing down TBone. It's definitely enough for an obstruction charge on Chill. It's clear he knew about TBone's actions."

"A slap on the wrist. He'll have to make the rounds of talk shows and confess—the stations of the media cross. It'll only enhance his cred. Win-win for Chill *and* the mayor."

"But not so much for TBone."

"Stick a fork in him."

"TBone is cooked."

"He'll do serious time."

"What about the bodyguards?"

"Maybe they get second degree or manslaughter, but it's weak," Ducksworth said. "The imminent threat of Sleeper brandishing his gun gives cause. Frick and Frack were both licensed to carry. Their paperwork is up to date. The bodyguards were basically doing their jobs."

"Who knows what we'll find when we see the rest of the footage," Wee said consolingly.

Ducksworth cracked a smile. "Maybe more of Angelika?"

"In high def?" Wee feigned a look of apoplexy.

39

Maybe not Such a Good Idea After All

Sulcov and Angelika drove in silence along the PCH. They passed the fabulous and historic Malibu Colony ... the palatial, palm-tree-lined plantation-on-a-bluff owned by the entertainer Cher ... the poshly situated (and insidiously conservative) Pepperdine University ... the hidden tropical oasis belonging to the rocker Tom Petty ... and high on a hill on the inland side, with commanding views of the ocean, the Malibu Heights RV Park, accommodating both tourists and long-term lessees.

Angelika tapped her fingernail on the passenger window. "I've always wanted to rent a little RV and stay up there with Eleanor," she said wistfully.

"You can take a girl out of her trailer, but you can't take the trailer out of the girl," Sulcov said, not meaning to be unkind—he'd done the expected research on her early life before she'd guest starred on the show. Getting to know her better, then and now, he'd found a simple, unspoiled quality beneath her shimmery, once-removed, megastar façade.

"For your information, we lived in a *double*-wide. It's pretty similar to a regular house."

Sulcov: "Did you know all of Malibu used to be privately owned until 1940?"

"No *way*."

"The guy who founded Union Oil owned the entire twenty-seven-mile coastline. There were fences and gates; armed guards on horseback patrolled the surrounding hills. It wasn't until his widow ran out of money that she started to invite wealthy celebrities to build vacation houses on her private beach. That was the beginnings of the Malibu Colony. Barbara Stanwyck, Clara Bow, Ronald Colman—those were the first generation of residents. They all had houses on the sand. They called them *shacks*. I'm sure your double-wide was a *mansion* in comparison."

"I *love* the Colony. Pam Anderson lives there. She really helped me stay grounded when the crap hit the fan with Christopher."

Pamela Anderson from Baywatch? *With the amazing pneumatic boobs?* "Contrary to the more popular notions about her best assets," he said, meaning to be amusing.

"So you know her *personally*?"

"Only from *Playboy* and from her sex video with Tommy Lee. Every time I see her on TV, I can't help but envision—" his voice trailed away. Much of the purloined film had been lensed from a POV one might call *gynecological.*

Cold silence filled the truck.

Sulcov: "I'm sorry. Wow. That was thoughtless of me."

"People think they know *everything* when they don't know *shit*." She looked out the passenger window.

Sulcov made a right turn off the PCH and headed up a winding road. At the top was a car park, a sign announcing their arrival at Solstice Canyon. Posted were the typical maps and warnings and notices of prohibition. Several groups of late-afternoon hikers—one pair equipped with oddly bent high-tech walking poles—were tramping in their colorful gear toward the head of the trail. The longest of the several available paths was less than four miles. With nearly two hours left until sunset, there was still plenty of time to burn some calories before dinner.

"I don't think I'm up for a hike," Angelika said preemptively. "My *ankle*—"

"We won't be hiking," Sulcov said.

He drove beyond the trailhead, made a right onto a dirt road, continued on past a small farmhouse. Soon they came to a secluded area, deep in shadow, overhung by alders and sycamore trees.

At a gate, he pulled to a stop, clambered down from the big-wheeled truck, using the provided jump step. He punched four digits into a combination lock, unwrapped a length of chain.

Set as it was, on the apex of a downhill slope, the gate swung open invitingly.

The Nissan angled obliquely downward. It was really more of a path than a road, two wheel ruts traversing the sun-dappled loam.

The forest was damp and fragrant, a green and leafy cocoon alive with critters and birdsong. The truck's cab jerked to and fro, the shocks squeaked and complained, the cargo of ground cover shifted in the bed. Angelika braced herself with hands and feet; Sulcov's knuckles were white on the steering wheel—so intent was he on driving that his talkative mind fell strangely silent.

He'd discovered the place the previous July, when he was here scouting locations for *HT*. The caretaker had ferried him along this route in an old Range Rover. At that time, the trip from the gate to the waterfall had been easy. But that was summer. The ground was hard and dry. This was the rainy season. Conditions had deteriorated noticeably.

Five minutes became ten. The going was slow. Then one of the tires got stuck in the mud. Angelika had to show him how to shift into four-wheel drive.

Maybe this wasn't such a good idea after all, Sulcov told himself.

At last they came to an old bridge.

Sulcov braked to a stop. The light was fading; he had his sunglasses perched atop his head. Bave's aviators were still in place on Angelika's porcelain doll face. The lenses were dark. Sulcov wondered how she could possibly see anything with them on.

Do celebrities' retinas adjust over time to accommodate the darkness of their sunglasses?

Do you think she remembers rehearsing that scene?

She was talking about it at Malibu Green's.

I mean the other part.

What do you think?

"Alright-y!" he enthused, sounding perhaps a tad too excited, a camp counselor on a difficult field trip trying to perk up the troops. "This is the stream that flows from the falls. Our destination is just around the bend. Hold onto *this*, will you?" He reached into his back pocket and pulled out a familiar orange cardboard folder.

She took the rolling papers, a pack of orange Zig-Zags. That she preferred the same style and brand was a stroke of pothead kismet. She wasn't exactly sure what she was doing here, in this truck with Sulcov, going to a secret place to smoke some Abusive. But one thing was clear: his point about being associated with whatever had gone down in front of Malibu Green's was well-taken.

The lawyer will deal with it.

Eleanor is home and safe.

I can't bear to face any more media.

There is no reason I can't escape for a few hours, is there?

It's not like he's a stranger. He's someone I've worked with before.

And kind of a good kisser.

They sat in silence for a few moments, listening to their own thoughts, the sound of the stream below, the water from the highlands cascading along the rocks.

"You ready?" Sulcov asked.

"I hope so."

"No guts no glory," he intoned.

She removed her shades. "That's what I said to Missy the morning I booked *Friends*."

"I tell it to my son all the time," Sulcov said. Her eyes made him think of s'mores around the campfire—melted chocolate centers with graham cracker-colored rims, delicious.

The bridge was fairly typical to high-end properties built in the 1940s, fifty feet from on-ramp to off, constructed of iron support beams and railroad ties. It rose to an apex in order to span the streambed, thirty feet below, and then dipped back to the level of terra firma.

Sulcov drove slowly. The truck's macho, oversize tires gripped the slimy surface; the old wood ties, treated more than a half century ago with creosote for preservation, were weathered now and covered with algae, broken down in spots, grasses and weeds growing out of cracks and crevasses, nature's slow but inexorable reclamation.

"Almost there," he sang.

The last six feet of the bridge were severely decomposed. As the truck rolled forward onto the final section, a distinct crunching sound could be heard. Suddenly, the cab lurched downward and to the right.

For one perilous instant, the big truck teetered on three wheels . . .

And then Sulcov gunned the man-sized V8 engine.

The trusty Xterra leapt to safety.

40

The Secret Celebrity Swimmin Hole

"Oh my God, Nathan. It's *beautiful*."

He tried to remember the last time he'd heard his name spoken in such fashion by a woman, with such genuine appreciation. He fought the urge to drop to his knees, to press his face against her taut, bejeweled belly."I decided not to shoot the scenes here because I didn't want to spoil it," he said. "Can you imagine a whole crew stomping around?"

After they'd cleared the bridge, the rutted path led to a small parking area. From there they followed a short trail to what was known to a select few as the Solstice Canyon Secret Celebrity Swimmin Hole. A fairytale hideaway on the back side of the waterfall, it was maintained by the county, known only to a select few. Well hidden and strictly VIP, it was an actual example of something the common man has always suspected: when you're rich and famous and in the know, a lot of swell, exclusive perks open up to you.

Motes of dust and mold spores danced in shafts of light slanting through the canopy of the trees. The air smelled of dirt and sage and mildew. Situated near the swimming hole was a huge boulder, eroded by time and the elements into a sort of poolside sofa, complete with arms and back. He led her to it, he in his Adidas, she in the pink flip-flops. The rocks were mossy and slick, as such places usually are, harboring the type of elemental slime that dwells at the nexus between water and earth. A smaller, secondary waterfall also fed the swimming hole, contributing to the symphony of percussive water sound.

"John and Yoko skinny-dipped here," Sulcov said. "Frank Sinatra used to come here. And Marilyn Monroe *may* have brought JFK. At least that's what the caretaker said."

"And this caretaker person just *gave* you the combination to the lock?"

He smirked. "Some people will do *anything* to get on TV."

"Have you told anyone about this place?"

"Just you. And my son. He and I hiked the public trail and approached from the front. There's a way around from the main falls, but it's engineered to appear impassable—basically, you have to know where you're going or you won't find it."

"You never brought your wife?"

In fact he'd invited Tish three different times over the course of the unseasonably warm summer, and once more as skinny-dipping season began to wane, in late September. On each occasion she'd had a ton of plans, a ton of excuses—a ton of fast talk, really, now that he thought about it . . . a ton of lies. As of last night, he wasn't sure anymore what was true and what she'd fabricated. Or how far back the files of his understanding had been corrupted, how often he'd been deceived and to what degree, how many times she'd told him one thing and then went somewhere else in order to "contemplate" fucking ex-Lakerboy.

Sulcov produced a small black container resembling a hockey puck; the cap carried Malibu Green's loopy logo. He screwed off the top, revealing a couple of fragrant, thumb-sized buds and some smaller nugs, one-eighth of an ounce of Abusive Kush Private Reserve. He handed it to Angelika.

"You wanna do the honors?"

"... So at this point, I don't know what will be," Sulcov was saying.

"I'm *sure* she'll come around," Angelika said soothingly.

Did you even *want* Christopher back after the whole bimbo-on-the-yacht business?"

"You don't know for sure yet that she actually *cheated*. Maybe she's telling the truth. Maybe you really did catch her *before* she had the chance to act."

"It's almost like, at this point, it doesn't even matter if it was consummated or not. What gets me is the lying. The systematic cover-up. The conspiracy. The treachery. The disloyalty. She might not have been fucking him, but she was lunching and flirting and daydreaming about him. She was texting him from our marital bed. *In the middle of a conversation with me.* We've been married fifteen years. How can someone who claims to love you deceive you like that? And so blithely?"

"When Christopher went on that so-called fishing trip, I was eight months pregnant. He made this huge deal about his buddy getting this special satellite phone on the boat just so he could call me."

"He was calling you while he was on the yacht with the bimbo?"

"Twice a day. Sometimes more. I was like, 'Oh, honey, you're so sweet. You don't have to call this much.' And he would make me put the phone on my belly so he could talk to the baby. And I would do it. *I would do it!* And I felt such love for him."

"The worst part for me is the *imagining*. I keep conjuring up mental film."

"Be glad nobody was filming *her*."

"You read all the time about these guys who kill their exes in a jealous rage," Sulcov said. "And you know what? Right now, I can *absolutely* understand that sentiment. Abso-*fuckin*-lutely. There's a little part of me that wants to kill her. *And* him. But mostly *her*. When I think of all the personal stuff she must have told him about us ... about me! What the *fuck*! You know? What did I do to deserve this?"

"Nobody deserves to have his heart broken," she said. "But it happens. Every day. Heartbreak is the opposite of love, just as decay is the opposite of life. With one you always have the other."

She patted his back as you would a child's, left her hand to linger, a warm and consoling weight on his shoulder.

". . . So the thing is, at the end of the day, what good are your triumphs if there's nobody to share it with?" Angelika was saying passionately. She was sitting Indian style on one end of the rock sofa. "You need someone to *celebrate* with. Someone who can be *genuinely happy* for you and be in your corner."

"You're telling me you can't hug your Oscar?"

Sulcov was standing at the other end of the sofa rock. One of his legs was propped up; he was in the process of stretching his hamstrings, which were still tight from their getaway run. Usually he stretched directly before and after exercising, which was better for his aging muscles and tendons, according to his trainer.

"You can hug Oscar, but he can't hug you back," she clarified.

"If you ask me, he looks kind of Ken-doll down there—is Oscar a eunuch?"

"Oscar is *above* sex," she laughed. She stood up and removed her long sweater-coat, folded it carefully into a seat cushion. She was still wearing the Juicy sweatsuit with KISS THIS stitched across her celebrated butt.

". . . I never wanted kids," Sulcov was saying, sitting now on the sofa rock, his feet propped on a smaller boulder that served nicely as a coffee table/hassock. "I didn't have the greatest childhood. I figured, why bring another miserable person into the world?"

"I couldn't wait to be a mom." Pink flip-flops abandoned, Angelika was doing a few stretches herself, using the arm of the sofa rock as a ballet barre, one leg extended. "I wanted to give her everything I didn't have."

HUMMMMMMMMMM!
HUMMMMMMMMMMM!
HUMMMMMMMMMMM!

The Edenic quietude was pierced by the loud buzzing of Sulcov's cell phone. The vibrating feature was designed to make the phone more discreet—in reality, it was annoyingly disruptive, a violent whining noise reminiscent of a cheap marital aide dialed to max. Once, in a restaurant, the piece of shit had actually vibrated itself right off the table.

"I still have your phone." She patted the zippered pocket above the cropped midriff of her Juicy sweatshirt. "You want it?"

"Let it go to voicemail." He picked up the joint and relit.

Gracefully she stretched her hands toward her foot; her torso bent forward at the waist until her forehead kissed her knee, exposing the small of her back. She held for several counts . . . slowly returned upright . . . extended her arm . . . accepted the joint from him.

The waterfall gurgled. Birds twittered in the trees. Standing there, one leg still resting on the sofa rock, sucking down a man-sized hit of Abusive, she seemed the embodiment of earthly perfection.

"Before I had Eleanor, I thought I understood the world so well," she said, exhaling a thick cloud of smoke. "Now I can't believe what an *idiot* I was."

Energized by the speedy effect of the strain—at the Farmacy they called it "rejuvenating cerebral qualities"—Angelika was moved to climb the sofa rock. Before coming to Hollywood, she'd been a consistent top finalist in the all-arounds in middle school club gymnastics. Now she pranced along the top of the curious and convenient rock formation, using it like a balance beam. Reaching the end of the improvised apparatus, she executed a half-pirouette, 180 degrees . . . and then another . . . her arms basketed in front of her, a ballerina atop a music box.

"I met this woman over Thanksgiving," Sulcov said, hitting the joint. "She was five months pregnant. And she was like, 'I can't wait to take maternity leave so I will have the time to write the novel I've always wanted to write.'"

Angelika laughed. "Like Missy says, 'You can't know what you ain't learned yet.'"

She jumped down onto the sofa rock's erstwhile seat cushion . . . and then down again onto the coffee table rock . . . and then down again to the level of the swimming hole—a deep, natural pool encircled with a natural coping of small boulders and rocks.

"Be careful, okay? It's slippery." Sulcov stubbed out the joint, walked over to the water, and knelt down protectively, as if being closer might keep her safe. "Whoa! This water is like *ice*. When I was here with my son it was *so warm*. It's totally pure, by the way. You can drink it. "

"I'm sure he'll never forget that day with you."

"I know I never will," he said. His face darkened. "I guess the only problem with kid love is that it's kind of one-way. You're there for them. But I don't think they're really supposed to be there for you in the same fashion. At least not while they're young."

She jumped to the next rock. "I know, right? You can't lean on your kid."

"Their bones are still soft. They can bend."

She laughed. "That's why we need other *adults* in our lives, daddy." She did another pirouette on the ball of her foot, this time a full revolution, 360 degrees.

"A partner," he said.

Jumping to the next rock. "In crime."

"A royal consort."

"I don't think we're really meant to be solitary creatures. *Believe* me. I *tried*."

She jumped to the next rock, landed on her right foot. Her previously sprained ankle gave way.

For one meticulous heartbeat the starlet seemed to be floating—a weightless action heroine frozen in midair.

And then she fell to earth.

The back of her head struck a rock—a sickening, hollow, resonant sound like a coconut hitting a pool deck.

She disappeared beneath the cold, fresh, potable waters of the Solstice Canyon Secret Celebrity Swimmin Hole.

41

I am Not a Fucking Doctor

Compressing her chest, the CPR techniques he'd *not* learned on so many occasions in so many different venues, including but not limited to, summer camps, scuba diver training, phys ed classes, coaching certification clinics, and, most recently, a refresher session for Writers Guild of America strike captains . . .

One, two, three, four, five.

How many compressions in a row?

How many breaths?

I am not a fucking doctor.

He tried to find a pulse on her neck. He couldn't remember which side to feel. He checked his own neck, both sides, found his pulse. Tried the same spot on Angelika. Nothing.

The superstarlet's melted chocolate and graham cracker-colored eyes were yawed open. Her pupils were dilated. One of his first *HT* teleplays had started exactly this way—tight shot on beautiful dead girl, eyes wide. In the lexicon of TV drama, it's called the teaser, a little establishing scene that cues the theme music and the first commercial. In his script the girl suddenly awakens—which totally *freaks* the seasoned detectives. It was a little twist that helped establish his writing chops around town.

One, two, three, four, five.

I am not a fucking doctor.

His heart sledgehammered against his chest. Her nipples were engorged and clearly outlined against the soft black material of her Juicy sweatshirt. He imagined having a heart attack and falling dead on top of her body.

I wonder what the police would conclude?

That you were deranged and kidnapped her?

Beat her to death with a blunt object?

That you were lovers?

Ha, the press would have a field day!

He bent awkwardly to her face, a Muslim in prayer. He pinched her nostrils closed. Affixed his lips over hers. She was cold. Her skin was ghostly white. He breathed himself into her. Her chest rose slightly and receded. He did it again with more force and felt a little dizzy.

What would I say if she woke up right now?

After a few more breaths, he placed his ear to her nose. Listened for what seemed like a long time.

The sun was low. The temperature was dropping. He was soaked to his underwear. He began to shake uncontrollably.

In contrast to her absolute stillness.

He gathered the superstarlet in his arms like a broken bride and made his way back to the truck, feet squishing in his soggy Adidas.

She was just a small thing, astonishingly light.

42

Murder in Malibu!

News helicopters circled the airspace above the Malibu Green's strip mall.

Three were dead. At least a million dollars in vehicles and real property were destroyed. There were still bodies *in situ* as police and evidence technicians processed the scene. Onlookers gathered a short distance away, behind the hastily erected barricades of yellow crime scene tape; traffic on the PCH had slowed to a crawl for miles in both directions as medical personnel and wrecking crews sorted out the injured and the damaged.

A dozen different news channels were already broadcasting live: *Murder in Malibu!* Given Calvin Scott's discovery of Angelika's leased beachfront house, just a mile down the PCH—the helicopters took turns buzzing up and down the coastline, collecting footage of her place. Of course this sensational new tragedy dovetailed nicely with the ongoing coverage of the Chillika sex tape, the shootings and the drive-by at RAP Records, and the subsequent courtroom drama following the arrests. *Crime Wave Hits Southland.* The perfect storm was growing larger and more perfect by the minute—and nobody yet had a clue that the stories were indeed related.

At this time, the only known facts were these:

On the strip mall asphalt, lying in a pool of blood, was the body of a white male, late thirties, well dressed. His New York driver's license identified him as Calvin Thomas Scott.

A sixties-vintage, baby blue metalflake Impala convertible had come to rest halfway inside the shattered frontage of a workout studio called The Pilates Place. The windshield was shattered, the hood was riddled with bullet holes, littered with dry wall and broken pieces of window glass and mirrors from the facility. The driver and the front-seat passenger—dressed and tattooed in typical SoCal Latino gangbanger style—were dead of gunshot wounds to the head and torso. Blood in the back seat seemed to indicate that another passenger or passengers may have fled the scene before police arrived.

Near Scott's body was some additional broken glass that appeared to be from another vehicle. Whoever had made the getaway appeared to have driven over a small messenger bag full electronic recording gear, squashing the contents.

An LA County Sheriff's Department spokeswoman on the scene held an impromptu press conference. She gave out a website and a phone number for tipsters. Uniformed officers proceeded to canvas door-to-door.

43

Headed for the Emergency Clinic

Sulcov floored it up the trail, headed for the twenty-four-hour emergency clinic in Malibu. The big truck's macho engine roared. The oversized tires gripped the loam.

He reached the bridge ramp going twenty-five or thirty.

And caught air...

And landed, front tires first, with a jarring *thud*.

The decomposing timbers gave way.

Judge Baverman's muscular and eco-friendly Nissan Xterra tumbled helplessly into the ravine.

44

I Ain't No Rat

An interview room in the County lockup. Chill was in his orange jumpsuit, shackled.

Detective Ducksworth was sitting across the table in his APC denims, wool vest, and corduroy blazer. His gold badge hung on a lanyard around his neck. His voice remained cool and impersonal as he reached his narrative climax.

"... acting on that information, we subsequently discovered your secret monitoring installation in a condo one floor beneath the penthouse offices."

Chill snickered. "Ain't no *secret*. The network pay for it. For the show. Ain't illegal, neither."

"That's really not the point. We've got the footage. We obtained it legally. And it shows exactly what happened in real time. William Jackson—you call him TBone? He's looking at murder. It's pretty cut and dry."

"That's the game, yo. That's one *version* of the facts. TBone will lawyer up and take his chances with *his own* version. Them tapes could get thrown out. A whole lotta shit could happen. Who knows?"

TBone was nine or ten when he started coming past Chill's grandmother's house, sniffin after his baby sister Bernice. That Chill had gone to prison instead of his senior year of prep school was on his own conscience; while he was away, Bernice had become pregnant. To his credit, TBone had always done right by Bernice—droop-eyed and loyal as the family basset hound for which he was nicknamed. After the second baby, the pair made it legal. Seemingly they were that rare couple who meet young and bond for life. Since he was able, Chill had made sure his unemployable brother-in-law was always employed, with money in his pocket, a roof over his family's head. As Chill saw it, he was the patriarch, the godfather, El Jefe, what have you. Like it or not, it was his responsibility. TBone was family.

"What's this got to do with me, anyway?" Chill said. "If you have the video, you know I'm innocent. You know that TBone acted on his own. I had nothing to do with this. Why am I still here? I still don't get why I was even *arrested*. Ain't the department had enough publicity off me yet?"

"To start with, obstruction of justice and all the related charges for lying in your initial interviews with myself. Then there's the murder charge. The DA can look at your role a bunch of different ways. There are chunks of time when neither you nor TBone are accounted for in any of the camera shots—plenty of time for a conspiracy to have been hatched."

"You think I *ordered* TBone to shoot up the room with a fuckin TEC and kill a motherfucker across the street?"

"It doesn't matter what I think. It's what the prosecutors can convince a judge and then a jury to believe."

Chill stared vacantly at Ducksworth. His head itched so bad he wanted to scream—trussed the way he was, he couldn't even scratch.

"So lay it on the table for me," the mogul said. "What's the what?"

"In exchange for immunity from prosecution, the DA wants you to agree to testify if necessary against Jackson."

"I already told my lawyer: I ain't no rat."

"I said *if necessary*. He might plead guilty. There could be a deal. There might not even be a trial."

"Why you need me?"

"Because four people were killed in the space of an hour by people who work for you?"

"Just another day in the music biz, yo."

"You can shuck and jive all you want. This comes straight down from the DA—which I'm sure comes straight from the mayor. He's Latino, remember? Your good pal? There's a shit-load of Mexicans and other Latinos who voted for him—and a lot of them want your head. *Los Vatos* has become a political football.

"And then you got that poor unlucky bastard across the street," Ducksworth continued. "Rich white lawyer, USC alum, thirty-nine, lived in Brentwood with his family. The tax base gets itchy when stuff like that happens. They want to feel safe. They don't want to feel they'll lose everything they've worked so hard for to a stray bullet. And you know how it go with white people—they don't have to march and boycott and agitate and shit. They just pick up a phone."

Chill sucked air impassively through his grill-less teeth.

Ducksworth leaned forward on his elbows.

"For some fucked up reason people look up to you. I got two teenage nephews. They live in Nowheresville, North Carolina. They play your music 24/7. They watch your show. They're always like, 'Did you see how Chill bought a piece of the New Jersey Nets? Did you see Chill's new line of shoes? Did you see Chill's house on *Cribs*?' Your fucked-up sense of values influences *millions*."

The fallen mogul raised his chin a notch. "*Hundreds* of millions."

"And now the whole world is watching. This is not a photo op. This is not a new album. You have the chance to make some good choices here, to make a truly positive statement. Something that really impacts society."

"You're tellin me I need to *Do The Right Thing*?

"If that's what you wanna call it. For yourself and everybody else."

Chill shook his head, no way. "Ain't no right thing to do in this situation."

"You can walk out of here a free man and say 'I told the truth.' Isn't that an amazing life lesson to convey to millions of kids?"

"How am I supposed to ask people to put theyselves on the line for me if I won't do the same for them? That's what a leader do."

"The captain gotta go down with his ship? Sounds good but you might wanna reconsider. You've got a lot of charges on the table here. They add up fast. Do you really wanna spend your Wonder Years living in a two-man cell with your shitter five feet from your bunk?"

45

Tears Flowing Upward

Nathan Sulcov awoke with a start, his face buried in the rumpled nest of his feather pillows. Birds sang in the fragrant eucalyptus trees outside his window. Waves pounded the beach a half-mile distant and echoed through the canyon—a muscular rolling crash followed by a muted roar, a two-part rhythm like a heartbeat. Even now, six years since he'd moved to the West Coast on a lark, it was a sound that never failed to thrill and comfort him.

The sheets felt warm and familiar, redolent of unscented All Concentrate and hypoallergenic Bounce. Sometimes, on his way to the studio, he'd discover one of the gauzy synthetic dryer squares clinging to the inside of his faded Levi's jeans. On any given morning there was no telling what he'd find down there . . . thongs, peds, toe covers, head bands—it was usually something stretchy and diaphanous and distinctly female; the glove box of his leased Bimmer harbored a colorful collection. Winding eastward through the sensuous tree-lined curves of Sunset Boulevard, his belt unbuckled, his zipper undone, his hand jammed down his pants to retrieve the foreign object du jour, he'd often wondered: *isn't the Bounce supposed to eliminate static cling?*

He loitered for a time in his cocoon of sleepy well-being, enjoying the weight of the down comforter, one of a half-dozen Tish rotated throughout the year. She was always rearranging something— the drawers, the closets, the furniture, even the pictures on the walls, which often meant repainting. It was her way of taking stock, he supposed, of making course corrections. Sulcov was more the type to worry the chair leg back into its familiar indentation in the Berber carpet; his own disordered battlefield was locked within.

He peered out tentatively through the curtain of his thick lashes, not quite ready to commit to the day. His clock was in its usual place on the night table, along with his books, his reading glasses, his framed picture of Tish and Jake, two peas in a pod, looking out mischievously from between the hand-turned oak balusters of the central staircase of their old place in Brooklyn.

At last, the pressure in his groin became urgent; the alarm was about to go off, it was time to get up—it was a school day, there was stuff to do, the usual routine, a clean page on the calendar, fresh with promise. He was the man of the house, first to rise, first to kindle the hearth. Two very special people loved and depended upon him. It was who he was. It was the only life he knew.

As he did nearly every day, he reached for his alarm; like a swimmer touching the wall, he had this thing about beating the ringer to the punch. (Leaving Tish undisturbed, big brownie points.)

But he couldn't move.

And he couldn't get up, either.

He felt as if he was being held down, pinned beneath a great weight.

What the fuck???

The smells of dirt and rot and gasoline came flooding back into his senses. The softness, the sheets, the bedroom faded away ... dissolved like one of the hazy, overlit dream sequences for which *High Tolerance* had been critically lauded.

And he was back inside Bave's Nissan Xterra.

It was dark and humid.

He was trapped.

The truck was planted hood first on a steep slope in a dense thicket of bushes and trees, near the bottom of a ravine, just above the streambed. The broken bridge was thirty feet above. Fire suppressant red apple ground cover was scattered everywhere around the wreckage.

Sulcov was hanging upside down in the driver's seat. His seatbelt was still hooked. His head was jammed against the crumpled ceiling; a ragged corner of the sunroof assembly was digging into his scalp. His chin was shoved uncomfortably into his chest, aggravating the bad disks in his neck, obstructing his airway, making it difficult to breathe. The smell of gasoline was intense; the sour taste of it coated his mouth and lungs.

For some reason, the air bags hadn't deployed. The herniated ruins of the dashboard—the glove box still harbored their respective purchases from Malibu Green's—were pinned against his lap; he couldn't move his legs. Thick branches intruded through the bent frame of the windshield and the driver's side window, impaling the vehicle against the slope, twisted under its weight. Tangled within the branches were Sulcov's left arm and shoulder. He felt as if he'd been crucified upside down, nailed by one arm. *An interesting fate for a Jew*, he'd told himself ironically at some point before passing out.

By now the sun had set. It was pitch black. He couldn't tell if his eyes were open or closed. He could hear the sounds of birds or small animals rooting around outside the wreckage. He wondered about Angelika. He'd secured her seemingly lifeless body with seatbelts to the bench in the passenger section of the extended crew cab. There was no telling where she was now.

Sulcov's arm throbbed. His head felt cleaved in two. The pain was unbearable. He felt loopy, like that time he'd taken too much Ambien. He wasn't sure anymore what was real and what he was hallucinating. *I'm hurt bad*, he told himself. *I probably don't have long.* He thought of Jake. He hadn't laid eyes on his son in two days. Or was it three now? *How can I die without saying goodbye to him?* He thought of his wife, who didn't love him anymore. Who took his manhood away. There were no words for this. He began to cry.

Tears flowed upward and puddled in his eye sockets, over-flowed into his brows. The unusual sensation arrested his attention.

What a wonderful detail: tears flowing upward.

You could put it in a script.

This whole crazy day would make a great episode.

Ha. Who would believe it?

Writing story is so much easier when you're borrowing from real life.

He thought about this for a few beats, how *High Tolerance's* "ripped from the headlines" approach had gotten the show so far. *There's nothing stranger than truth.* He'd said it to Zondo on their very first night together in LA, over cocktails at the SkyBar. He'd said it in every pitch meeting. And to himself a zillion times.

And then something else strange occurred to him, a little bit of a plot twist:

Maybe I'm already dead.

46

DONUT RETRN CALL THIS #!!!!

Drawing on his experience playing commando with Airsoft guns in the canyon behind their house, Jake Sulcov low-crawled across the cold concrete floor of Big Gato's *abuela's* garage.

His target was the cell phone sitting on the lamp table beside the Barcalounger. It belonged to their minder, a *veterano* named Diego. About an hour ago, under strict orders not to leave his post, Diego had modestly turned his back on the boys and cooked up a spoonful of *chiva*. Now he was in the land of Nod.

Jake snatched the battered flip phone, retreated to the farthest spot in the garage, behind a lawnmower, where they'd been given a bucket in which to piss. Deeply yellow, it smelled bad.

He changed the settings to silent mode, then set about thumb-toggling a text to his father's cell—the only number he knew by heart. (All the rest were on speed dial.)

HELP. THIS JAKE. NO JOKE. ME N Z KIDNAPED IN VENICE. REMBER HOUSE W BBALL FIGHT? CALL DET. DUCKSWORTH. 323-650-8999. DONUT RETRN CALL THIS #!!!!

47

Maybe Her Pocket Ripped As She Was Being Ejected

Tish with ex-Lakerboy.

On the big screen.

Doing things she would never do with Sulcov.

Full color. High def. Surround sound.

Familiar parts of her moving in unfamiliar ways—this woman, his wife, the mother of his son.

All the channels. One hundred screens. A fly's-eye view: CNN. ABC. CBS. ESPN, MTV, VH1, Bravo. Fox News Network. Larry King Live.

And Oprah.

Who is titillated by the super-realistic footage.

"You go girlfriend!"

The studio audience applauds.

HUMMMMMMMMMMMMM!!!!

The obnoxious, marital-aid whine of Sulcov's outmoded flip phone, piercing the blind silence within the wreckage.

Followed immediately by a pert tri-tone:

do Re MI.

Even in his semiconscious state, this combination of sounds, announcing the receipt of a text message, brought Sulcov to attention. By far the majority of the texts he received were from Jake. More often than not, the messages included some pressing demand for immediate parental attention—TRANFER $ TO ACCT ASAP PLS; FRGOT BBALL SHOES PLS BRING NOW!

If something was particularly dire, it was Jake's practice to re-text the same message a number of times until he was answered. As a baby he'd been the same. Might as well just go pick him up.

HUMMMMMMMMMMMMMM!!!!

do Re MI.

Sulcov struggled to gather his wits, to pinpoint the source of the sound, to figure out the spatial relationships in his topsy turvy state. His head was pounding. Hot pain flowed along the tributaries of his cervical nerves, into his shoulders. His brain felt glitched; it was hard to think. He wondered if he was getting enough oxygen.

The phone was in her pocket, he told himself.

In the waterproof zipper pocket of her prototype Juicy top, new swag from the *Surf's Up!* line, just arrived from the company ... the partner to the bottoms she'd painstakingly customized: KISS THIS.

If she's still tied to the bench ... she's above me, facing down.

But the sound seems to be coming from lower, beneath your head.

Maybe she came loose and "fell" onto the interior of the roof.

Maybe she's still tied and the phone fell out of her pocket.

Or maybe, given the amount of damage to the truck—they'd rolled several times on the way down—Was it possible the phone was still inside the wreck but Angelika wasn't?

Maybe her pocket ripped as she was being ejected.

HUMMMMMMMMMMMMMM!!!!!!!!!!!!!

do re MI

This time followed by a strange rustling noise from within the wreckage, the distinct sound of movement, something rooting around, something alive.

It's bigger than a bird.

Could be rats.

Opossum.

Raccoon? Skunk?

I'm pretty sure they have mountain lions around here.

Years ago, when Sulcov's house was owned by the actor James Caan—during his ascendant period, when he'd starred in *The Godfather* series—*Los Angeles* magazine had written up the place as part of a roundup of "Extreme LA Homes." The writer called the banyan tree in the courtyard, "a living presence that unites the family of man indoors with Nature's family outdoors."

Given its perch on the edge of the canyon and its proximity to Topanga State Park, the banyan had more than lived up to its review over the years, playing host to all manner of birds, insects, reptiles, rats, and large climbing mammals that found their way through the neighborhood and over the roof, bringing with them the attendant scat and tsoris. Since Sulcov's terrifying run-in one evening with a pair of brawling raccoons—fur and shit literally flying as they roiled across the Mexican ceramic tile floor like two Hollywood stuntmen—trespass into the courtyard had been forbidden on a regular basis to all but the gardener, who entered twice a month to sweep up leaves and excrement and to dispose of any carnage.

Born and raised a city boy, Sulcov had lived most of his life in the realm of man. The five boroughs of New York City stood as a monument to the ascendance on this planet of crafty *Homo sapiens*. There were breathtaking feats of engineering—skyscrapers, bridges, tunnels, elaborate seawalls—but little was left of the natural habitat; the earthly order of things was nowhere apparent. Mankind had occupied and prevailed.

In Los Angeles, nature was everywhere ascendant. There were beautiful days, spectacular sunsets, starry nights. And there were fires, earthquakes, torrential rains, and mudslides. Despite what his tree-hugging friends in the neighborhood were always saying, despite all the claptrap from the NPR liberals about the peaceful order of Mother Earth's green universe, Sulcov was beginning to understand things differently.

Inspiring is the sight of a red-tailed hawk in the middle distance, holding its position in the cloudless blue sky, wings backpedaling so majestically . . .

But what of the field mouse about to become dinner?

For the first time he prayed: *please God, don't let her body be eaten.*

He rummaged around with his free hand, seeking a suitable weapon. His fingers found an empty water bottle, a box of Kleenex, a magazine. Judging by the thickness, it was a woman's title. He held the binder facing outward, thinking to use the corner as the business end.

"SCAT!" he screamed hoarsely. "GO ON, *GET! LEAVE!*"

And then: "*HELLLLLLLLP!*

"*SOMEBODY, PLEASE.*

"*HELLLLLLLLLLLLLLLLLLP!*"

Startled by the sudden outburst, the surrounding forest went mute. The chirping birds, the singing insects, the entire soundtrack of routine terrestrial night life . . . everything became still.

He listened acutely; all he could hear was his own ragged breathing. He could no longer feel the pins and needles in his trapped arm; he couldn't feel anything anymore, just dead weight tugging against his shoulder. Briefly, he imagined himself in one of those minimalist productions of *Godot.*

An actor on a dark stage, surrounded by all of eternity.

You're stuck, he told himself. *There's nothing more to do. There's no way anybody's ever gonna find you out here.*

More movement inside the truck. It sounded very close. He gripped his magazine/weapon. . . .

And then a small sound, a voice: "Where am I?"

48

The Celebrity Use Curve

Detective Kenyatta Ducksworth was sitting at his desk in the suitably frayed and multiethnicly inhabited squad room of the Hollywood Station precinct house, keyboarding the usual forms into his computer. Phones rang, printers ground out paperwork, handcuffs and gun butts and other martial hardware thunked and clanked against furniture; suspects and complainants came and went with their flopsweat and tales of woe, adding to the general din.

Ducksworth's sleeves were rolled midway to his elbows; against the advice of *GQ* magazine, his corduroy blazer was parked over the back of his chair. The last few days had been as brutal as any he'd served as a cop. Yet somehow he still looked fresh in his tweed vest and designer jeans; he had about him the stunned but triumphant air of a calf-roping contestant who's tied up all his loose limbs in a winning time, hands raised overhead.

Of course, with glory in the field—ferreting out the truth, exonerating the innocent, sticking it to the politicos, bringing the guilty to justice . . . not to mention leading a major celeb on a televised perp walk through the very epicenter of Hollywood—there is always the attendant messy afterbirth of paperwork. Ducksworth was hoping to get out of here at a decent hour. His cell phone had been blowing up all afternoon with good tidings from friends who'd seen him on CNN, E!, and the rest. With any luck, there was a victory lap in his immediate future.

But he couldn't leave just yet.

Absent a suspect (or even any clues) in the drive-by at Sunset and Vine—and with no apparent evidence linking it to the shooting of *Los Vatos*, or to anything else for that matter—the entire squad of detectives had been ordered to stay overtime to work their contacts.

Across the room, a fortyish detective named Sullivan popped up from his cubicle. Similarly dejacketed, he was tall and ruddy with a beachball of a gut. A telephone receiver was cradled against his shoulder.

The television mounted on the wall behind him was tuned to live coverage of this afternoon's latest carnage, an apparent drive-by shooting . . . *in Malibu?* A real puzzler, this one, the first *ever* such incident within the corporate limits of the storied enclave by the sea. Despite the best efforts of the press to connect all the dots—the two drive-bys, the deaths of *Los Vatos*, and the Chillika sex tape—there was no evidence . . . as of this time. Newscopters continued to circle the crime scene (and to buzz Angelika's place), relieved at intervals for refueling by fresh craft. Traffic was still tied up, one lane in either direction.

"Hey, Ducksworth," Sullivan called, loud enough to put the room on pause. "I've got *Angelika Collette* on the line for you."

All ears in the place twitched awake, recalibrating focus like so many satellite dishes—perp, protestant, and police officer. Maybe they hated her because they used to love her and she'd betrayed their conceptual image—the beautiful and chaste single mom next door had taken up with a Mandingo. Or maybe they were more fascinated with her now because of the lurid turn of affairs—*Wow, little miss sweetness likes big black rapper dick!* Or maybe there is just a genetic need for humans to create heroes, only to later tear them down when they turn out to be so disappointingly . . . human—richer and more beautiful and more fabulous than most, yes, but basically subject to the same foibles and ill winds as their fellow earthlings. After we've built them up to such lofty heights, after we've studied with such intense fascination everything they do and say and own . . . maybe we start to feel humdrum by comparison? Inferior even?

Maybe we become . . . *resentful?*

In any case, to love or to hate is equally diverting, which is the purpose of entertainment, one would suppose. Call it The Celebrity Use Curve. If you're lucky, the third act brings redemption.

Even as Duckworth's friends e-mailed and texted encouragement in the wake of his newly kindled fame, his coworkers had been subjecting him to endless tons of grief. *Angelika on the phone? Give me a fuckin break.* He kept his eyes on his computer screen, continued to type. "Fuck you, Sullivan."

"I'm not bullshitting," the veteran detective protested. "Seriously. She *insists* she's Angelika. The caller ID comes up—" checking the display—"Nathan Sulcov?"

"Deal with her. I'm busy here doing *real* police work."

"She's asking for you by *name.*"

"Kunta-Kenyatta?" This was Sullivan's long-time partner, popping up out of the adjoining cubicle like a Whack-a-Mole on the midway. The partner's midnight black skin was contrasted by a trim white beard, a kind of yin and yang of appearance that suited his hot and cold style. He'd been up Ducksworth's ass from day one, self-elected to supply this promising new jack the appropriate load of tough love, the legacy of all the mean black fathers who'd preceded him.

Ducksworth searched the ceiling for signs of his maker. All he saw were dirty acoustical tiles.

Up popped a junior detective, eager to be heard. His name was Norman Patel. "Wasn't Angelika the first to *publically* mention the existence of the video facilities at Chill's place? Maybe it really *is* her."

Ordinarily, given this kind of suggestion by the nerdy South Asian kid, Sullivan would have belched out something suitably distasteful.

But this time, well . . . a lot of strange shit was going down. He returned to his caller, spoke a few sentences, listened intently. After a few beats, he covered the receiver.

Not sure yet whether to be cynical or alarmed, Sullivan's voice assumed a neutral tone. "She's speaking from a vehicle. There's been a wreck. They're trapped," he told the room at large.

Then he indicated Ducksworth. "She says she got your number from a student at Santa Monica Prep. Ring any bells?"

49

Listening In on History

"Put it on speaker," Sulcov said. His voice was raw; his mouth tasted of blood and gasoline. He was still hanging upside down, his left arm intermingled with the limbs of uncountable bushes and trees.

Angelika was behind him and below, prone against the upturned ceiling. The glow from the flip phone illuminated her famous face, which was swollen and bloody almost beyond recognition. As the truck had tumbled down the hill, the dead weight of the starlet's unconscious body had worked itself loose from the jerry-rigged arrangement of seatbelts. For at least one revolution she'd been in free fall, rolled and tossed with the other flotsam—the various pairs of flip-flops and sunglasses, empty water bottles, magazines, textbooks, collected shells, and fine grains of sand—that lived in Judge Baverman's Xterra. At last she'd face-planted on the thinly upholstered metal ceiling of the rear-most section of the passenger cabin, which had survived intact—unlike the forward driver's portion of the roof, which had caved inward and was impacting unfavorably against Sulcov's bloody head.

From her position, the groggy starlet could have reached up and tapped the hapless striking screenwriter on the shoulder. As it was, her presence in the moment was tenuous at best. Everything was jumbled. Everything hurt. Her face throbbed. It was difficult to speak. She sounded like someone who'd just been wheeled out of dental surgery. "Can you hear me, officer?", she asked.

Sulcov shouted hoarsely into the void. "I'm here too—can you hear me?" Though he couldn't actually see the light from his cell phone, the degree of the darkness in his part of the wreckage had leavened a bit, as the night sky does imperceptibly in the hours before dawn.

"I can hear you both," Ducksworth assured them—as could every detective in the room, all of them having conferenced into the call from their respective desks. Obviously it took something unusual to capture the attention of this crew of cynical vets. Everyone had the sense that they were listening in on history (or viewing it, in the case of the suspects handcuffed to chairs). *Where were you when Angelika called the squad room?*

"We're trapped," the starlet reiterated, marble-mouthed.

"My son—do you know him?" Sulcov projected hoarsely. "Jake Sulcov. He's thirteen. He told me to call you."

"We are aware that he's friends with Zeke Garcia, the brother of the deceased rapper," Ducksworth said.

"The boys have been kidnapped by the Venice Gang."

"Do you have a suspect and a location?"

"The guy's name is Big Gato. They're at his grandmother's house on Brooks Street, near Seventh. He just got out of prison. I don't know his real name. I think he drives a blue Chevy Impala. It's vintage. A '63, I think. A real cherry. It shouldn't be hard to find."

On the TV screen behind Sullivan's head there could be seen a jittery supertelephoto closeup of the parking lot/shooting scene in Malibu, taken from a helicopter—Big Gato's totaled Impala. A muscular tow truck was pulled up behind the vehicle's curvaceous rear end. Bellowing black smoke from twin exhaust pipes, it was attempting to couple. The scroll running across the bottom of the screen informed viewers of the vehicle's connection with the film *Boyz N the Hood*.

At that moment, every detective in the room was thinking the same thing: *I hope I don't have to drive out to Malibu at this hour.*

"What about you?" Ducksworth asked. "Is anyone injured? Can you give me your exact location?"

"We're upside down," Angelika offered.

"We're in a Nissan XTerra truck in Solstice Canyon in Malibu." Sulcov clarified. "On the private road that leads to the Secret Celebrity Swimmin Hole. A small bridge collapsed and we fell into a ravine. There's gasoline everywhere. This whole truck could blow any minute. Please hurry!"

"The Secret Celebrity Swimmin Hole?" Ducksworth repeated.

Around the squad room, brows beetled.

The Secret Celebrity what?

50

The Next-of-Kin Awaiting Word

Thanks to procedures developed after the terrorist attacks on 9/11, a task force was hastily dispatched.

With Ducksworth in command, a full complement of uniformed police officers—along with a SWAT team, members of the gang squad, and a hostage negotiator—were sent to the house in Venice. When the situation was explained by a translator, Big Gato's *abuelita* charged back toward her garage spewing colorful colloquialisms—even the non-Spanish speaking officers could make out the words *machete* and *pinga*.

Jake and Z were promptly surrendered by their homeboy/jailer; given the old woman's rage, he seemed content to be handcuffed and taken away by police.

Meanwhile, in Malibu, the LA Sheriff's Department, which had jurisdiction by agreement over the incorporated area, was joined by personnel from the LAPD, the California Highway Patrol, the U.S. Forest Service, and the U.S. Coast Guard, the latter for additional heavy air support. An environmental impact coordinator was loaned by the Getty Trust. The dual mission: to secure the parking lot/crime

scene at the Malibu Green's strip mall and to mount a full-scale rescue operation at nearby Solstice Canyon. As the evening deepened, as
the press got wind of the expanded story, more newscopters and journos and curiosity seekers converged.

After Jake and Z were cleared by medical personnel on the scene
in Venice, Ducksworth drove the boys out to the rescue operation,
where they were joined by Tish Sulcov, Missy Collette, and Sulcov's
old friend Judge Baverman, whose truck was innocently (and embarrassingly) ensnared within this infotainment clusterfuck. They stood
inside the hastily erected canopy of the on-scene command post, just
beyond the police line. Absent other viewable action, all cameras
were trained in their direction: the tense next-of-kin awaiting word
on the fate of their loved ones. As the drama extended into the golden
hours of prime time television, commercial rates were bumped expo-
nentially higher. Somewhere in this strike-besieged town, the suits
were celebrating.

The CEO of RAP Records sat with his boyz around a picnic-style table, all of the parts fabricated of nearly-indestructible materials and
anchored into the cement floor of the common room in the southeast wing of Bradley Memorial County Jail, an hour east of downtown
Los Angeles.

Because special treatment exists everywhere, the posse was allowed to stay together on the inside. The two bodyguards were room-
ing together; Clevon and Eddie were scheduled to be released in the
morning. Chill and TBone were also together, as it had been for so
many years. Their futures were not yet clear.

At the moment, all attention was focused on the TV screen
mounted high on a wall. A giant crane—trucked down from Santa
Barbara, a donation from an oil drilling company—was being maneuvered into position to aid a combined team of Navy Seals and firefighters who were reportedly waiting in position beside the Xterra, beneath
the splintered bridge, in the deepest declivity of the streambed.
According to closed captioning, the condition of the starlet and her
unnamed companion had been characterized by rescuers as "grave."

The overhead lights in the common room began to blink—time for lockdown. The brilliantly colored TV screen went abruptly dark. As they were conditioned to do, all the inmates stood and proceeded to shuffle toward their cells.

Chill remained seated, continued to watch the dark screen. Without his hater blockers and the attention of his regular barber, without his hundred K smile, the internationally famous music mogul looked pitiably human. His crew stood around him uncomfortably, not quite sure what to do.

"We gotta go boss," Clevon urged.

"You don't wanna piss off nobody in here," Eddie added.

EPILOGUE

51

High Tolerance Is Something You Develop Over Time

Her hair long now and in curlers, tied up in a scarf, Angelika Collette plopped herself down in the makeup chair in her luxury StarCarriage mobile dressing room.

"Did you see the dailies last night?" she asked Kisha. "I was afraid to look."

The makeup artist/confidant took the starlet's face in her hands and examined it closely, turning it this way and that. "You've healed *so* nicely. I remember when I first saw you at the hospital. I was like— *Oh my God!*"

"You look *amazing*," assured JamieLynn. The long-time personal assistant sat at the dinette table behind her ever-present Mac computer.

"Thanks to Dr. Cohen—and to my *girl*, here."

"Like I said," Kisha stressed, "there *ain't* much to cover."

"You *are* ready for your close-up, Miss Collette!" JamieLynn bubbled. She raised a fist, cheerleader-style.

Angelika tilted her head this way and that, considering her image in the unforgiving light of the three-way mirror. "I'm still getting used to the new nose."

"Honestly, to me it look the same—like every other white-people nose."

"The new one or the old one?"

"Both?"

"Are you trying to tell me all *white people noses* look alike?"

"No. I'm trying to tell you white people *got* no noses."

"It's like God was stingy with us *whities*," Angelika said, still appraising her renovated whiffer. "He gave us small noses, thin lips . . ."

"And teeny-tiny booties."

"I *wish*," Angelika groaned.

Kisha rolled her eyes. "Are you kidding?"

JamieLynn, emphatic: "Are you *kidding*?"

"But I feel so *fat* after being home *doing nothing* for so long. I just started working out again!"

"You still have the *Ass of the Ages*," JamieLynn pronounced, somewhat covetously.

"More like an *ass that's aging*," Angelika said.

The three women dissolved into laughter . . .

A knock on the screen door. The CEO of RAP Records peered inside the StarCarriage. The late afternoon sunlight reflected off his platinum and diamond grills. "What's all the cacklin? You havin another one of yo secret sorority meetins up in here?"

"Hey, *Thomas*," Angelika sang.

"What up, Chill," Kisha said.

"Hey Chil-lll," JamieLynn drawled, managing to stretch his name into two syllables.

The mogul was wearing an NBA-style warm-up suit and brand new Kobe-brand Nikes. The spring-loaded door banged unexpectedly behind him, bringing another round of giggles. He leaned down and planted a kiss on the superstarlet. "You ready to do this *thang*?"

"*You're* the one who's about to have his acting cherry popped."

"You sayin a reality show ain't acting?" His tone was a mixture of braggadocio and defensiveness—in this woman he'd surely met his match; she'd even volunteered to accompany him when he appeared on Jay Leno to issue his measured *mea culpa* regarding the deaths of *Los Vatos* and the unlucky attorney. When Oprah offered to host the couple on her show for a frank discussion of interracial dating, the nation swooned—everybody could see how right they were together. (Well, they'd already seen a pretty good demonstration of *that*, but it was nice to observe, in a more sedate and public setting, how well they got along, how these two seeming opposites were actually complementary. Like Liz and Dick or Brad and Angie, their relationship made perfect sense; who else could handle their oversize lives?)

The object of the most recent frenzied run of headlines was secured at the moment in the StarCarriage valuables safe: a five-karat (blood-free) emerald cut diamond engagement ring. The couple's decision to make it official may or may not have had to do with the scheduled court appearance of William "TBone" Jackson. As he'd agreed, Chill was on standby to testify for the prosecution against his brother-in-law should the need arrive. As it happened, on the day in question, TBone decided to avoid a trial by pleading guilty to a lesser charge. No doubt he would be released and back home before his children graduated high school. Uncle Chill would see to their care in the meantime.

Angelika held out her hand toward her man, palm up. She wiggled her fingers . . . *Gimme.*

He looked at her, like, *What?*

She pushed her hand higher, toward his mouth—a mother demanding the removal of an offending piece of gum (from a much-taller child).

Without protest he removed the upper and lower pieces of his hundred K smile and surrendered them.

Walking purposefully, Nate Sulcov entered Heston Arena at Santa Monica Prep.

Although it was September and still hot outside, it was cool inside the cavernous space and typically fragrant; balls bounced, whistles blew, sneakers squeaked—another set of sensory treats that never failed to thrill and comfort him. Alloyed with these pleasant feelings was a new and profound sadness; in all likelihood, he'd never again play the game he loved.

Before he could reach the court he was mobbed by a bumptious contingent. Led by Jake and Z, the incoming freshman team was outfitted from head to toe in NBA-style gear and Kobe-brand Nikes. The warm-up jackets had shiny satin hoods—Little Red Riding Hood meets the Harlem Globetrotters.

"Dad! These uniforms are *sick!*" Jake raised his arms, palms facing inward, as if to mirror his own magnificence.

"Thanks, Mr. Sulcov," Z added.

All the other boys in unison: "Thank you, Mr. Suuuul-coooov."

"Don't thank me *yet*," he said with mock severity. "You still have *work* to do, remember?"

"You call this work?" Jake gestured to indicate the gym behind them: the well-worn bleachers, the banners in the rafters, the racks of basketballs . . . And the several tons of camera, sound, lighting, and craft service equipment . . . And nearly five hundred people—the cast and production crew of *High Tolerance* and four hundred student, teacher, and parent extras—here at Prep's gym to shoot scenes for a new episode of the award-winning show, which was finally back in production.

The screenwriter's strike had lasted one hundred days. The writers won some points and lost some. Looking back, it seems a shame that all the brilliant, liberal-minded fruits and nuts who populate the industry couldn't have found a better way to compromise without flushing billions of dollars of revenue down the toilet.

"Basketball is *never* work," confirmed Z.

"Unless we're running suicides," added Wes, a beanpole with a big Afro bubbling out from beneath his hood.

All the boys agreed. They slapped palms and elbowed one another, made various noises of enthusiastic agreement.

If Sulcov's love for Jake was supreme, if Z was like a son to him, these others were his favorite nephews. For years now he'd coached, driven, tied shoes, hosted sleepovers, supplied snacks, organized hotel rooms, even conspired with them from time to time against the smothering tyranny of their tiger moms and overbearing dads. He'd nursed them through the first intense and frightening moments of physical injuries both trivial and severe; he'd carried them off courts and fields, dried their tears, kissed their foreheads, triaged their breaks and sprains and bloody cuts, driven them to the emergency room.

And how they'd grown from year to year, their bodies filling and elongating, their voices dipping, their personas taking shape. Even relegated as he was these days to the bleachers, Sulcov was still their biggest fan, if not the most vocal. (He wished some of these parents would learn to shut up! *Do you really think you're helping your kid?*) When Jake hit a sweet three or delivered a perfect no-look pass. When Z executed a perfect drop-step for a layup or countered with the hook. When Wes drove hard to the basket with either hand from the top of the key. When Luke calmly handed the ball back to the referee after a bad call instead of melting down . . . these were the things he'd taught them, pieces of his own game they'd taken up and made their own. In this way he'd always be a part of their lives. On the scrim of his memory he could still see Jake, age three at the local court, commandeering Sulcov's big-guy basketball and toddling drunkenly toward the hoop, a little man attempting to hoist the moon.

"Does everybody know their lines?" His voice came out strained. *Do not cry!* he commanded himself.

"We *got* this, Dad. *Trust* me. We've rehearsed *a zillion* times!"

"One hundred zillion," assured Z. The others chorused their agreement.

Sulcov raised his hands in surrender. "Okay. *Sor-ry.* As long as we get these scenes shot today, I'm—"

"*Whoa!*" Jake interrupted. "You got the new Z-Tech prototype."

Sulcov beamed like . . . a father whose teenage son has noticed him. "Just fitted this morning," he said proudly. "What do you think?"

The boys *oohed* and *ahhed,* captivated by Sulcov's cool new prosthetic hand/forearm. As a group, and individually with their parents, they'd visited Sulcov in the hospital and at home as he'd recovered over the months from his various surgeries—somebody's little sister had even made him a get-well bear dressed in a tiny reproduction of a Prep basketball uniform.

"It looks a little like C3PO," Z said of the new mechanical hand, recalling the neurotic bipedal robot from *Star Wars.*

"Except it's not *gold*," Wes corrected, the straight-A student in the bunch.

"This one's a *loaner.* It's just the guts, basically," Sulcov explained. "The final version will have 'skin.' Check it out. All the fingers work independently."

Via the magic of implanted electrodes and tiny computerized components, Sulcov's nerve impulses traveled from his brain to his mechanical digits, which wiggle-waggled playfully, accompanied by a fine motorized whine. "They say I'll even be able to learn to *type.*"

Sulcov made a monster-hand of the expensive device—*It's aliiiiiiiiive!*—and thrust it into the crowd of awkward and be-pimpled teens, who set about kibbitzing joyfully, bumping and colliding, boy-molecules in motion.

"How's it going, guys?" asked Angelika Collette, interrupting the fun.

"Whatup, playas?" added Chill.

Everyone froze in place. Faces slack, eyes wide . . . *Holy shit!*

Sulcov: "Close your gob, Luke, you're attracting flies."

Everyone cracked up. Another round of shoving and teasing ensued, a spontaneous overload of hormones and excitement.

Jake and Z held back a bit. By the look on their faces, you could see they weren't so sure yet how they felt about the man responsible (at least in part) for Sleeper's death. They'd already met Angelika—the first time was in the hospital, right after the rescues.

It had taken six hours to extricate the odd couple from the twisted remains of Judge Baverman's trusty XTerra. (A less rugged vehicle may well have pancaked; fortunately nobody thought to use the Jaws of Life on the glove box.) Sulcov and Angelika supported and coached each other during the long and painful ordeal. That Sulcov had fished her out of the Secret Celebrity Swimmin Hole and saved her life well overshadowed the fact of the truck accident, which was arguably his

fault—in his panic, he'd driven too fast up the ramp to the decomposing bridge; he'd admitted as much to her and she'd forgiven him. He
was already on board to write the next installment of Ozone Jungle,
the plot and details of which had been fleshed out during the frequent chatty phone calls that marked their joint convalescence.

Now Sulcov air-kissed the starlet so as not to muss her makeup.
With the mogul he made the appropriate series of hand clasps and
fist bumps, ending with a hug-and-back pat-combination, part of this
business performed with the new prosthetic hand, albeit gingerly.

"Meet your new coach," Sulcov told the team.

Chill laughed modestly. "Remember guys—I played *football*. I
have no idea what I'm doing. You have to go gentle on me, k?"

"That's why they call it *acting*," Angelika joked, a smurf in a
stand of tall trees.

"I think they're just about ready for you guys," Sulcov said, indicating center court.

The show was slated to run as the season opener in January—
the much-heralded return to the air of *High Tolerance*. This super-
sized lineup of guest stars was still top secret. You should have seen
Zondo's face when Sulcov brought him the treatment—followed by
his list of demands.

Sulcov to Angelika: "You wanna hang with me? You're in the
next scene with the kids and Chill. This won't take long."

"Famous last words," she trilled.

As the boys and the mogul took their places on the court,
Sulcov and Angelika walked over to the production command post
set up in the corner of the gym. In the trade they call it the video village—two folding tables lined with laptops, a medusa's head of elec-
trical cords, several large monitors on rolling carts, and a collection of
folding camp chairs common to movie and television sets . . . all of it
crowned with a soccer-mom-style awning overhead, standard operating procedure, indoors or out.

In attendance was a typical Hollywood assortment of valuable
functionaries and extraneous onlookers: the script supervisor, the director of photography, several network suits, the wife and son of an

investor, Troy the press agent, Morrie the agent, the parents of one of the *HT* cast members. Also present, putting in a rare appearance on the front lines, was Sulcov's former roommate and current boss, the show runner, M. Kelley Elizondo. As Sulcov approached the encampment with the starlet in tow, Zondo rose and hurried over to greet them, nearly tripping over a cable in his haste to be gracious.

To commemorate the start of their sixth season—during which they would reach the magic number of episodes necessary for worldwide syndication, the fifth season having been foreshortened by the strike—new camp chairs had been ordered for the set.

Sulcov showed Angelika to one of the empty chairs; they were the taller variety for a better view, oak with extra-sturdy black canvas slings. On the backs had been embroidered the familiar logo from *High Tolerance*. Sulcov took his own chair. Along with the logo was his name and his new, twice-a-season title: DIRECTOR.

He nodded to the assistant director, known as the AD, who called out "Set!"—indicating that everyone on the set should make ready.

And then the AD called out "Background!"—meaning the extras could start doing their business. The whistle blew, the basketball game started up, Chill began coaching his team.

Sulcov took a moment to survey carefully the panoply before him—the court, the actors, the two teams of boys and their respective coaches, the cheerleaders, the four hundred or so students, faculty, and parents who'd volunteered to be extras in the stands—all of it exactly as he'd typed . . . letter by letter . . . word by word . . . with the fingers of his remaining right hand.

He spotted Tish sitting with the other parents in what used to be their regular spot, at the crown of the ancient varnished bleachers—you could use the wall for back support, prime real estate. She looked beautiful, her hair expensively straightened and augmented, her clothes and accessories as typically enviable as her wealth and connections. He'd spent nearly two months in the hospital, four surgeries in all, including the amputation, a two-level cervical spinal fusion, and a pair of stump reductions. Once he arrived home and he'd established a reasonable routine, his wife of fifteen years decamped from the household, leaving behind, to his surprise, a quitclaim deed to the Arnold Stevenson Treehouse. An amicable divorce was in process; he'd be receiving a settlement, as per their prenuptial agreement.

Thereafter they'd shared custody of Jake equally, the boy's best interests uppermost, the adult details of the plotline left for him to wonder about or not, the damage to his perfect childhood irrevocable, come what may. Probably the greatest wound was Sulcov's loss of full custody. Because she wanted to move on, how was it fair that she could take his son away from him half the time?

What became of his soon-to-be ex-wife ... who she contemplated sleeping with or actually slept with ... where she moved, to which rung of Hell ... none of that really matters. This part of the story was never about her, anyway. It was about Sulcov and his need to be with someone like her in order to himself feel whole—and about his realization that living a good life doesn't mean living a life filled only with good.

Sooner or later, shit will splat in your face. Some might get in your mouth. You may not deserve it but there it is.

It's how you cope that takes your measure.

MIKE SAGER is a best-selling author and award-winning reporter. A former *Washington Post* staff writer under Watergate investigator Bob Woodward, he worked closely, during his years as a contributing editor to *Rolling Stone*, with gonzo journalist Hunter S. Thompson. Sager is the author of four collections of non-fiction, two novels, and one biography. He has served for more than fifteen years as a writer at large for *Esquire*. In 2010 he won the American Society of Magazine Editors' National Magazine Award for profile writing for his article "The Man Who Never Was." Many of his stories have inspired films, including *Boogie Nights*, with Mark Wahlberg, and *Veronica Guerin*, with Cate Blanchett. For more information, please see www.MikeSager.com.

About the Publisher

The Sager Group was founded in 1984. In 2012 it was chartered as a multi-media artists' and writers' consortium, with the intent of empowering those who make art—an umbrella beneath which makers can pursue, and profit from, their craft directly, without gatekeepers. TSG publishes eBooks and paper books; manages musical acts and produces live shows; ministers to artists and provides modest grants; and produces documentary, feature and web-based films. By harnessing the means of production, The Sager Group helps artists help themselves. For more information, please see www.TheSagerGroup.Net.

www.ingramcontent.com/pod-product-compliance
Lightning Source LLC
Chambersburg PA
CBHW020308200626
46814CB00006BA/2141